ISBN 978-1-330-87736-4
PIBN 10115984

FB &c Ltd, Dalton House, 60 Windsor Avenue, London, SW19 2RR.
Company number 08720141. Registered in England and Wales.

The Gates of Kut

BY

LINDSAY RUSSELL

CASSELL AND COMPANY, LTD
London, New York, Toronto and Melbourne

First published 1917

To

AIN JAMES MACALLAN

WHO DIED OF WOUNDS
IN MESOPOTAMIA
ON FEBRUARY 9, 1917

*"Better lo'ed ye canna be—
Will ye no come back again?"*

CONTENTS

Contents

THE GATES OF KUT

PROLOGUE

NIGHT, like a dark and bloated buzzard, was winging its way slowly and uneasily over Mesopotamia.

In Kut-el-Amara, in that grim, tongue-shaped loop of the Tigris, the broken jumble of mud huts began to merge into strange, distorted shapes. The scraggy tamarinds and liquorice trees made a fretful murmuring. The stifled moans of the sick and the dying rose for a little space, faltered, and fell away again into silence.

Thin, skeleton fingers plucked aimlessly at the sand, and voices murmured and muttered deliriously of the white cliffs of Dover, of England and home, of London—gay, laughing, lamp-jewelled London, dancing down the roads of the world.

Towards the great marshes, stern and sinister in the growing darkness, isolated flares of light betokened the Turkish lines of investment and the redoubts of the enemy.

North, south, east and west they were merging into a circle, slowly narrowing, ever creeping closer.

Now and then, to the besieged camp at Kut, the wind brought strange, distant voices, or that desolate Eastern cry of the Arab, echoing eerily across the night. Then silence fell again, broken only by the low, threatening mutter of the flood-swollen Tigris, and hoarse, delirious voices in the broken mud-brick huts.

In one of these huts a man rose abruptly and, walking to the door, looked out for a moment. The dark wings of night folded close about the village. The collection of mud huts loomed strange and shapeless before him. Shrouded lights flickered, marking here and there the way along the winding alleys and roofless passages open alike to the chill of night and the heat of day.

He swung out into the night and made his way towards the black shadow of the fortifications. Gaunt-faced, emaciated men lifted hollow eyes and sprang stiffly to the salute at sight of him, and strove to stand upright on limbs that were almost too weak to perform the office.

With doglike fidelity their eyes followed him. Many of them had served under him at Chitral Fort. A glow came into their hearts; where Townshend of Chitral led they would follow—ay, to the end. Hope rose anew in hearts that at the coming of that night had begun to quail. Hands clenched and faces turned, grim and determined, towards the distant glare of lights.

The General swung on his way. The night was dark and very silent. The very stillness presaged trouble. What danger skulked and crept stealthily on the slow heels of the passing hours?

Hunger stalked along the narrow, tortuous passages. Gaunt starvation, bony of cheek and wolfish-eyed, peered into the broken huts. In a wan, flickering square of light a group of men, with backs bent to the spade, were shovelling up the sand into mounds. The General came to a pause, stood by with bared head, lips set. . . . Death was taking its toll, man after man. . . . Perhaps there came into his mind, as he stood there, broken fragments of Tennyson's undying poem:

> "Someone had blundered . . .
> Theirs not to reason why,
> Theirs but to do and die. . . ."

He returned abruptly into the darkness, but the words followed him out into the night. Along the winding alley-ways, in some of the huts, men were crying for water, babbling of water, pleading for water.

"*Water! Water!*" The pitiful plea rose and fell from parched, delirious lips that had learned the utter uselessness of crying for food.

The thick, muddy liquid of the Tigris was all that was to be had. Here and there beside a number of crude, earthenware jars men were striving to filter it in Arab fashion, gaunt, terrible caricatures of men.

When the relieving force came there would be food and water to spare. . . . It might come to-night, to-morrow. . . . Who knew? Somewhere, surely, in God's name, a relieving force was on the way.

The General set his lips tight as he went his rounds. The men who had been at Chitral Fort knew that look well, that haggard face, steadily growing thinner day by day, but the eyes always dogged and resolute, the mouth set in lines of determination. A cheer rose and followed him as he went, dying away in sheer weakness.

Something else came to him out of the night—the peal of happy laughter. It broke and cracked suddenly on a high note. A weak voice followed it.

". . . Cool running water," it babbled in rapture, ". . . cool running water . . . rippling past . . . and here's Teddington Lock already. . . . See how the water is surging against the gates . . . and the band is playing, and there are tears in your eyes. What is it, dear? . . . Oh! that old thing that always made you weep lately. . . . But one must go, dear—one must play the game."

The voice stopped for a moment, then the sick man began to sing, in a weak, quavering way:

"We've watched you playin' cricket . . .
And every kind of game.
At football . . . golf and . . . polo
You men . . . have made . . . your name.
But now your country calls you
To play your part in war,
And . . . no matter . . . what befalls you——"

The voice faltered suddenly and dropped into silence. Then it rose again.

"Cool running water . . . and the boat slipping through at last . . . and the gates of the lock opening . . . ever so slowly . . . ever . . . so——"

The voice broke suddenly like a snapped string. The gates of the Great Lock against which surge the waters of the River of Death had opened. The frail boat of one man's soul passed through. Far away it seemed as if one heard the voice of a woman sobbing in the dark.

The wildfowl fluttered from the marshes beyond Kut-el-Amara with a sudden startled cry. Men instinctively turned their faces in that direction, wondering what it presaged.

The lonely figure of one man stood very still, listening. But no further sound came. He turned his face towards far-off England. By now they must have received his urgent message. The slow, cumbrous machinery of State would begin to move—help would be already on the way; but if help should not come, after all—— He thought of his tried and trusty men, of the wistful question lurking ever in their eyes.

Dogged, resolute, he stood there and faced the facts. No news had come, no supplies could reach him. Starvation, long kept at bay, stalked familiarly through the camp. His men—skeleton figures that wrung his heart—grew steadily weaker. Over in England—what were they thinking? What were they doing? Were they going to leave him and his to starve and die like forgotten cattle? The murmurs of the sick men cut deep into his heart. His hands clenched. Would to God those men over there, in far-away England, might hear it! If they heard, would they understand? If they acted, would it be in time?

Kut was far away—a name to men—a column perchance in the papers.

What did England know of the desperate fight, of foes worse than the Turk, of disease and pestilence and starvation, of the struggle to keep closed the gates of Kut, those low-walled gates, built up of and fortified with the dogged spirit of Britain, stained with the blood of Britain, but still held?

"And held to the last." Through set teeth he said it. For the pride of the race that beat within him, for the blood that surged through his veins; it throbbed in the hearts of his men, too. They stood shoulder to shoulder, side by side, the faces of the living and the dying turned towards England—faces yearning, watching, questioning, worn to emaciation, yet dogged and unafraid.

* * * * *

Where the fretted pile of Westminster lifted its square tower against the grey sky, and the last of the dying sun glittered on the windows of the Houses of Parliament, an urbane and portly gentleman rose in answer to a question. He polished his glasses, set them firmly in place. Men leaned forward breathlessly to listen.

"The prospects of Kut," he announced, "have never been brighter."

Wild cheering drowned his voice. A moment afterwards and members rose and surged out into the lobbies, laughing and talking, nodding cheerfully, discussing everything, it seemed, but the war.

It was near the dinner-hour, and clubs and restaurants beckoned, gay with light and flowers, and music and tempting dishes.

* * * * *

The sun had set and the theatre crowds were flocking into the restaurants for dinner—beautifully-gowned women, immaculately-attired men. Ragtime music pulsed and beat out into the roar of traffic.

London, gay and laughing, tripped on her way. Here a luxuriously-fitted motor rolled by, with the glimpse of a white arm, bare shoulders and flashing jewels, there a khaki-clad line of men marching, full kit, towards a station. . . . Women, too—shabby, white-faced—marched by them, silent, beating back the tears. The mud of the passing, pleasure-seeking motors splashed on them as they marched.

Newspaper boys flashed across the road, in and out of the traffic, crying aloud:

"Latest news of Kut! Latest news of Kut!"

There was exactly an eighth of a column in the paper. The Ministry's message to the nation was in the stop-press column—a few sentences.

A whole column was devoted to foolish, dribbling nonsense about restaurants and anecdotes about third-rate actresses, and what Lady So-and-so said to the scribe, and what the exalted scribe said to her, and what to eat and the latest fashionable drinks. . . . Someone clamoured for more races, more sport, more light in the streets, lest the war prove too depressing. . . . Crowds of people were pouring into the latest revues, where fortunes were spent in decorative effects, and half-naked women danced to the accompaniment of the blare of a band and clapping hands.

Kut! What was Kut beside the latest revue?

Far away, over Kut, hung silence, black and deep as the grave.

CHAPTER I

The Rivers of Destiny

FROM where young Mrs. Marcourt sat, at the head of the long, exquisitely decorated table in her brilliantly lighted dining-room, she could, by lifting her head ever so slightly, look out over the bald, good-natured head of her legal lord and master, and see the shining waters of the old, old Thames, flowing soundlessly past, or swirling stormily under the arched bridges, with a passing freight of light and laughter and music.

Caught in the eddies of the wind was the plash of a pleasure-boat, or the muttering of deep voices from a dark barge, with its green and red lights blinking like tired eyes, as it drifted slowly on in the wake of the flowing river—the old river that flowed on like life, destined, inexorable. . . .

To the guests gathered at the dining-table in that long, dark-panelled room, with its hubbub of chatter and laughter, its pleasant tumult of well-bred argument, this visioning of Enid Marcourt's would have seemed a strange and inexplicable thing.

Had they followed the direction of her grey eyes, they would have seen only the heavy brown curtains—artistic enough, to be sure—draped closely at the windows in deference to the war-time order for lighting regulations; they would have turned back the more appreciatively to the well furnished room, the glitter of silver and cut glass, the cheerfulness of the masses of red roses piled high in the bronze bowls, the well trained servants hovering in the background, and the bubbling of wine in the slender-stemmed glasses.

But Enid Marcourt's vision was not barred by blinds. She had the gift of imagination that could throng the loneliest sea with ships, with tall masts swaying to the rhythm of tumbled waters, an imagination that could people vast plains and great open spaces, and that, last but not least, did not fail her in the limited circle of domesticity, where it filled in the interstices between prosy speeches and the fatuous or epigrammatic remarks that pass nowadays for wit.

Before the war, and before blinds were drawn over windows, Enid Marcourt could see in reality, from her place in that room, the Thames water flowing past. With the eyes of her soul she had followed the course of the river—a river that had seemingly no ending, for where it lost itself in the earth it mingled with far seas, swept in with incoming tides on far beaches, was part of the rain spattering on wet leaves in great forests in strange countries.

That night, just before the first guest had been announced, she had gone to the window, had drawn the curtains aside and looked out over the river. A great dark shape moved slowly past, its lights just glimmering. She watched it come from under the arches of the distant bridge. It seemed to draw her with it out into the night, with its monk-hooded lights and the passionately restless wash of a mighty river; and the barge went by, slowly, cumbrously, merging into the drifting mist.

"The Barge of Fate," she said, with a quick, indrawn breath. "It is like life——" And she turned a little despairingly from the window.

Around her now were the ripple of laughter, a woman's chirruping voice, the deeper tones of a man's voice in answer, the shallow stream of modern conversation frothing lightly over the grim stones in the bed of the river of Life.

A woman's voice said plaintively: "My dear General, I'm almost worn to a thread. These flag days are really so wearing. It took me quite a week to think out appropriate costumes."

The cracked tone of the old General's voice, a little grim: "But can't you sell flags without costumes, my dear lady?"

Another woman's light laughter tinkled out, provocative, expostulating.

"Naughty, naughty! My *dear* General——"

Elephantine in its heavy playfulness, Marcourt's voice protested from the far end of the table.

"You are making the General blush in his old age. He didn't mean what you meant. Oh! you didn't mean what you thought he meant. Ah, ha!" His big, blustering laugh filled the room. "Ah, ha, ha!"

The General had either blushed—or flushed. He turned somewhat abruptly to Mrs. Marcourt, who apparently had not heard. Under his shaggy white brows his eyes still burned with the fire of youth, but also with the cynical knowledge that age brings.

"So Territt is back with us again," he said, more with a desire to change the conversation than from interest in the subject.

"Yes." And then: "George met him at the club. He had just come back from India. He was needed here, I suppose."

He nodded. "I suppose so. Did he say anything?"

She hesitated. "I really do not know." She began mechanically to crumble her bread into tiny pieces. "I was so busy; I had not a chance to talk to him before dinner. He looks older, I believe. But then life in India does age one quicker than here. The climate is so different." She spoke with less effort now than when she first answered him.

"Let me see"—he wrinkled his brows—"I think it was here that he last dined before leaving for India. Five years ago, wasn't it?"

"Yes; five years," she said in a low voice.

"I often wondered what took him there." He lifted his head, glanced down at Captain Territt, who was listening intently to a stout lady in black who had views on the suffrage question and aired them at any and every opportunity. "It was his own desire, I understand."

"Yes. I believe so." She did not seem very interested in the subject.

Philip Territt looked up at the same moment, caught the General's eye and smiled. Then his eyes rested on his hostess, who was not looking at him, but at the little mound of crumbs her long white fingers were making and unmaking. Philip Territt looked at the mound, symbolic in its shape. She was burying even remembrance.

Her little bronze head was bent. He noted how the hair lifted and waved back from her ears, how it curled in one particular place at the nape of her white neck. It struck him with a sudden foolish pang, and he turned hurriedly and somewhat incoherently to a review of the suffrage problem, and the necessity for a woman as Prime Minister.

"The war would have been waged in a far different way had we a woman at the head of affairs," asserted the stout lady. Her very diamonds vibrated with excitement.

"I am quite sure it would," he agreed.

She glanced at him somewhat suspiciously, but his lean, sun-tanned face held no derision. His eyes were quite thoughtful. He was apparently pondering deeply.

"A woman would first of all have had a spring cleaning. She would have vigorously wielded the Broom of Reform. There are only two implements needed in the House of Commons—the broom and the spade." She paused for breath, for stout ladies can seldom be eloquent without discomfort. "The broom would have swept all the dust out of the corners, the cobwebs off the ceilings."

"You mean," he asked, "the mental ceilings?"

"Of the members? Yes."

"And the spade?"

"Oh! I haven't come to the spade yet, my dear man. One must do the sweeping before the delving. Have you ever seen Sam Mayo?"

She shot the question at him with such suddenness that it hounded him abruptly out of the kennel of abstraction where he had been gnawing the bone of old memories.

"Mayo, Sam Mayo? No! Is he to be the next Premier?"

"No!" she said indignantly. And a girl in white and silver, a little farther along the table, who was much interested in the conversation, or the conversationalists, laughed lightly and said:

"Do not forget, mamma, that Captain Territt has buried himself in India for a century or two. Captain Territt! Sam Mayo is a comedian."

"And what have comedians," asked Captain Territt, with a quick smile at the white-and-silver vision, "to do with politics?"

"A very great deal sometimes," drawled someone, and a quick flash of laughter followed.

"You are all missing the point," said the stout lady indignantly. "Sam Mayo has made his name by his particular method of singing songs or telling a story as if he were asleep, just out of bed, as it were. On the posters he is represented as being fettered with spiders' webs."

"Ah! I begin to see now," said Captain Territt. "And that is the symbol?"

"Of the House of Commons," added the stout lady with satisfaction. "So now you see why the broom is needed. They are all asleep."

"For a sleepy government," he remarked casually, "they have managed to do some big things, all the same. You must admit that."

She shrugged her plump shoulders. "Why? Because they have been hounded on at every step. One section of the Press chases them with a sledge-hammer, and hits them on the head with suggestions."

Territt laughed heartily. "And when they are unconscious the other section waits around with hot bottles, and comforting words, and a-little-drop-of-what-killed-auntie. Is that it? Well, well! And to think that over in India we have been thinking that everything was going all right." He turned that finely modelled head of his, with its grey hair waving back from the temples.

"That reminds me"—and his companion lowered her voice with evident interest—"a great many of you have been sent for, haven't you?"

"If we tell tales out of school," he asserted solemnly, "we get spanked."

The girl in white and silver giggled. Her partner, a prosy front-bench parliamentarian, frowned. He liked young society, and he wished the exquisite little section of it next him would show less interest in that long, lanky chap Territt, with his sun-tanned face and hands, his prematurely grey hair, and his air of altogether popping out of a backwoods novel, or entering the stage, with a background of great mountains and wide plains behind him, and a vista of white clapping hands in front of him. "Confound such fellows!" he said crossly.

At the far end of the table Mrs. Marcourt was playing her part of hostess to perfection—a smile here, a nod there, eyes lifted in interest, dropped in thought. She seemed very interested in all that the fatherly old General was saying. Her long, black, up-curling lashes hid her grey eyes as she listened.

He talked to her as he would have talked to no other woman at that table, because he had known her from childhood, or more likely because when he told Mrs. Marcourt anything she never referred to it in any way afterwards.

The General knew a great many of the other Society women as well from their childhood, but he did not talk to them as he did to young Mrs. Marcourt. He knew only too well how many of them loved to air their knowledge, or want of it, in fashionable restaurants and theatres. Even if a very attentive and generally foreign waiter of dubious nationality hovered near, it gave only a piquant flavour to the sauce of forbidden conversations.

So he said now, "Territt has been in Australia, too, hasn't he? If Gallipoli was on the slate still he would be sent there. I suppose that is why he came home, to find the wet sponge of unforeseen circumstance had been at work."

She raised her eyes. "Yes." And then, rather unusual for her, asked a question: "You think, then—it will not be France?"

He was watching Captain Territt from under his shaggy brows. "I think it will be wherever the Australians go."

Her hands made a fluttering movement. "Ah! Then there will be danger." She spoke involuntarily.

He turned and looked at her quizzically, but her hands were quite steady now, her face expressionless. Its grave sweetness was unaltered, save that in the glare of the electric bulbs he thought she looked a little older, a little paler.

"Danger? Why do you say that? There has been danger everywhere. War isn't a parlour game."

"Well—because the Australians have been in some especially dangerous places, haven't they? In some big and hazardous things, with Death keeping step ever beside them——" She broke off with a shudder.

It seemed so strange to talk of Death there, in that brilliant room, with its happy, laughing company. Down the room the young, slim girl in white and silver was laughing so merrily.

"Death stalks on every battlefield," he said gravely. "In France as well as Gallipoli."

There was a little silence. Across it broke a rapturous voice.

"And dear Matilda is having the time of her life. She says Paris is still bright enough to satisfy *anyone!* That you would never think war was on at all. She is one of the V.A.D.'s at the Influential Hospital, don't you know, so she should know all about it."

A lazy drawl, with hidden meaning in it, said: "She certainly looks very sweet in that get-up of hers; white kid-boots, too, eh? Does anyone happen to know if there are diamonds in the heels?"

"How absurd!" A laugh that tinkled like empty glass. "Of course there wouldn't be!"

"But why? Aren't they the very latest in fashion? Does she think the Tommies might pick them out when she wasn't looking?"

Everybody laughed. Someone protested, "But dear Matilda doesn't nurse *Tommies.* It is a hospital for officers only."

"Ah! I see!" The drawl had a note of contempt in it. "I had forgotten that the Tommies have nothing to do with winning the war."

"I wonder what the real nurses think," said Mrs. Marcourt, in a low voice.

"*I* know," said the General grimly; and somewhat wearily he added: "Enid, child, is this what we are fighting for? To keep the cotton-woolled thoughts of the bric-à-brac woman intact, with all her distorted ideas of the meaning of life, the relations of the classes? Good God! are we fighting for only such things?"

She lifted her face; her eyes were very grave and very sweet.

"No! We, too—the sisters and mothers of men who made England—are fighting for England, for our own country, for the dear deep things that are of England. This is but the froth on the surface, the decadent weed that has sprung up from wasted ground: You have seen neglected fruit trees, how the suckers grew up from the old roots, in a new, strange growth of their own, barren of good fruit."

"But the suckers kill the old trees in time, Enid, and so, too, the old great aristocracy will die out. I don't mean the beer-and-bun aristocracy that would buy a place in the heavens as well as the earth. But the old, fine people, with their ideas of honour."

"They are living in an aristocracy yet to be," she

said. "The aristocracy of the incorruptible class that has left its suburban homes and gone out into the trenches, and is writing the imperishable history of England on the field of Flanders. Scotland wrote it large at Loos, Ireland at Festubert, Australia at Suvla Bay. Even our Bond Street Brigade has not failed us." She ran rapidly over a list of names, well known in most cases.

He made a gesture of contempt.

"Yes, they are at the front. But those of whom we read so much in the papers—Lord Somebody's sons, and Lady Something's nephews—what are they doing? I can tell you. Running messages like errand-boys, dressed up in staff uniforms, comfortably out of the firing-zone. The Turkey-carpet and the Armchair Brigade, I call them. I tell you, Enid, that it is these popinjays who are always in the limelight. But the brave boys who have died in the trenches, like the Master of Kinnaird, for instance, what of him and his kind? A line in the paper, a name here and there in the casualty lists, graves over which alien feet may tramp. Yet these are men who scorned the soft jobs. They died in the trenches, facing the foe, and Kinnaird died as a Kinnaird would wish to die." He brought his hand down on the table. His voice trembled, for he had loved the lad of whom he spoke.

"Enid, I am an old man, and perhaps I am an old fool, but had I my own way, I'd run every staff *aide* into the trenches, where he is needed; and I'd use one trained boy scout for every six of them. I've been through it. And I know. I'd lay down my life for one of my soldiers, but for one of these staff supers. *No!*"

She was silent. She who unostentatiously played her woman's part in the war understood only too well all that he meant.

"Now, Territt is different," said the old General. "You won't catch him content to flutter aimlessly around headquarters, getting under one's feet and in one's road. You'll find Territt where we found Kinnaird, and other men like him."

She went quite pale. "You think—have you a premonition——"

"Premonition," growled the General cheerfully. "I'm not talking about premonitions, although God knows we could do with some second sight in this business. But we'll find Territt useful." He looked around the room at the strong sprinkling of military men present. "To think," he added in grim admiration, "that every man jack of us here, for all our laughter, has one ear listening for a summons that may come from the W.O. at any moment."

"Where will Captain Territt go?" she asked.

"I think," said the General, and he lowered his voice, "he will go to Kut."

The plaintive voice of his neighbour, the pretty, flirtatious widow, intervened. She tapped him lightly with her plumed fan.

"You haven't talked to me for ages," she complained. "I never knew you could be so interested in any one of our sex. Won't you talk to poor little me for a while?"

"With pleasure!" He turned with courteous

alacrity. "What shall we talk about? Of Matilda and her playing at nursing, and having all her *lingerie* embroidered with red crosses in rubies? Isn't that the latest?"

She gave a little squeak, like a startled mouse. "How witty of you!" She tapped him with her fan again. "And how naughty of you! Matilda would die if she heard you. And Kate would have a fit! But I wanted to ask you if I couldn't be a V.A.D. nurse—not exactly a nurse, you know, dear man. I would much rather be the matron. That is if a matron can do just as she likes?"

"Quite so! Would you like," he asked carefully, "to be the boss of the whole show? A super-superintendent, or something like that?"

She turned a delighted, delicately-powdered face towards him. "Why, yes! It sounds splendid." She leaned towards him eagerly. "Do tell me! What are the duties?"

"Oh, nothing at all!" he replied, with a wave of his hand that swept serious nursing into a limbo of its own. "All you have to do is first and foremost to get the right costume. The most fashionable *costumière!* You would, of course, see to that!"

She clapped her hands. "I know the *very* place. The very creature! She has perfectly rippin' ideas."

"And then," explained the General carefully, and lifting his port and watching its red glow against the electric light with an enigmatical light in his rheumy old eyes and a quizzical expression on his gnarled face, "then you embroider a huge red cross on it, or have one dangling from your neck. It is not yet definitely decided, I believe, which is the more fashionable."

She was quite breathless. "Oh! that will be too lovely. Just imagine it!"

"I can imagine it. I've seen it," the General admitted. He sipped his wine. "If you have the cross in rubies I believe it is more effective."

Her eyes sparkled. Her little vain, powdered face peered up at him. To have a real live officer, and a General at that, who always caused a crowd in the street when he passed, to give one such advice! She ran over the list of calls she really must pay to-morrow. She saw in imagination the interested circle that she could gather about her with a *résumé* of these very conversations. Generals were just generals—before the war, of course; now they were a combination of George and the Dragon and Michael the Archangel in one. It was really too lovely for words.

"A ruby cross? How perfectly sweet! And what else? Do hurry and tell me what else, for the butler is bringing something that looks like the fag-end of things. And I have to go on somewhere else immediately after. What next would I have to do—with the nursing, I mean?"

"The chief thing is to get your photograph in the papers." He told her this quite solemnly. "It's no use, you know, unless you go out of the country to nurse the wounded, for, of course, there is no romantic interest in nursing them in England. And you must always remember to have your photo taken on any and every opportunity; the halfpenny pictorials have grown to expect it."

He leaned back in his chair while a servant dexterously removed his plate and substituted another.

"If you can't become famous, become notorious. At least that is what the ultra-smart believe. And I give you this suggestion free, gratis, and for nothing. Take your own pet photographer with you. It saves a lot of trouble. Then deluge the papers with photographs. The favourite positions, always garbed in your nursing attire and the Red Cross well in evidence, are many, but some of them have their drawbacks."

"But won't that cost a lot?" she asked anxiously, after a surreptitious glance up at him. He seemed too serious to be serious!

He shrugged his shoulders.

"It is advertisement. What more do the modern angels of mercy want?"

She frowned, flashed an inquiring and more thoughtful glance at him, but he was eating the sweet quite calmly.

"You mentioned there were certain drawbacks. What are they, then?"

"In the photography line? Well, for instance, one of the favourite positions is to have oneself posed between rows of beds with wounded soldiers, or among a group of nurses."

"I should like that. What are the drawbacks to either of those poses?"

"Well, it depends. The nurses should be compelled to turn their faces sideways. In fact, I suggest that only their backs be turned to the camera. So with the soldiers."

"But why?" She was frankly amazed. She paused with the sweet suspended on the slender silver fork she held.

"Because the eyes of legitimate nurses and soldiers are apt to mirror their thoughts, my dear lady."

She pouted. "Now you are making fun of me."

"I am not, I assure you. But I want you to see the side of the thing as the people see it, as the real nurses, not the *poseurs,* see it, as the wounded soldiers, racked with pain, see it."

He was going out to the Front again at any moment. Perhaps even here at the dinner-table a ring at the door might herald a summons. So he spoke his mind bluntly, albeit he was always more or less blunt in speech.

"My dear lady, I regret to say there is little or no real charity in nursing such as you want to go in for, and many of our mutual friends are already doing, or misdoing. Nor is there any real charity in these flag days. They give something to charity I know. One can be thankful for that. But I know only too well that the fluttering after a new sensation is behind it all. Do you think that the masses of the people don't realise that the dressing-up for the part is of more interest to most of the promoters than the actual part in the charity itself?"

"Oh! the *masses!*" she said, and her lip curled a little. They were outside her life, a pale, distant blur in the scheme of humanity. "Why should we care what they think?"

"You should care," said the General quietly, "because it is the Masses who are making the destiny of England. It is the Masses who will save England. It is, incidentally, for the vast auditorium of the Masses that the notoriety-seeking women prance about on their gilded stage, and hover around the doors of ha'penny newspapers flourishing their latest photographs."

"I believe you are one of those dreadful iconoclasts, Socialists!" she cried. "The war has changed you, surely."

The General was not exactly a religious man in the accepted sense of the term, but he spoke devoutly now. "Pray God," he said, "that He will change all of us."

She thought it very plebeian for anyone to talk about God at a dinner-table. God was for Sundays, for such churches as St. Paul's at Knightsbridge, or any fashionable church where in the hour between a late breakfast and an interesting lunch one could devoutly trail one's best garments along a cool, dim aisle and kneel, because kneeling had now become fashionable, on a dainty and often exquisitely monogrammed cushion.

And sometimes the minister, or the dear canon, or the dearest bishop, would come to lunch, and be treated with charming patronage, or be gushed over according to one's mood or the dear, devout thing's position.

But for a General to drag God into a most interesting discussion on nursing, or across a flirtation that at the beginning had flared up most promisingly, e end fizzled out as if it fell into wet mud! :d reflectively and a little resentfully to the :lba.

', one did not know what the world was , nowadays!

CHAPTER II

Straws on the Stream

THE shallow, pleasant brook of conversation was still babbling lightly over the stones.

Its thin stream began to widen out, to become more discursive, a little vague and wandering, for dinner was coming to an end. At any moment Mrs. Marcourt's grey eyes would make a quick inventory of the table, and then her slightest nod to the women present would result in the room's being left to the men folk. George Marcourt had the reputation of being a fine after-dinner speaker. People had been known to say that it was the only time he could speak. But for the most part he was amusing enough. And always he was good-natured and jovial, hospitable to a degree.

On Mrs. Marcourt had fallen in these last few minutes of grace, one of those inexplicable, detached moods that would descend on her sometimes when at her gayest, at times when light and laughter and music rioted round her, and other people's feet beat in rhythm to the pulsing tune of the moment.

Yet her lips smiled and her head turned at the first word from any of her guests, but all the while her eyes brooded behind their dark-lashed, half-closed lids, and her thoughts went soaring out and away, through decorously drawn blinds and the prim, closed windows of convention.

Once or twice those eyes, very grey, almost too large in the setting of her pale, rather thin face, lifted from the red glow of the roses, the gleam of silver, the flash of jewels, and looked instead at the flowing river which the darkest blinds might not hide from the eyes of her mind.

Mrs. George Marcourt was not pretty in the accepted sense of the term; she had hair of a wonderful coppery shade, that curled about her face, and she was slim and tall and pale. That was the first impression one gained of her. And then one saw that her eyes were beautiful, extraordinarily so at times, for their colouring seemed to change with the hue of the gown she wore. She wore grey to-night, grey with a cluster of violets at her breast—and her eyes had that same soft grey sheen and shimmer of light in them.

Her face was uncommonly sweet in expression rather than pretty. Between her and that lovely young creature in white and silver at the far end of the table near Captain Territt, there was, for example, a distinct difference. And yet, strangely enough, it was on Mrs. Marcourt's face that one's eyes would perhaps rest longest.

The last eddy of a discussion was whirling about the table. It swept everyone but Mrs. Marcourt into its whirlpool. She was content, it seemed, to sit there smiling and listening, while confused fragments of the discussion of how to run a war were in progress. Everybody, of course, knew all about it, and how to do it, except the Government! That was distinctly understood.

"A lot of old men who ought to be in bath-chairs," someone described them, with a note of contempt.

"Or in heaven, playing harps," added someone.

Someone else interposed, "Some of them are playing the Jews' harp as it is," and a chorus of laughter followed the sally. It was the thing to abuse the Government, especially after dinner, when one's ego waxed large and important, and one flung out brilliant suggestions, any one of which might stop the war at an instant's notice—and again might not!

Mrs. Marcourt was looking at the amber curtains, a wrinkle between her brows, as if she were worried slightly over the way they were draped, as if she did not like their arrangement, one would have said. But she was thinking only that there was a blurred path of light on the water, reflected downwards from the hooded lamps on the river bank; dark, monk-like lights with cowled heads, peering into the Thames with its muttered litany.

The lights were strung on the water like rosary beads. The dark bridge flung a great cross of shadow. Even as she watched, a huge black shape came silently into view from under the farthest bridge. Unlighted, with no herald of its warning, it drifted by. She heard the muffled sound of the engines, like padded feet in a forest. She watched it go slowly by, blotting out even the blurred lights.

"Like Fate," said Enid Marcourt, rather wearily, and she turned for a moment quickly to the guest at her left, Captain Spane, thinking he had spoken. But he was looking down the table thoughtfully, perhaps at his friend Territt, or that pretty young creature in white and silver. It was because he was Philip Territt's friend, she remembered, that she had asked young Spane at the last moment to complete the dinner-party. Spane, on a night five years ago, had come with Philip Territt to say good-bye.

Mrs. Marcourt's small dinners could always be depended on as a success. One met the right people, one always sat next to somebody who held one's own views and agreed with one in every particular. Perhaps the true secret of her success as a hostess was that Enid Marcourt incidentally sank her own individuality. Modern hostesses as a rule are not content to do that. The desire to dominate, to preen oneself in one's own carefully-chosen limelight, is too big a temptation nowadays. Less intellectually brilliant women than Enid Marcourt undoubtedly was perhaps found that it was only at their own tables, with the polite listeners roped in, that they could hold forth on the pet topic of the moment, and promulgate their mysterious and constantly-changing doctrines and variegated ideas.

Enid Marcourt had begun by tossing the ball of conversation from one to the other, quietly, but so dexterously that one began immediately and eagerly to talk to one's fellow-guest about it, just as if it had been one's own idea and that of no one else. And perhaps on these occasions no one enjoyed Mrs. Marcourt's little dinner more than Mrs. Marcourt herself. For she was left minding the goal-posts of interest, with the players far in the centre of the field, and George acting as jovial, if rather prosy umpire.

The Gates of Kut

The dinner to-night was on the surface just like other dinners at Marcourt Place, successful, bright, cosy and intimate in the dark-panelled, comfortable room, with the world outside the barred windows, and a pleasant company of well-pleased people within. Even the pretty but *passée* widow had forgotten her momentary displeasure, and was talking eagerly to the General.

Yet it was not an ordinary dinner, after all. The prearranged order of things had been upset. The fourteen people invited had eventually numbered eighteen. The fat lady in black and the girl in white and silver, obliging mother and pretty daughter who was just out, had been telephoned for at the last moment. Mrs. Marcourt had said that one or two soldier-friends of her husband had come back from India. When Mrs. Byndham had asked their names, torn between desire to be at one of *the* quiet little dinners of the season and just resentment that she had not been included in the earlier list, and when her hostess-to-be had said, "Captain Spane and Captain Territt," one of these names brought an immediate answer. Mrs. Byndham had been more than pleased to accept Mrs. Marcourt's invitation.

So, at the last moment, an extra leaf had been added to the hospitable table. At eight o'clock that night you would not have known that at five o'clock the whole plan of dinner had been upset. Nor would you have known now that the whole plan of a life, of two lives and maybe three, was also upset and disarranged, flung out of their usual reckoning. Who knew if ever they would settle quietly in their old places again? Tragedy was in the air.

At a quarter to five o'clock of that afternoon George Marcourt had gone to his club. At five o'clock he bellowed into the 'phone an intimation to his wife that Territt was home from India—good old Territt, mind you—brown as a berry, just tumbled into the club. He was makin' all sorts of excuses why he couldn't come to dinner, to a quiet little dinner at Marcourt Place.

Would not she, Enid, insist, yes, insist, that Territt should come? Marcourt roared. Of course, he must come! Had not Marcourt Place been like Territt's own home before he went to India? What need had he to stand on ceremony? Dash it all, friendship was friendship!

All this through the 'phone, while Enid Marcourt leaned against the wall holding the receiver nervelessly, only half hearing. But she heard one thing very plainly. Captain Philip Territt, who had gone away for ever and a day, was back in England. Marcourt called her twice before he heard. When she answered, her voice sounded so far away, so muffled and strange, that Marcourt in his blustering impatience shook the receiver and bellowed execrations at the unoffending exchange.

"Worst system in the world!" he stormed. "Never saw the like in my life. Always something going wrong. What do those attendants do, I wonder? Sleep and read penny novelettes all day. Until the villain's dead or murdered or the heroine gets married, one can't get an answer!"

The shaking and the storming had apparently done the telephone good. Presumably the villain was dead, and the hero triumphant, for Marcourt heard his wife's voice again, quite clearly this time.

It said, "Halloa! Yes, George! Territt? Oh! you mean Captain Philip Territt, who went to India some years ago? Yes! I would be pleased if he would dine with us. Tell him there is just a small party of us, fourteen or so."

Marcourt thought his wife's voice rather cold. Perhaps she was tired. She worked hard on these Red Cross organisations. He flung instructions into the telephone.

"*You* ask him, Enid. *Insist* on his coming to us," Marcourt was saying. "Tell him he *must* come. Yes! Your voice sounds tired, dear" (a little anxiously); "hope you haven't been overdoing things. I'll send Territt to the 'phone now. Wish you could have a peep at him. Brown as a berry, lean as the kine that came into Egypt. Or did they go out? Anyhow, he says he's as fit as a fiddle. But he's gone a bit grey. These young chaps don't wear as well as us old married men, after all. Here y'are, Territt, Mrs. Marcourt wants to speak to you."

She told herself dumbly that it was the last thing in the world she desired to do. She had not answered Territt's call as quickly and calmly as she had intended. At the first sound of his grave, rather quiet voice, she shrank back against the wall and closed her eyes as if in pain.

She heard his voice again, quieter than of old,

but unmistakable. He said, "Halloa! Halloa! Are you there? Halloa!"

"Shake the damn thing!" advised Marcourt. He began to fume again. "Rotten system! No use talking to them! Pay in advance, and then grin and bear it!"

"I think it is all right now," said Territt quietly. He did not shake the receiver. "Probably the wires are crossed. Ah, is that you, Mrs. Marcourt? Yes, Philip Territt speaking. How are you? So glad to hear it. Quite wonderful weather, isn't it? Yes, I just got back, and George pounced on me straight away. Thanks so much for your invitation! It is good of you. I really should not inflict myself on you at such short notice."

She said, "I will be so pleased if you would dine with us. Yes, come home with George. I'm sorry I won't be able to see you until dinner-time, but this happens to be a day crowded with appointments. But you'll understand." Despite herself there had come a little shake in her voice.

"Yes," said Philip Territt. "I think I—understand." Something in that dear, well-remembered voice gripped him by the throat.

There came a brief silence. "Then we shall expect you, Captain Territt." He heard the clang of the receiver on its hook ere he could answer. But he answered as if she were still there.

Perhaps Captain Territt had the gift of imagination, too—after all, it is more common than one supposes—for he thought he saw Mrs. Marcourt leaning against the oak-panelled wall by the telephone.

He had even a premonition that it was in the hall at Marcourt Place, that old-fashioned hall with its deep, tawny carpet, and polished floor and dark-hued walls. He wondered whether she wore that leaf-green dress in which he had last seen her, with her little shining head bent over a deep bronze bowl full of yellow daffodils.

Because of those important appointments that crowded her afternoon, as she had said, he did not see Mrs. Marcourt until the moment the guests were due, when she came into the drawing-room, where George and he already were.

The flush of exertion still burned brightly in her cheeks. She talked hurriedly of the day's doings, asked him many questions about India, and rippled on without waiting for answers to them. She was very gay and feverishly bright, but Philip saw with a shock that she had grown much thinner. For all her laughter wistfulness clung to her.

George Marcourt was very fond of his wife and never chary of hiding the fact. He stood by her, leaning his back against the mantelshelf. His hair was still dark at the temples and towards the back of his neck, the two places where he had any hair to boast of. He was short and growing very stout. His waistcoat had a most comfortable, well-fed appearance. He was the epitome of prosperity.

George spoke about the telephone system at some length. With him discussion developed into wordy lectures. They were both very interested in his description, and he waxed large and important on the question. It was, indeed, a very nice feeling to know that your listeners were so intent on what you were saying that they looked at you and you only, and were too engrossed in your eloquence to reply. It gave one a fine sense of satisfaction and incidentally of one's own importance in the scheme of a badly organised world that has very few such important people in it.

George was a bore, without doubt, sometimes. When he rode a topic he used spurs, and flogged it past the winning-post, dismounting to acknowledge the admiring, if occasionally feeble, plaudits of the crowd. He was a weighty adjunct, in more senses than one, on many a platform. George, then, had his faults; but he had none of the faults with which, were he but a character in a novel, one might endow him. He should have drank heavily, have neglected or beaten his wife, have shown a *penchant* for the footlight fairies, but instead he did none of these things.

He was simply an honest, prosy, English gentleman, plethoric in person, dogmatic in debate, but intensely loyal.

If George had only been different—and at that Territt pulled himself up with a sense of shock. Good God! What was he thinking? George was his best friend.

Then the bell tangled in the hall, and the telephone system was banished with a wave of Marcourt's plump white hand. People began to surge into the room, laughing and chattering. The stout, elderly lady in black, after greeting Mrs. Marcourt, made straight for Territt, followed by a fluttering, blushing vision in a white and silver creation almost too elaborate for the occasion. They had met once in India, it appeared.

"Such a surprise!" Mrs. Byndham said afterwards to Mrs. Marcourt. "We met at one of the hill stations, you know! Fancy, Captain Territt never mentioned that he knew you, though we talked of heaps of home people."

She laughed in a pleased way as she looked over at her daughter, to whom the said Captain Territt was talking so earnestly.

Mrs. Marcourt glanced involuntarily in their direction.

"I always say we saved his life," Mrs. Byndham resumed cheerfully. "He was ill, down with low fever. Wretched thing that everyone seems to get at Kasmapur. Beatrice and I volunteered to nurse him! Of course, Beatrice did not do any of the actual nursing. Only cheered him up when he was better, you see."

"I see," said Mrs. Marcourt.

"Then we met him again in Australia. He went for a trip there afterwards; to the Buffalo Mountains. Wonderful and wildly fascinating place, you know. If it were only in England or the Continent we could make it the rage. And we met him there. Quite a coincidence, wasn't it?"

"Quite," agreed Mrs. Marcourt politely. She knew Mrs. Byndham well, so that she could understand the coincidence. Coincidences of this nature were apt to loom large on Sophie Byndham's horizon. Sophie was like the fatalistic fisherman who, when playing his line in a satisfactory pool, would consider it a coincidence that the bait and the fish met at the same instant.

Then dinner began. Now it was ending, and Mrs. Marcourt lifted her head, but no one was looking in her direction at the moment. The conversation still raged about the Government policy. She waited, dumbly, a trifle impatiently. She was so weary, she said. When they had all trooped out into the night, and the door was barred, she would go into her own room and close the door, and sleep—sleep. . . . She told herself, very wearily, that at twenty-seven, when youth is gone, one is too wise to stay awake and stare into the dark and think. Think? That way madness lay. Five years ago she had given up thinking.

She turned with a start to Captain Spane, who had called her twice before she heard.

"I'm so sorry! The girl in white? Where?" She followed the direction of his eyes vaguely, as if she became aware for the first time that there was only one white gown among those soft satins. "Oh, she is a Byndham—Beatrice Byndham. She is just out, the last of the family——" She stopped abruptly; she had almost found herself adding—"on the market." People were so apt to use the term.

"She seems very sweet," he said. He was an ordinary-looking man, fair-skinned, with nothing very distinctive about him, except his eyeglass, and the moustache, like a moth-eaten tooth-brush, affected by officers.

"She is very sweet—and young," Mrs. Marcourt said. She sighed involuntarily. "She is just at the age to enjoy life. And she will. Unless she marries too soon."

"Does marriage put an end, then, to joy?" he asked her, laughing. He turned to her. "Now just fancy you, one of the happiest married women one can meet, talking like that."

She had laughed, too, albeit somewhat nervously, and caught hérself up. "I was trying to be smart, you see," she said lightly. "It is the fashion to perpetrate epigrams. Does not every love story end with a peal of wedding bells and the scent of orange blossoms?"

He nodded. He was looking again at Miss Byndham.

"I thought her face was familiar," he remarked. "I remember now. I saw her photo."

"Yes? She sent it to me only recently. It is very sweet. That large picture on one of the tables in my drawing-room you mean, of course, Captain Spàne?"

"No, I didn't see it here"; and then, confidentially, "I saw it in old Territt's digs. in India." His eyes went back to Beatrice as if to make quite sure. "Yes, it is she without a doubt."

Mrs. Marcourt did not answer. Her face changed in some indescribable way. When he turned again the smile still hovered about her mouth. But it was not in her eyes. She was touching with the tips of her fingers the little pile of crumbled bread that she had broken earlier in the evening. Her fingers mechanically formed it into a mound like a grave.

"Is the engagement announced yet?" Spane asked

casually. "I haven't seen Territt for over six months, you know. He didn't take his leave."

After a little while Mrs. Marcourt said, "I had not heard. George would know about the engagement, of course. I haven't had time for more than a word with Captain Territt since he arrived. One's days are so crowded now! So many things to do. I just got back before dinner." She launched forth into an explanation of how busy one's days could be. She did not say that she had been sitting in Hyde Park for two hours of that day watching the children under the trees, the riders in the Row, with eyes that never saw anything. Then the Park began to empty, a mist to curl among the trees, and one knew it was time to go home, that one must catch up the dropped stitch and weave it into the pattern, lest all go awry and the labour of years be in vain.

"Yes, your husband tells me you have been working specially hard. You are certainly looking much paler than when I saw you last. The war is telling on the women as well as the men. It is harder, perhaps, in some ways, for those who stand and wait than for those who serve."

"Yes." Her fingers made and unmade and remade again the mound of crumbs, and then, "Captain Territt and Miss Byndham are engaged? I wonder whether they will be married before he goes to the Front. War marriages are very fashionable," she added, laughing lightly. "One's friends call on one in the morning, drag one off in the afternoon as a spectator to her or his wedding, and expect one to be waving a handkerchief at a troop train the following morning. Now, I hope that, if Captain Territt is going to do that, he will give us at least a day's grace, for I have three weddings on my hands to-morrow."

Spane shook his head. But a woman's thoughts always raced ahead.

"I don't think there's anything so definitely settled as that, Mrs. Marcourt. After all, it's little more than guesswork on my part, a sort of mental arithmetic, you know. Adding up little things."

"Putting two and two together—matrimonially," she said, with a twinkle. She laughed, caught at last the eyes of her guests, and with a nod rose. A new note flashed into her laughter, a glint of colour.

In the pleasant tumult of departure she laughed often. Her cheeks were flushed, and she was very gay.

One of her girl-friends patted her hand. "Dear Enid! You are looking better to-night than I've seen you for a long time. Always wear pearl-grey. It suits you. I felt inclined once or twice to stand up at the table and begin an oration to you. 'My pearl-pale-Margaret' sort of thing. But you were flirting with the General."

Mrs. Marcourt shook her head, and laughed. "Di! You are incorrigible. The poor man only turned to me when he remembered that famous advice to bachelors and widowers."

"And that, my dear?"

"'Samivel, bevare of vidders.'"

Di laughed. "She will catch him yet, you'll see!"

They all trooped out at last, with a word here, a

light jest there—flung back over a white, delicately-powdered shoulder from which the cloak half slipped. Most of them were going on somewhere else. The war had not altogether wiped, like a wet sponge, the gaiety and the joy of living off the slate. There was less glare and ostentation. The blinds were down, that was all.

Mrs. Marcourt was not going on somewhere else. Neither she nor her husband was to be found among the gaiety-seeking crowd to whom the war meant only darkened lights in the streets, which were rather boring, but after all concerned the chauffeur more than the occupants in the snug, roomy car; a lack of men at theatres, restaurants, and receptions—which set the heads of the chaperons shaking dolorously and their eyes gleaming in predatory fashion; and the prices of commodities rising. One could always economise in the basement. For upstairs there were war profits as well as peace profits. Some incomes went up instead of down during wars.

Truly someone suffered. The poorer classes, as a matter of course. The middle classes were reputed to be finding things especially hard. Now and again one met a crank who talked about it at dinners. It sometimes made a most interesting discussion. It was as fascinating, really, as peering into a fashionable doctor's laboratory and seeing those funny sorts of things that apparently grow out of nothing, and are quite too fascinating to be diseases.

But this is drifting away from Marcourt Place, for all that it has some bearing on it and on the people who lived there.

Mrs. Marcourt, then, had said good night to her departing guests. She had socially, for all intents and purposes, said good night to the few men who lingered in the dining-room. She could hear George, who was speaking a little thickly, for he was fond of good wine, and the deep murmur of answering voices.

Enid Marcourt lingered in the hall for a moment. She was thinking that at the War Office the hum of work went on, like the war in the trenches, men working like bees in the hive. Outside in the darkened streets shadowy figures passing by would look up at the darker shadow of the War Office looming out of the night. And they would say, as no doubt George was saying and a million other Georges in the world, how they would run the war and incidentally the universe.

But behind closed blinds a swarm of men worked in silence, men whose names would never flare forth from the press, small bee-men, whose brains yielded the God-given honey of intellect.

The men over them, the politicians, stood in the limelight. The bee-men worked on and the politicians gracefully purloined the honey from the hives. What would you? The politician could take his week-end in comfort, could snore in the lethal chamber of the House of Commons, could even get out of the country for good and all while the war was waged, and in reality you wouldn't miss him. The bee-men would work on just the same, the great hives would buzz with industry, with labour that went from the day into night, and throughout the long night into day again.

But you must have a plate on which to put your honey. You must have a figurehead on which to drape the laurels of success. If politicians are, after all, little more than dummy figures in a shop-window, at least, as the Americans put it, you can hang the goods on them.

No one knew this better than Mrs. Marcourt. She was the daughter-in-law of a once famous politician, whose fathers had been politicians before him. She had a husband who was aspiring to be one and would be one as soon as a safe seat was found for him.

As George Marcourt was saying now, "Confound it all! No seat is safe in these times! Look at Pemberton Billing! Look at the men who are following Billing! I tell you that soon there won't be a seat left in the House if we're not careful. One doesn't know where this sort of thing may end. God knows, it may result in a Labour Government eventually! One's got to hang on like grim death and play the game."

"And the present game," said Spane dryly, "seems to be known as 'Follow my leader.' There's too much of the sheep-track about the House of Commons for my liking."

The smoking-room door was open, and his voice floated out. As Mrs. Marcourt stood lingering, hesitant in the hall, the door bell rang shrilly. Out of the shadows a manservant moved and opened it. A messenger stood there. He said crisply, interrogatively, "Territt? Spane?"

The manservant answered in the affirmative, took the letters and signed for them.

Mrs. Marcourt held her hand out for them, looked at them, and gave them back to him. They were marked "Immediate." The War Office seal was unmistakable.

"Take them to the smoking-room, Jevons!" she said, and then she turned quickly and passed along the corridor. But she did not go far. The door of the nearest room was open and she entered it.

It was half picture-gallery, half music-room. Deep-seated chairs were scattered round, and she sank into one of them. The yellow-shaded lights blazed only in the centre of the room. They hurt her eyes. Her fingers groped for the gilt knob in the wall near her. The lights died instantly.

In the smoking-room George's authoritative voice had stopped. There was a confused murmur of voices, following on the significant silence when Jevons handed those sealed letters to the two men.

She heard Spane cry excitedly, "Hurray!" and then Territt's voice.

It said distinctly, "Report in the morning at ten! Leave the same evening!"

And then George's voice, "Mesopotamia, of course."

And then Territt again, non-committal, quiet. "I do not know. One can never be sure, but I hope so." And again, "Townshend! God bless him!"

A babble of voices rose. They took up the question of whether a relief force could reach Townshend in time, whether the man there with his remnant of army, in a loop of the marshy Tigris, with the sun blazing on the dreary monotony of the sandhills, with the invisible wall of treachery about Kut-el-Amara, could hold out.

And in the music-room Mrs. Marcourt saw that scene as plainly as if she were there. She had seen it ever since the moment when the old white-haired General said, "I think it will be Kut."

Following on that, from the open smoking-room door came words that seemed cruel in their relentless dictation:

"Leaving to-morrow evening for a destination unknown."

And at that moment her husband, followed by Territt and Spane and the General, who was just going, came out. Her husband called her at the foot of the stairs.

"Enid! Where are you, dear?"

Her fingers groped for the gilt knob, found it, hesitated, then forced it upwards. The light flashed out from the central cluster, under the pale yellow of the silken shades.

"I am here," said Mrs. Marcourt in her quiet voice.

CHAPTER III

Masks and Faces

MARCOURT came bustling into the music-room, followed by the two men. The General had gone. They found Mrs. Marcourt down at the far end of the room, where the great organ towered to the ceiling, its gilded pipes gleaming in the electric light. The music-cabinet was open, and Mrs. Marcourt, kneeling by it, had some sheets of music in her hand as if she had been searching for a particular song; but she laid them down immediately at their entrance and came forward to greet them. Marcourt told her the news. Both Spane and Territt were off to-morrow evening.

Her quiet eyes, dark-shadowed as if with the fatigue of the day, went from one face to another. She smiled and said to them in her level voice:

"That is what one must expect nowadays, is it not? A sudden call, and the destination unknown."

Spane plunged boyishly into an answer. "Officially," he said, "we don't know where we are going. But of course we do know. They gave us an inkling this morning."

"And Captain Territt and you will go out together," she smiled at the boy with something of maternal and protective tenderness in her eyes. "That will be nice for you both."

Someone came with a message for Marcourt and he bustled away.

"Were you playing?" asked Captain Territt abruptly. He looked from her to the gilt pipes of the great organ climbing into shadow.

She shook her head. "No! But I had promised Miss Byndham some old songs I had which she liked. They are out of print now."

"Won't you sing for us?" asked Spane eagerly. "Or are you too tired?"

She did say she was rather tired. Captain Territt pushed forward a chair at once and begged her to sit down.

"Forgive me," he said. "But somehow one never associates weariness with you. Once——" and then he stopped abruptly and crimsoned. But Mrs. Marcourt had her face turned to Captain Spane.

"Will you do something else that will not tire you, and that would give us more pleasure, if possible, than hearing you sing?" Spane was saying in his impulsive way. He was but a stripling, after all, very boyish at times when he forgot that he was Captain Spane, for promotion was rapid and he was very young. "It is something special."

"Am I to promise," she asked, "before I am to know what it is? Something special? Now what could that possibly be? I haven't any little parlour-tricks."

He leaned forward eagerly. "It is just to come and sit with us in the smoking-den for an hour, Mrs. Marcourt. You see, we are privileged folk for to-night. This time to-morrow Territt and I may be out of England. When we were last here, it seems just yesterday, I remember how your husband and Territt and I used often to stay behind after dinner, and how sometimes you used to sit and have a cigarette with us. It was ever so chummy."

She shook her head gently. "But I am five years older, a more settled and more serious person." She laughed a little breathlessly. "You couldn't expect the president of the Womanly Girls' Society to do such things." She looked from young Spane to Territt, who had got up and was studying a full-length picture that hung on the wall. She addressed her laughing question to him. "It would hardly do, would it, Captain Territt?"

"Now, Phil *would* approve, Mrs. Marcourt," Spane broke in triumphantly. "For I remember his once, when we were talking of England, speaking of it, and how cosy and homey the den seemed when you were in it."

She looked at young Spane oddly. Somehow her lips smiled.

"Then you did think of—of us, in India?" she addressed her question directly to him.

Spane nodded. "Why, this is the very last house one would forget. George Marcourt is such a good sort, the very best of good fellows. Lots of folk must have told you that, Mrs. Marcourt——"

She said, "Yes! Lots of folk have told me that," and then, "I am glad to hear you speak like that of him, and to—to think that you had not forgotten us."

Spane blundered on while Territt gazed at the

picture and Mrs. Marcourt looked down at her hands and wondered how long George would be.

"And of course you were always so good to us. Why, we practically lived here, didn't we, Territt? It was only natural that we should speak of Marcourt Place. Now, Territt, come and do your piece! Tell of that dark night when we were hemmed in the hills, and the treacherous tribe from Banshari nearly finished us—and what you said about Marcourt Place."

Mrs. Marcourt went a little white. But she did not speak. Territt swung abruptly back.

"Don't talk rot, Spane!" he said. "We got through all right. That is all one remembers."

"That's old Phil all over," reiterated Spane affectionately. "Never will admit his share in anything. But the War Office knows. And that's why Captain Philip Territt is not to be left kicking his heels in England when there's big work ahead."

Marcourt came to the door at that moment and called Territt. Someone had come unexpectedly who wished to see Territt. They went off together to George's sanctum.

"We won't be long, Enid," Marcourt said over his shoulder. "We'll get rid of him in no time. Are you coming into the den for a chat?"

His wife nodded. When they had quite gone she said to Spane:

"But you didn't tell me, after all, what—what happened at Banshari."

He told her then of all the hours of suspense, the stiff fighting towards the grey dawn, of the handful of troops whose courage blazed up to heights of heroism almost unparalleled even in the history of India.

Mrs. Marcourt listened. She waited, too, for something that had not yet been said. At last it came.

"It was that night," said Spane, and he spoke now in a hushed voice, for the scene rose vividly before him, "in the darkest hour, when all seemed lost, when it seemed impossible that we could break through that overwhelming horde, that Territt spoke of this house and the hours we had spent here together. Curiously enough, he seldom speaks of anybody or anything, as you know. He is always reserved. But I suppose in an hour like that, when in one second one may face eternity, one's thoughts go to one's own country. Mine went to Scotland, to puir auld Scotland. Sir Walter's ditty was running incongruously through my mind. You know it, of course:

> "Ere the King's crown go down there are crowns to be broke,
> So let each Cavalier who loves honour and me
> Come follow the bonnets of Bonnie Dundee."

Strange how that should ring through one's mind."

She agreed in a hurried affirmative.

"And old Phil must have thought of England, not of the horde waiting, of dark forms creeping near, ready to pounce, but of London—and here."

"And—here?" she said.

"Yes! He said only a few words, as if they were involuntarily wrung from him. They were, 'and I can see the smoking-room plainly, and the four of us sitting there, and how quickly time passed——' Queer, wasn't it?"

"Very." She began to laugh, fought against hysteria, and rose. "I suppose that means, as he is fond of his old pipe, that his thoughts had gone back to the place where he could smoke in comfort without endangering the lives of everybody with the flare of a match. Your vision was certainly much more picturesque." She rose abruptly. "I can hear them coming. Let us go into the smoking-room."

They passed the picture at which Territt had been looking. Spane stopped involuntarily.

"Why, it's you!" he cried. "A new portrait? It is lovely!"

She paused beside him and gazed at the woman in the portrait whose painted eyes stared back at her. The artist had given a wistfulness to the face instead of the laughter that Mrs. Marcourt's circle of friends would have told you was much more characteristic. The artist seemed to have missed this altogether, and George had been righteously angry. He had said candidly, "And I paid him a pretty stiff price, too. He doesn't get a commission from me again. Fellow raves about painting the soul or some such rot; and the result is a bunch of dead violets and a nunlike expression, when my wife isn't a bit like it. I don't see any likeness."

Young Spane hesitated before it. He frowned. His eyes looked puzzled. Mrs. Marcourt said to him, "Do you like it?"

He answered in a perplexed way, "I don't know! It is like you and yet unlike. You are always so bright and all that sort of thing. And yet, it *is* you. But I don't like it, somehow."

She smiled her bright-and-all-that-sort-of-thing smile. "George doesn't like it either. He says that it isn't a bit like the healthy, happy sort of woman I am. And, after all, one's husband should know."

Spane assented. They came into the smoking-room just as Marcourt and Territt entered it by another door. Spane began immediately to talk to Marcourt about the portrait.

"These new chaps!" Marcourt averred patronisingly. "They're all out for something out of the ordinary. I suppose I should be glad that he didn't send me six zig-zag lines and a triangle and tell me that was Enid." He laughed heartily at his own joke.

"And you?" said Mrs. Marcourt in her level voice to Territt, "What do you think of it?"

And Territt answered, in a moment when Spane and George Marcourt were plunging deep into a discussion on Futurism.

"I think," he said, "that he held the brush of revelation. He painted you—*you*——" he drew a deep breath.

Mrs. Marcourt began to talk quickly of other things. She spoke of the weddings she had to attend on the morrow. Then she came back casually to the question of another wedding.

"When," she asked, "will your engagement be announced?"

He turned his head quickly towards her, that striking lionlike head, with its grey hair waving back from the temples. Her eyes rested on the grey for a moment. Her lips twitched as if a nerve quiver passed over them.

"*My* engagement?" Territt said. For the first time his eyes rested directly on her face. For the first time Mrs. Marcourt's eyes met his, then dropped suddenly. She drew a quick breath. The match had burned down to Territt's fingers. He tossed it into the tray.

"To whom," asked Territt, "am I to be engaged?"

And Mrs. Marcourt, looking away, said, "I understood it was to Beatrice Byndham."

"Ah!" said Territt, and that was all for a moment. He leaned over for the match-stand, lit a match, and held it out to her.

She puffed at her cigarette several times before it lighted. His fingers accidentally touched hers. The contact shook her heart with a thousand memories. Under his tan Territt went pale.

"My God!" he whispered. "Do *you* think I have forgotten?"

His hands clenched. Around them in the air was the incense of wreathing smoke, and Marcourt was coming to an end of his denunciation of what he termed tomfoolery arts and brain-storms of the art world.

He dragged Enid and Territt now into the whirlpool of his criticisms. They went helter-skelter after him, agreeing with everything he said without knowing quite what they were agreeing to, not very sure indeed that either knew what he was talking about.

Mrs. Marcourt had finished her one cigarette. She

was making signs of departure. Spane and Territt would stay late into the night. Marcourt, indeed, was insisting they should stay the night. There was plenty of room, and he thrashed out the question of unaired hotel sheets then and there.

Territt went to the door with Mrs. Marcourt. At Marcourt's invitation he took another look at the offending portrait on the wall of the room beyond.

"Enid," said Territt, and he was white to the lips. "I go away to-morrow. God knows when, if ever, I may return. Men are doing strange, mad things at the moment. They are saying strange, mad things. Even men like myself who can hold their thoughts in their hearts for years, who can go out of a woman's life lest they bring pain to it. Enid! My God! Why did he paint you like that? Wherever I am it will haunt me. Why did you let him paint you like that?"

They were standing before the portrait. Her hands were at her side, clenched tight.

"It was no use," she said. "The artist-soul of him looked into the souls of others. He painted as he saw. He is dead now," and then she laughed a queer, empty laugh. "He died of starvation. At first he went up to the pinnacle of fame. When he painted Society his downfall began. He would paint only what he saw; and here and there he saw some terrible things! Society began to whisper he was mad. Some of the women burned his portraits of them as soon as they saw them. It made some of them quite ill. But he said he must paint only what he saw."

She hesitated for a moment.

"I went to him, smiling, laughing happily. It was a glorious day, I remember. The parks were full of people. And everyone seemed so happy. And I—I felt happy, too, for a little while. I—wanted him to paint me like that."

His eyes stared at the picture, not at her.

"I told him how happy everybody looked. I said to him, 'Monsieur, Spring is in the world and the hearts of the people. It has crept into my heart. Will you not paint something of the Spring, all that I have brought in with me?'"

She turned her face towards Territt. "And he said to me, 'Yes, I will paint you with all of the Spring that has touched your soul. It is of the soul only that I paint, madame. And all that you have brought me of the Spring, madame, is the bunch of violets you wear. And they already are wilting.'"

There was a silence.

She pointed to the picture. "And this is what he painted! For all the laughter on my lips, for all the echo of the Spring song that seemed in my heart! He swept those aside. They were to him but as leaves rustling in the wind, turning gold or russet, as the sun shone on them, but rustling past like emotions of the moment. He painted Margaret"—and she named a certain woman, high-placed and much-discussed, whom they both knew well. "He was told by well-meaning people that her influence could make or break him. He listened and said nothing. She had a lovely gown, designed specially for the occasion, barbarically beautiful, dazzling in its splendour. She told him if it pleased her he would become quite famous. He just listened. He was a peculiar man, Philip."

She paused as if in thought, and then resumed.

"And he went on painting. Then her portrait was sent home. She was so sure of the result that without looking at the portrait she gave a private view in the nature of a reception. Could she not make or break him? Everybody was there. I was quite near when the portrait was unpacked and placed on the easel. She fainted straight away."

"How had he painted her?"

She hesitated. "Well—just as people who see behind the veil of outward appearances might have sometimes thought of her. But they would never have voiced the thought. But there it was on canvas. The wonderful purple robe was there, too. It was thrown carelessly over a great gilt chair as if it were but part of the decorative scheme. From behind the tall back of the chair her face showed, empty, smirking, terribly soulless. One bare withering arm held up a cluster of those jangling Japanese wind-bells. In some queer way he had made her part of them and their tuneless, jangling emptiness. She was furious afterwards. She went to him about it and raved. She asked him to look at her face, and compare it with the picture. And he answered patiently, 'You paint your face, madame. I paint the soul.'"

For a few moments both were sunk in reflection. Then Territt turned abruptly to her.

"He at least gave you your soul, Enid. That dear, beautiful soul of yours. It shines through all the wistfulness that looks through the eyes. And the violets? Did they mean all of the Spring you might ever know? Is it in the violets that one looks for the title of the picture?"

She shook her head and bent forward. Her fingers pointed to the left hand lying idly half open. In the painted shadows it was barely visible. But as he stooped nearer he saw one thing which had escaped him, and which a great many other people, indeed, had never noticed. In the half-closed palm, at first sight was just a deeper shadow, and then one saw that it was fine dust. He bent nearer. With an exclamation he lifted his head.

"What is it?" he said sharply.

In a low voice and without moving she answered:

"Ashes!"

They were both quite silent and very still for a moment. She had her head half turned so that he could not see her face. Territt moved suddenly and walked down the room, head inclined, hands thrust deep in his pockets.

Mrs. Marcourt sank into a chair. He came back to her and stood beside her.

"In the dining-room to-night you asked me whether I was engaged."

"Yes."

"Once, five years ago, I told you, Enid, that there was only one woman whom I ever cared for, whom I will care for until the very last hour of my life."

Her lips moved soundlessly.

"I went away because you asked me to. For a while, you said, until life seemed easier. It has not been easier for me. I have come to the conclusion that it never will be."

He spoke in the steady voice of one stating a simple fact that no argument could shake.

"I have a feeling that we are not going to see each other again," he went on, and Mrs. Marcourt caught her breath in pain. "To-morrow night I shall sail. Because of that I ask you and I want you to tell me. Dear, has life been any easier for you since I last saw you?"

She leaned forward, elbows on knees, her chin resting on the palms of her hands. Now they hid her face. She shook her head. Words refused to come.

Territt stood staring in front of him. Then, hoarsely, he added:

"After all, Kut may be the happiest way out. I love you. You love me. But we are parted irrevocably. I would not drag you down even if it lay in my power to do so. Because I love you. But also because between us stands one man, big-hearted, trusting, loving—my friend and your husband. There is no way out save through dishonour, and that neither I nor you would take. Enid, I was a fool to come here to-night. I thought that it would no longer mean pain to you. That you had forgotten——"

She spoke then. "I am glad you came. No, I, too, do not easily forget. But in other circumstances I would have donned the mask that I have schooled myself to wear. I would have worn it, even for you, until the last. But"—and a cry escaped her—"you are going to-morrow—oh, Phil!"

Territt was unable to trust himself to answer. Mrs. Marcourt rose. She turned her face towards the door as one calculating how long it would take to cover those few steps and if one had strength to endure them.

That involuntary cry shook Territt's heart. He came to her and caught her hands in his. For an instant they stared at each other. Once, once only before, had a moment fraught with so much emotion held them. It was the day before he left London for India five years ago, and Territt spoke of it now.

"We had tea, do you remember, in a little restaurant in Soho, where no one knew us, where we sat and drank tea and talked platitudes and of the people about us, and all the while with the thought of parting beating like hammers on the brain? And then we went out into the dingy street and walked together, aimlessly here and there, only half-conscious of where we were going. Often in India I have walked through those streets, sat in the little place in Soho——"

He stopped abruptly, turned his face, haggard under the tan, towards her.

"Men are doing strange, mad things," he repeated. "And the maddest and strangest thing of all, after all the resolves we have made, is the one I shall ask you now. Will you dine with me to-morrow, Enid, before the boat sails, at the little restaurant in Soho? We will be two friends who love each other, who will say good-bye to each other as dear friends do, and no more. But to me it will mean something that life has hitherto not given me.

It will give us one hour together that nothing in life afterwards can take from us."

She drew a deep breath. Her eyes looked past him. From the smoking-room they heard Marcourt's loud, goodnatured voice.

He was saying: "I'd like awfully much to come, Spane, but to-morrow I have a most pressing engagement for dinner. It's awfully good of you. You see, it's like this——" and he dropped his voice.

In the music-room they looked at each other.

"I will come," she said. "But—oh Philip! Philip——"

But whatever she was going to say she did not finish. She went suddenly out of the room and left him standing there.

CHAPTER IV

Whispering Spring

On either side of the Row the trees were donning the full green kirtle of a late Spring. April was passing swiftly, a month of tears and little laughter, but May, trembling on the border of the morrow, was prodigal with blossom and promise of belated sunshine.

Somewhere in the Park, as Enid Marcourt and Beatrice Byndham cantered down the tan track, a thrush was filling that corner of the world with melody. Children were playing happily under the trees, sailing paper-boats or gaily-coloured seaplanes on the Serpentine, or racing joyously up and down the yellow-sanded strip beside the sun-shimmered water. The laughter of the little children floated across to them. Involuntarily both drew rein. The horses went more soberly along the track.

"Spring is here again," said Enid Marcourt, with a lilt in her voice. Exertion had brought a faint flush to her cheeks, her hair, escaping in tendrils, blew about her face, ruffled in the slight wind.

"Spring is here again," Beatrice Byndham echoed wistfully. In her neat, dark habit she looked older than in her white-and-silver gown of the night before. The morning sunshine showed tiny fretted lines near her eyes. But she was still young and very lovely.

The Gates of Kut

"Always it seems more wonderful," and Enid lifted her face to the breeze. It brought with it the perfume of the golden daffodils blazing under the trees by Bayswater Road, of hyacinth, tulips, and the glory of primroses in full bloom and fragrance.

Beatrice looked at her enviously. "You are always so happy. You have everything you desire. Spring comes to you without an ache under its laughter. But Spring whispers to me of something I have never really known, and may never know."

She stopped abruptly. Her eyes were full of unshed tears and her tan-gloved hand clenched on the bridle.

Enid turned quickly. She saw the glimmer of tears that were not far away, and her ready sympathy flowed forth. She leaned over and touched the girl's hand gently. Perhaps Spring whispered also to her.

"What is it, dear? You are unhappy over something."

"When I think," said Beatrice Byndham bitterly, "I am always unhappy. And always I end by asking myself why can I not be like my sisters who do not think at all, but just float ahead on any rainbow-hued bubble of the moment? After all, they are wiser than I. If the bubble breaks—well, one has at least had the illusion. I—I have nothing, because my eyes have seen too clearly."

They rode for a while in silence. There seemed nothing that could be said, by Enid at any rate. Revolt against something had forced the girl's young heart open. The torrent of revelation might pour forth at any moment. One can only help with silence.

"You know," said Beatrice, "so there is no need to hide anything from you. Your eyes have a way of looking through all the flaunting veils with which one may strive to hide things. When I first saw you, Mrs. Marcourt, I realised that. I saw you look at mother, *through* mother, I should have said. I watched you, and your eyes spoke."

"Beatrice dear——" Enid began, but the girl made a weary gesture.

"What does it matter? You only look that which, after all, many others have not been slow to voice. You see mother playing her pitiful game of make-believe, you know how she has hustled four of us into the marriage market, and has secured satisfactory bargains."

"Dear! Is it wise to say these things to me?"

"You are the only woman to whom I could say them. You are loyal and true as I have found few women. And it does me good to speak. You know quite well that I am gowned and manicured and taken round as if on parade. The tragedy is that I, too, know it."

"One would not put it so bluntly as that, Beatrice." Her voice was very gentle. "There is no use fencing with you, or I would not say that much. But I think you exaggerate how people look at these things, which, after all, are part and parcel of any rank of society. You might really say the same of a very great many people."

"But there is a difference," Beatrice maintained

stubbornly. Her eyes were full of pain. "We dance always on the edge of things. Because we are poor we are used as 'fill places'——"

Mrs. Marcourt went suddenly red, thinking of last night's dinner-party and its late invitations.

"Oh! I don't mean that." Beatrice was genuinely distressed. "You knew without doubt that we had met Captain Territt in India, and it was sweet of you, when he came unexpectedly, to ring us up. I did appreciate that. To think, if he had been only one night in London and I had not seen him—surely Fate would not have been so unkind."

Mrs. Marcourt was curiously silent. Beatrice waited a moment, then went on.

"I came out in a mood of revolt against everybody and everything to-day, Mrs. Marcourt. Against everybody but you, that is; I knew you would understand. And I wanted to talk to you."

They were walking their horses very slowly. They had come to the end of the Row. On a primitive stand an enthusiastic preacher was pouring forth impassioned views to three or four listeners, a couple of chattering nurse-girls and a crying baby. A motor-car swept by with a stout lady lolling luxuriously against her cushions and a Pomeranian beside her, a monogram embroidered in diamonds on its collar. She bowed to Mrs. Marcourt, lifted her lorgnette and stared at Beatrice; then, recognising her, bowed stiffly.

They turned back along the tan track, still slowly, under the arching trees. Beatrice's words came with sudden passion.

"The world—our little world, that is—shrugged its shoulders at my mother and her struggle on a small pittance to establish her daughters. It was amusing, a topic of unflagging interest. And now I am the subject of discussion. Mothers with sons of marriageable age but little prospects carefully manœuvre to keep them out of the danger zone. We Byndhams were always considered dangerous. We have always had the jealousy of others to contend with. Especially my sisters."

"*They* were all very pretty and charming," said Mrs. Marcourt sincerely. "And they were very witty."

"They had the gift of humour," Beatrice assented. "Other people and their views amused them a thousand times more than they amused other people. The girls never noticed snubs. They had made up their mind that it was better, with apparent innocence, to let a snub rebound, like a boomerang, on the head of the enemy. They had a definite goal before them, and no means of attaining it save by a perfectly good marriage. I don't remember any of them ever shedding a tear over anything. They laughed where I weep. And yet I am not melodramatic."

"You are hypersensitive, dear. And a sensitive nature suffers acutely." And there came to Mrs. Marcourt's face for the flash of an instant the look the portrait wore in the gallery in Marcourt Place. "One imagines things to be worse than they are. One sees things in a mercilessly clear perspective, with microscopic vision, as it were. You must remember that, Beatrice."

"Yes, I do. But it doesn't lessen one's sufferings. One learns to hide it, that is all, lest we cause others suffering." She turned her young face towards Enid.

"Mrs. Marcourt, I never speak of these things to my mother because I understand that she, too, sees far more than she will ever admit. I see the pitifulness of the struggle, the necessity for it, and I know that it is the love for her children that makes her do the things she has done. With her head in the sand of determination she is blind to the fact of how I feel our position. Practically poverty-stricken, we struggle on for the sake of an old name, that only people who bear it can understand how much it means, especially in these days when one must rub elbows with all sorts of folk whose sole claim to recognition is their enormous wealth. It is all money, money, money nowadays. Even the faith of Christ is in the market."

She touched the mare with her whip and it sprang forward. Mrs. Marcourt followed, a little glad of the interruption, wondering what all this portended, and to what Beatrice, winding in and out of the many ramifications of her thoughts, was definitely leading.

They galloped down the avenue, and many eyes looked at these two women, undoubtedly the handsomest and best-gowned in the Row.

They were turning for a final gallop before heading homewards ere Beatrice spoke again. The horses walked slowly, heads bent. Across the distance they heard the raucous voice of the box-orator, the words indistinguishable.

"Life is often like that," said Beatrice, in bitter

weariness. "A jangling of sound, a harsh voice, half-heard, crying out vainly, and the world surging past, unlistening."

"And yet under it all," said Enid Marcourt, "is the message of hope. It is like life, too, is it not, that it is at a distance that the meaning is vague, and that we misunderstand? When one comes closer, to the heart of things, as it were, one finds the true meaning."

The horses plodded nearer, almost soundlessly on the dark, soft turf. They heard the voice now distinctly, crying aloud with terrible fervour and persistence.

" . . . 'Though I speak with the tongues of men and of angels, and have not charity, I am become as sounding brass or a tinkling cymbal.' "

And as they came nearer yet, "Love is charity. Love seeketh not itself. . . ."

The last words followed them as they turned, striking deeply into the hearts of at least two listeners in the Park that morning, words fraught to each with meaning, words that to one woman at least, in an hour of which she thought not, would rend her very life in twain.

But this Enid could not then foresee. Overhead in the trees birds sang happily of the spring of life, the mating of loving hearts. Only the thrush mocked. In the flood of melody he echoed and re-echoed the voices around him; blended them into one song of exquisite mockery.

"O Love, Love!" said Beatrice Byndham, in a queer, hushed way, and she lifted up her young face to the warm radiance of the sun. A little chill wind went by, but it seemed not to touch her. But it blew in Mrs. Marcourt's face with the sudden chill of storm that had been and storms yet to be.

Beatrice was speaking passionately now. The pain had come back to her eyes. "Why can't a woman who loves a man very dearly tell him so? Why are we so hidebound by convention, lisping our little lies, playing at half-truths? Why can't we come out into the open? Men can voice the love of their hearts without shame. Why not women?"

Mrs. Marcourt gave a sudden start at the first sound of the girl's voice, that held no longer its usual quietness. It throbbed with emotion, with suppressed passion.

"I love someone—very dearly," Beatrice said. She spoke in a lower voice now, and something thrilling, exultant, ran through her words. "If he hadn't a penny it would make no difference. At a word I would follow him throughout the world. That is love, isn't it?"

"Yes," said Enid Marcourt, "that is love."

A little child, following its playfellow, ran out of the trees by the tan track, hesitated a moment, and then scurried across, scrambling under the railings. It waved its fat hand to them, and Mrs. Marcourt waved back.

Beatrice pointed to it with her whip. "To be the mother of children like that—little, fat, chubby-faced children with yellow hair and pippin-red cheeks! And the rest of life with a man one loved! What could one want more? What would money matter?"

And she swung back again to where she had begun. "I love someone—very dearly. And yet because convention wills it, I cannot tell him so. I know he likes me. I believe that he does not care for anyone. I could easily make him love me."

"Perhaps some day, dear, he will speak."

"Some day," Beatrice flung out her hands. "Some day will be too late. He leaves England to-night. I may never see Philip Territt again."

"Captain Territt?" The cry leaped suddenly from Enid Marcourt. She stared at Beatrice for an instant, then turned her face abruptly away. But Beatrice, looking at the blue sky, the feather-white clouds, did not see.

"Yes," said Beatrice resolutely. "And I don't care whether the whole world knows. I have courage to tell the whole world. And yet not him."

The little breeze, for all the warmth of the morning, blew coldly in Mrs. Marcourt's face. Somewhat vaguely she put up her hand and lifted back the tendril of hair that seemed to blind her eyes. Even then she did not see quite as clearly as before.

"We met in India, as you know," Beatrice was saying in that thrilled new voice, which to Mrs. Marcourt sounded strangely thin and far away. "I cared from the very first moment, as I never believed I could care for any man. I said to myself, 'Here is a man among men, a man of whom a woman could be proud, for whom she could well sacrifice everything, and glory in the sacrifice.'"

There spoke modern Youth, glorious, armoured in innocence, Don Quixote ready to storm the gates of the citadel that generations had built up out of the wisdom of previous generations. Youth, with its lance atilt, poised ready for conflict, preparing to leap all the barriers of convention.

Beatrice Byndham glowed, apostle of the new cult whose cause modern Youth so eagerly champions, armoured with Omar Khayyám instead of the epistles of St. Paul, and a sheaf of Suffragette literature in place of the sampler.

Enid Marcourt had the vision of Beatrice striding on, head high, trampling underfoot the old, wise, grandmotherly saws upon which Youth, fresh from the doors of its new school, looks with scorn and rebellion. The darning-needle had given place to the lance, the chair by the hearth to a soap-box or primitive stand in the Park.

In the Park near by women clad in khaki were drilling. They raised their hands to the salute to a hard-faced woman in uniform and addressed her as "sir." Beyond them, outlined against a low slope, men were drilling in earnest, preparing for the morrow of eventualities. Beside them the women in khaki were like characters in a farce.

But the hazel eyes of Beatrice never looked at the men. They looked instead with pride at that company of women. She pointed with her riding-whip.

"See!" she cried exultantly. "We no longer sit at home and strangle our individuality in the arena of pots and pans. We no longer thread slow, placid thoughts about nothing into our darning. There is revolution. A new world in the making. You see the spirit of it. We are weaving great things into the woof of our destiny. Can you not see it?"

They had paused for a moment. Enid Marcourt looked at the women. They all stood at the salute as two of the women officers swaggered past them. The whole thing looked rather grotesque and absurd.

"No," said Enid suddenly. "I cannot see it, Beatrice; I see instead a hideous travesty those women are making of the real thing. The real thing is there," and she pointed to the slope where the men were training. "They are to fight for us, those men, to lay down their lives for us. And here before them are these monkey-women, aping the ways of men who are facing the supreme sacrifice. I have no patience with them."

A flush came to Beatrice's cheeks. Indignant reply was on her lips, but Mrs. Marcourt swept on.

"Why are they here in the sunlight, playing spectacularly at the game of war? Why are they not in the slums where poor sick children are moaning, where hollowed faces are bent over tasks that will never be finished? Don't talk to me of these women weaving anything but mockery into the great scheme of life. Their very uniform, by its blatant advertisement, is an insult to the spirit in which our men are fighting and dying. Come away! I feel sick when I look at them."

And this time Beatrice followed her wordlessly. They went on under the arching, swaying trees. At the gateway leading to Bayswater Road they paused. Beatrice Byndham's home was in the street almost opposite.

"I am sorry if I have hurt you in any way, Beatrice," Enid said. "But at nineteen I know one makes ideals out of things like that, which one finds in after years to be but coloured balloons, flaunting in the wind. I do not want to preach, dear, and to you my views may seem old-fashioned, but the true ideal of womanhood is the old sweet type that we scorn as grandmotherly. But it was those women who made nations, who made England."

"You think, then," said Beatrice a little resentfully, "that laws unjust to women should be left as they are?"

"No, Beatrice, I do not. But will all this sort of thing alter them? No! While we are fighting for ourselves we are forgetting the most vital fact of all."

"And that?"

"That the children of to-day make the nation of to-morrow. It is only from the home itself that women will ever strike out at unjust laws. Mould well the mind of the little son of to-day, and then the man of to-morrow, seeing with clearer vision, will, for the sake of his higher ideal of womanhood, make better laws."

Beatrice with bent head and puzzled brows was looking down at the gravel that her horse was pawing restlessly. She did not very clearly follow Enid Marcourt's line of thought. At nineteen one does not think of nations and to-morrows and children. These lie on the distant horizon, obscured by one's ego. For at nineteen one is apt to think of the world in relation solely to oneself, not oneself in relation to the world.

Whispering Spring

Between nineteen and twenty-seven the eight years build generally a bridge of experience that spans the sea of knowledge. The piles of the bridge are sometimes built of suffering.

But this nineteen could not yet know. It spoke impetuously, missing the wider issues, picking up the pin-point of argument.

"Then, you are shocked at me because of what I said about—about Captain Territt? If you have these—these old-fashioned ideas you will think me bold, unmaidenly."

Mrs. Marcourt answered without a second's hesitation. "No! Such a thought as yours beat at many a woman's heart, even in pre-war days. Now it has but attained a more poignant point of view."

She lifted her eyes and looked from the strip of the road, with its passing traffic of swift motor-cars and heavy rumbling buses, to the soft blue sky, like a sea with fleecy clouds as white yachts drifting before the wind.

One's heart went like the cloud-yachts these days, sailing on to unknown distances. Her lips trembled slightly and trouble came into her eyes.

It seemed a strange thing that she should sit so quietly there, talking to Beatrice in a level, emotionless voice, while her heart ached almost intolerably or rocked with a fierce, wild joy. And Beatrice spoke and said again that which she had said more than once, only now it voiced the thought that had sent the trouble to Mrs. Marcourt's eyes and the throbbing pain to her heart.

Beatrice said: "And Philip goes to-night?" And

her eyes, too, lifted and soared above the dusty road, but they saw only her own life, suddenly bereft of something she loved and desired, and her hands still and quiet that might hold so much for the asking.

She began to speak quickly. "Oh, why should I not?" The voice was a cry, half pleading, half rebellious. She swung round to Enid. "Mrs. Marcourt, if anything should happen to Philip, if he should go out of my life and I should never see him again, I think it would be the end of everything. I feel things so intensely. I am innately so rebellious against conventionality. It seems to me that I stand now at the very cross-roads of my life, that I shall either make or break it."

Enid turned, her own face a little white. Her eyes went to the girl's strained face, her nervy hands clenched tight on the bridle. All at once she began to tremble.

"If Philip loved me as I love him, everything would be different. Even if he died I could go on, my face to the heights always because of him. But if he turned from me I—oh! I do not know what I would do. Only I know I would dance to the tune of the moment whatever it might be. That is the temperament we Byndhams are cursed with. It seems to have passed my sisters by. To me it is given in full measure, pressed down and running over. What am I to do?"

"One can only wait," said Mrs. Marcourt in a low voice. She spoke with difficulty. Her eyes looked beyond Beatrice as if they saw a ghost. "That is all we women can do at times like this."

"Oh, no!" cried Beatrice. "I cannot! I must put my all on the toss of the coin. To win or lose! Only one must know! One must know!"

And then:

"He didn't care for anyone out in India. And presumably nowhere else. For there was no portrait of any woman save his dead mother and married sister. When I—I gave him my portrait and that of mother, of course he thanked me and placed them among the others. But"—and she turned again to Mrs. Marcourt—"if there had been anyone else, any woman whom he loved, her portrait surely would have been there."

The pain in her voice was a question. And Mrs. Marcourt, looking anywhere but at Beatrice, answered:

"One would think so."

"If he had loved anyone," pursued Beatrice, "or believed that he had when he was younger, he must have forgotten, or had schooled himself to forget. You see, I have thought all these things out. I have thought, too, that if it were anyone in England he would have come back, and at this crisis either married her straight away or announced the engagement. It is better, say I, to be the last woman rather than the first. I am not boring you, am I?" with sudden remorse. "You look so tired!"

"No. You are not boring me," said Mrs. Marcourt. Her eyes were on the white yachts on the sea-sky again. "I am more than interested, because I am thinking how I can help you."

"Oh! if you would," impulsively. "You see,

I am utterly without false shame in the matter. You and Mr. Marcourt know Philip so well. You would have told me had there been anybody. You were so sweet about asking me to dine just because he was coming."

Her face was flushing like a child's now. She was a child indeed at that moment, eager, enthralled by a vision that hope conjured up.

"Listen! I shall tell you something,' she said, half whispering, and she leaned forward. "One night in India, at a dance, we elected to sit it out. It was hot, and the conservatory cool. The band was playing a waltz, '*Quand l'amour meurt.*' You know it, perhaps?"

"Yes," said Mrs. Marcourt, "I know it."

She knew it very well. It was from a song she had been wont to sing five years ago. All the words came back to her.

"'*Quand l'amour meurt.*'" repeated Beatrice. "'When love dies.' It is very sweet but sad, and that night Philip quoted the words of the song for me. It drew us nearer somehow. I—I thought he was going to speak."

"You—thought that," said Mrs. Marcourt, and she gave a start.

Beatrice nodded. "I felt sure. And I felt, too, intuitively that his thoughts had gone to someone else, to someone perhaps whom he had once believed he loved, and that he said to himself, as the song said that night, that when love is dead or dying one may not call it back, that it is over and done with, and that it was for the best."

The little cloudy yachts were scudding now. A breeze had sprung up and blew them before it, as human craft in the wind of destiny. And Beatrice's voice went on until the end.

"Then the waltz ended. It ended too soon. People rushed into our little world and gabbled of ices and claret-cup and how really too hot it was for dancing. And a fat man I hated came up and reminded me that our dance was beginning. And in the morning Captain Territt had gone—up into the hill country somewhere. I never saw him again until last night. And then you—brought us together. If I had not loved you before I should always have loved you for that. You brought us together again."

CHAPTER V

Honour and Arms

MRS. MARCOURT rode back through the Park, absorbed in thought.

Beyond the iron railings Park Lane was crowded, noisy with traffic. On the other side of her, perched in his impromptu pulpit, the preacher was still holding forth. His voice followed Mrs. Marcourt for a long way.

Long after it had died to silence she seemed to hear it. Four words echoed over and over in her brain, mechanically meaningless just then.

"'*Love seeketh not her own.*'"

Her way lay across the Park. She came to the great gates and turned by the statue of Achilles. Here and there on the seats under the tremulous green of the trees in the open spaces, warm and sunshiny, were people she knew, bowing to her as she passed.

But to-day Mrs. Marcourt did not see them. Head bent she rode on, turning mechanically to the right and out again to the gateway. And it was there that Territt and she met. He spoke twice before she heard. And then she lifted her head, and the lovely colour flashed into her cheeks and light into her eyes. Involuntarily she drew rein. She looked down at him standing there in his uniform, his eager, tanned face upturned.

"It's really—*you*," he said.

"Really I!" she cried. She held out her hand to him. "Were you hoping it would be someone else?"

He was still holding her gloved hand. His rare smile came to his face.

"Do I look as if I were?"

She raised her eyes, and they rested on his sunburnt face. She saw the grave tenderness in his eyes, the flash that came into them when they met hers. It set her heart beating wildly, her pulses thrilling beneath his fingers. She drew her hand away. The colour fluttered into her cheeks.

"I saw you coming down the track," he said. "Indeed I almost kept pace beside you, outside the railings." He waved his hand towards a big grey touring car in the street beyond, with a chauffeur in uniform beside it. "I wanted to ask you if you would like to hand your mount over to Smith while we investigated the tea-châlet."

She gave a nervous laugh, hesitated, and: "I—I am afraid I ought to go straight home. So many preparations for to-morrow."

He lifted his face. "There will be all the Tomorrows," he reminded her very gently.

Some of the warm colour went from her face. She drew a deep breath, spoke quickly, "Yes; let us go."

For a moment she turned her beautiful head away from him lest he should see the shimmer of tears that came into her eyes. But he did see them, and he trembled suddenly.

"Enid," he said, and he stretched out his hand

as if to take hers again, but she drew hers away quickly. Her grey eyes looked down into his, and saw the trouble and the pain in them.

He held out his hand and helped her alight. Together they walked to the gateway. The sunshine, flooding through the leaves of the chestnut under which they passed, patterned her with dancing shadows and touched the coppery brownness of her hair with red.

"If Smith would take the horse to the mews," he snuggested, "he could drive you home in the car afterwards."

"I should like that," she answered quickly. "There is a mews just across the way."

They waited there by the grey car while Smith took the horse in charge. They talked of all else but those things that had roots deep in each heart. They spoke of people they knew, of incidents and rumours, and, last but not least, of far-away Kut, of brave Townshend waiting for help, holding out against unknown odds. The newspapers were optimistic then. Hope burned high still in many hearts in England.

"But there are many things yet to do," Territt said, "and always one must reckon on the inevitable delays. And if the Tigris floods—— But we will not think of the possibility of failure."

"Because we dare not think of it?" she queried.

He nodded silently.

"And you—go—to-night?" she said, and her lips pressed tightly and her eyes looked away.

"To-night. I go to the W.O. straight from here."

There came a silence as they walked on. Then Territt spoke suddenly, passionately.

"Ah, Enid!" he cried, "how hard it is to go to-night! If I had only a few days—a few days of my England, something to hold and remember when one is out there——" His hands clenched. His eyes were full of pain. He broke off suddenly. When he spoke again it was in a different voice.

"Forgive me, Enid," said he. "Did I make you unhappy? I must not do that. I want to bring you happiness, not to take it from you, God knows."

They walked down the white path that, twisting under the trees, began to slant like a ribbon across the green turf. The breeze blew them the fragrant perfume of budding flower, of leaf, of young, dew-wet grass. For the most part they walked in silence.

Once Territt spoke of Bussorah-Basra, with its collection of mud huts, its clustering palaces, its winding alley-ways crowded with Arabs, the quaint dhows and *bellums* drifting on the thick, muddy water of the Tigris.

They had tea under the trees at one of the tiny tables, with its white cloth fluttering idly in the faint breeze. The cheeky sparrows fluttered round, chattering incessantly, hopping beside them unconcernedly. Overhead the great boughs murmured, casting alternate shadow and leaf-patterned sunshine.

Enid had removed her bowler-hat and gloves, and sat leaning back in her chair as she sipped her tea. On the table in front of them a cluster of daffodils nodded in a tall, slender vase.

"Daffodils," said Territt suddenly, "always remind me of Miss Byndham."

At that Mrs. Marcourt, who had been very silent, gave a start, and the hand that held the cup shook.

"Of Beatrice?"

He nodded. "Yes; just as violets always make me think of you. Perhaps because violets seem to me to hold all the garnered sweetness of all other flowers."

Her lips trembled.

"Of flowers that have passed their season," she said, and sighed.

But he shook his head. "No, no! You know I do not mean that; but violets, fresh with the dew of dawn still on them, fragrant——" And he paused, and his eyes rested on her face with a world of tenderness in them.

"And—daffodils?" she queried, and drew a sudden breath. "What of them? How do they remind you of Beatrice?"

"I hardly know." He pondered for a moment. "I have never analysed the thought really. Probably because she is golden-haired and full of the love of life. You know the picture:

'Slender, golden daffodil . . .
Golden, dancing daffodil.'"

She was looking up at him thoughtfully.

"And—you find Beatrice like that?"

"Don't you?"

She thought a moment, then shook her head. "No. I think I should have likened Beatrice to something stronger, less ephemeral. There is more character in her than meets the eye."

"I know that, God bless her!" said Territt with enthusiasm. "Did she tell you about India?"

She nodded, flushing.

"They, both she and her mother, were exceptionally kind," he said, "and I was practically a stranger to them."

She had turned her face away and was looking over the green sward. He could just see the soft curve of her cheek.

"It is a wonder to me," she said in a low voice, "that you did not fall in love with Beatrice. Most men would have done so in the circumstances."

"One can only fall in love once, Enid."

She drew a quick breath. "Ah! but you might easily have forgotten. Other men would have done so."

He shook his head.

"Other men, dear, not I."

She began passionately. "Ah! but why not you? Surely, sooner or later——"

"*Enid!*" he cried, stretching out his hand to hers and holding it tight in his warm grasp. He forced her to look at him. "Dear," he said, "don't talk like that. It hurts. There can only be you. As long as you live——"

She repeated the words, "As long as I live——"

His hands held hers so tightly then that pain silenced her.

"Don't!" he whispered; and again, "Don't, dear."

She drew her hand from his and passed it across her eyes as if the dancing sunlight blinded her.

"I wish," she began, "oh! I wish so many things, and it is all in vain. Philip, why do we sit here, you and I, when it is all so futile? Why do you sit here talking to me when there are hundreds of places open to you, hundreds of young and lovely creatures who could bring you happiness? Ah! don't speak just yet, dear. Let me finish. It is all so sad and impossible. Why don't you get up, and go away now, and leave me?"

"Because I love you," he said. "Because I shall always love you."

He spoke a little hoarsely. "And because," he added, "it is my last day in London for a long time—perhaps, maybe, for ever. Give a man, on a day such as this, his choice of what he would do, and he would spend every minute of it with the woman he loves."

"But—it is not right——"

"Ah! I know," and he closed his eyes momentarily. "None knows that better than myself. But I am not a cold, halo-seeking saint, Enid, I am a man of flesh and blood. A year ago, before I went to India, I loved you with just as much intensity as now. But tradition held me with her chains, honour pointed out the way."

She said, half sobbing: "The way now is as clear as then."

He shook his head. "The war has torn up a great many of our old conceptions by the roots. It has shaken us off our feet. We look at the world with new eyes."

"But—honour," she whispered.

"Honour," he said, "will always be honour. But the war, too, has shown man his littleness as well as his greatness."

He turned to her gravely:

"And my littleness," he cried, "is this, that I can sit here with you, another man's wife, and love you, and be proud of loving you."

She turned her head and looked at him in a strange way. "And I? Oh! I do not think I would care if George came to us across the grass now, and asked me why I sat here with you. I would tell him," and she beat her little clenched hand on the table between them. "I would glory in telling him. She was right after all."

"She?" he said questioningly.

"Beatrice! She said so only this morning as we rode through the Park. And I thought her wrong, but now I know she was right." She gave a cry of remembrance then and shrank back. She was thinking of other things that Beatrice had said.

He saw the shadow that came over her face.

"Don't let us think of Beatrice," he said impulsively. "What has she to do with us? She stands outside of our lives."

"Ah! I wonder," said Mrs. Marcourt. She turned to him, smiling pitifully. "Think! Was there never once, once," she cried, "that a thought did not come to you about—about any girl, lovely and sweet as Beatrice is—a thought of home and children—of all life might mean to you?"

"More than once," he said slowly, "I have had that thought."

And suddenly Enid Marcourt winced, for she heard Beatrice's young, passionate voice again, saw that ballroom in far-away India, the nook amid the palms. It unfolded before her eyes like a film.

"But," his voice was saying, "it was only in relation to you. I thought of how the river of our destiny flows on, carrying us with it. Somewhere in the world were you. And we were destined not to meet until you had married another."

He leaned forward. "In all the world are there no such lines that hold so much meaning as these two :

> 'I could not love thee, dear, so much,
> Loved I not honour more.' "

"And that," he went on, "is how things stand with us. We are for each other clearly, but honour is first with us both. This little hour—ah! would George begrudge it to us, even if he knew? If he were anything different from what he is, big-hearted, generous George Marcourt, could I sit so calmly here? No! I would run off with you whether you would or no. I would take you, to have and to hold, for always—*always*."

She shrank back before the force of his words, the passionate light that leaped to his eyes.

"That's love," he cried, and then, "but honour keeps guard also."

She turned wet eyes to his.

"Had *he* been different," she whispered, "I would have gone. Ah! so gladly."

He looked at her, bent forward, took her two hands in his for a moment.

"I wonder, Dear Eyes," he said, "if I should also have added, 'had *you* been different.' You are so white and wonderful."

She broke sharply across his words.

"Ah! no! You must not enshrine me. I am only a woman, playing a pitiful little part when all is said. I sit out here with you, and when I go home, if George is there, I will talk to him of the weather and the trees in the Park and how lovely were the flowers; but of you I shall not talk, unless by chance he heard that we were here."

She drew her hands away.

"And we will go on through life together," she said, "through all the days—the months and the years—that are left to us; and his very kindness will torture me, his very sympathy for suffering he cannot understand, but in some dim way comprehends. Oh! I went through it five years ago. I thought I could not suffer like that again."

She rose and blindly began to search for her hat. He brought it for her, and with fumbling fingers she put it on. For a moment they stood together, both very pale.

"Oh, Life!" she said, with a sob. "How hard it is! It does not seem right that there should be so much suffering."

He would have taken her to his arms then, before all the world had they been present, but she moved quickly.

"Sometimes," she said in a low voice, "when you

were out there in India, I used to think that I could not bear it any longer; that I could not go on, day after day, year after year, in an aimless circle; that I must run away, go out to you. But there was *his* career and your career."

A waitress came to them across the grass. She had stared curiously from under heavy, stolid brows at the lady in the riding-habit who looked so sad and the officer who gazed before him as if he were terribly angry over something. She thought they were quarrelling. She yawned as she went back, complacently clinking the generous tip Territt had given. Someone else, unknown to them, stared at them, too.

"Sometimes," said Mrs. Marcourt, in a hopeless way that was infinitely more pathetic than tears, "I prayed to God that He would take memory from me, or that He would let me die. But He did not heed. There are so many sorrows in the world, perhaps, that He cannot give heed to them all. I should have thought of that. And you——"

"Yes," said Territt, and his jaw set, "I suffered, too."

They began to walk slowly away, neither with any very definite idea where they were going. Only one thought throbbed in her brain. To-night he would be going away, and this time one knew that he might not return. Had she not had a premonition of that, that she would never, never see him again?

It forced a cry from her lips. Instinctively he had taken her arm, began to pilot her through the trees, away from the paths. His lips were set. Repression of the thoughts that surged within him brought the sweat in great beads on his brow.

They walked under the trees, arm in arm, as lovers walk, and all else was for the moment forgotten.

Nursemaids sitting under the trees and people passing them looked at them—this tall soldier, bronzed with a fiercer sun than that of England, his head bent, his eyes on the slight, swaying figure by his side.

"Once," said Mrs. Marcourt, in a strange voice, "I went to the aviary and let loose all the birds there. That is why not even a canary is at our house in Chelsea, or at our place in the country. And I said to the birds as they flew away: 'O birds, birds, you are free, *you* can go where you will. But I know of no hand that this side of the grave can set me free.'"

She passed a hand across her eyes and straightened herself then as if she would rid herself, for a while at least, of thoughts that beat at the breast.

"Why do we walk here like this, you and I?" she said in a half-whisper. "This is only the place for happy people, for little children from whom all signs or tokens of sorrow should be kept."

"Enid! Enid!" cried Philip Territt in a shaking voice. "What can I say? I must keep silent or betray my trust. If I spoke now, God knows what I should say. I would ask you to come away with me now, I know——"

"And I—I would not go," she whispered. "I did not go before. I sent you away. It is only the moment, the knowledge that to-morrow we shall be parted one from the other, makes us think otherwise. Oh!" and she leaned against him as they walked, "let us pretend for a little while, Phil. Let us pretend that we are free, that we are two lovers walking here, with nothing to make us unhappy."

"Ay," he echoed, "let us pretend! We will sit down on the grass as some of those other couples are sitting, and whispering and planning of a home to be."

They walked on blindly, past a stout lady, dressed like a charwoman in holiday garb. The stout lady, who had just dismissed her electric brougham, and who had been staring at them for some time, lifted her lorgnette to her eyes. She did not go after them and voice the thoughts that raged within her. There are some things that some people do not do.

These two desperately unhappy people went on under the arching trees, and came at last to seats in a quiet corner. They began to pretend that they were part of the cosmopolitan passing world about them. She rested her cheek for a moment against his sleeve. The tears sparkled on her lashes.

"And we would have a little cottage in the country, just a little cottage, Phil, not a great house full of servants, and we would build us a great green hedge that would shut out the world." A tear dropped and fell on her hand, and he pressed her arm tightly against his side.

The great love that he bore for Enid Marcourt surged over him in a flood, threatening to carry him away with it.

"Why cannot we go—now?" he cried. "Let's have done with pretending. Let us gather the roses of life while we may." And then suddenly he stopped and turned back with a hopeless gesture, his head bent. "But—my country——" he began, and then stopped again.

Her arm trembled within his. She raised her head and looked at him. She repeated very softly the two lines he had quoted before. The tears were still in her eyes.

"Ah! I know all that you would say, dear heart," she whispered. "You go to-night because your country needs you. It is something greater than you or I——" And then she, too, stopped speaking; they rose without a word and went on in silence.

In all the days to come these two would surely remember that day. The breeze was dying down. The sun lay warm on the grass. The great trees, slowly nodding their heads, whispered and whispered. The children under the trees, the lovers seated on the benches or wandering across the grass, one dear woman's face very near to one's own, it was all part of a picture for a man to carry away to the barren plains and dreary marshes of Mesopotamia.

Often and often, then, and in time to come, would that picture present itself. They knew that the hour of parting was inevitable, these two, and they knew also that never again might one look on the other. The dark shadow of War flung its black wing over them, blotted out for the while the sun of hope.

Philip Territt's head drooped. Lines of pain gathered about his mouth. He fought in that hour in the Park a great battle, the battle between love and honour. The storm of passion swept over him and shook him in its passing.

They had paused by the path that led beyond the shrubbery to the gateway where the grey car waited. For the moment they were alone. Only the green trees stood witness. Deep in his eyes she saw such an expression of pain as she had never seen in any man's eyes.

"I know that I should say to you that it is best for us to part when we come to the end of the pathway," he said. "But I can't say it. Dear, to-night before I go will you give me one thing you have not yet given me? I ask one thing that I shall always have, no matter what else be taken from me."

"And—that?" she whispered very low.

He put his hands on her shoulders and looked down into her eyes.

"That, to-night, ere I go, you will kiss me," he said. "Not now, and here, where anyone may come and break into our little world. But to-night before I go. Ah! Enid, how I love you! And after to-night I shall have nothing left of you but memories."

Even this passing moment might not be theirs, for footsteps sounded on the path beyond the shrubbery.

They turned and went on, he and she, walking more and more slowly as the gateway came in view. He turned to her then.

"And to-night—you will come. Dear heart, am I mad to ask you? I am mad, perhaps, but not bad. It will be a little while together, to ourselves, such as we could not have in other restaurants where our world moves, and would criticise and judge us wrongly. But in a restaurant where no one knows us, where we can talk to each other——"

She drew a long breath.

"I will come."

"And if you do not—if anything should happen to prevent your coming?"

He went white under his tan at the thought.

She shook her head. Her heart was beating wildly.

"What can prevent it? Why should I stay away? Is it not all that I may have to last me in the years to come?"

"I would know if you did not come that only one of two things had stopped you."

"And these, Philip?"

"One is—Death. The other"—and he hesitated—"the other a thought that has haunted me; that haunts me now."

She raised her eyes in question. His voice trembled as he spoke.

"That you may think differently when you reach home. We are both unstrung now. Calmer thoughts may come to you, Enid. You might say to yourself that the thing I ask of you is too much. Yet, after all, what is it? An hour in an out-of-the-way restaurant. No more and no less. Yet, when you go back, you might change your mind. Dear"—and he turned to her—"if you do I shall not blame you. I shall only understand that—that you thought it best that we should not see each other again."

"I shall come," she whispered; "I shall not fail you."

They went out of the gate to the waiting car. The chauffeur jumped down, opened the tonneau door for Enid, looked at his master inquiringly.

"I am going to the Club," said Territt. "After leaving Mrs. Marcourt you can call back for me."

When the chauffeur climbed into his seat again, Territt held out his hand to Enid.

"Good-bye," she said.

"Not good-bye," he said, in a low voice, "only *au revoir* until to-night."

His hand tightened on hers. He could feel the pulse leaping under his fingers. His own heart beat fast. So for a second they looked at each other in silence, and then Territt stepped back, his hand to the salute.

So she saw him standing there in the glorious sunshine, his eyes following the car as it turned. He saw her face again for a fleeting moment and the flutter of her hand, then the car rolled swiftly out of sight.

"To-night," he said to himself as he turned, and he squared his broad shoulders and went his way, for there was much to be done.

"To-night," whispered Enid Marcourt to herself, and she hid her face in her hands.

And it was well, perhaps, for both that the god of happiness, touching each with his magic wand, hid the future from them.

CHAPTER VI

Anniversary

At a quarter to six that evening George Marcourt, whistling softly but with much cheerfulness, came up the steps of his mansion, and let himself quietly in with his latchkey.

As he entered the hall he stopped abruptly and listened. Upstairs, moving about her room, Mrs. Marcourt was singing. The words floated down to him, with a lilt and a freshness for the sheer joy in them. She was singing very happily:

> "I will arise and go now,
> And go to Innisfree."

Marcourt's face beamed. It was a long while since he had heard Enid sing like that. The thought that to-day of all days, the anniversary of their wedding, she was happy added to his pleasure. He feared she had forgotten all about their anniversary, for she had not spoken of it that morning.

His round, pleasant face positively beamed. It enveloped even the hovering footman in its radiance. His face, at such moments, was like a good-natured sun grinning cheerfully over the mountains at the world below.

"So Mrs. Marcourt is at home," he said to the footman, who was divesting him of his light coat after confiscating tall hat and gloves. The footman volunteered the information that he thought Mrs. Marcourt was going out. She was dressing apparently for that purpose.

Marcourt's eyes twinkled. Going out, of course she wasn't! She was dressing to surprise him! Wasn't this the anniversary of their wedding-day! So he told himself and strutted cheerfully into his smoking-room.

He would wait there and surprise her when she came downstairs. She would not have heard him come in. He had purposely used the latchkey, for the door bell had a habit of ringing with disconcerting and arresting shrillness. So he threw himself contentedly into a chair, stretched out his legs comfortably and lit a cigar.

What could man ask more of life, after all, than this? A comfortable chair, a good cigar, and a special dinner impending—and one's wife singing happily upstairs. George Marcourt leant back and puffed away in a haze of contentment.

Enid had not forgotten, God bless her! He might have known she would not. Few women, surely, forget the anniversary of that momentous day in their lives. And yet—for an instant he pondered—Enid had changed in the last five years or so, somehow. That was perhaps to be expected. They had been married just eight years. A woman of twenty-seven cannot be expected to remain a girl of nineteen always! And Enid at nineteen was very young, almost too ignorant of the world. She had come from a country vicarage where the main worry of life was how an overworked and ill-paid parson and his not over-strong wife could maintain themselves and a brood of small folk on the annual dole that a wealthy Church thought meet and proper.

But then the Church of England quite naturally looked at it this way: You can't pay your bishops high salaries and your small fry, in the shape of the submerged thousands of the clergy, as well. One has to economise somewhere. The rule of life, in other things as well as religion apparently, is to pay the figureheads handsomely and divide the little that is left over among the men who do the work.

Bishops of any creed, as we all know, are lordly people who are of different clay from struggling parsons. A bishop to work! Why, the very statues in up-to-date churches would hold up their hands in horror at the thought. Bishops have only, at the worst, to drive about among the poor, in luxuriously-upholstered cars, and, wearing a bland the-poor-are-always-with-us expression, exhort the people to be humble of heart and not riotous in living; and then, with a sorrowful shake of the head and much display of gaitered and often none too symmetrical leg, climb with dignity into the carriage or motor and be whirled away again. Perhaps, because Christ walks among the slums clad often in other garb than that of a cleric, the people accept the visit of such august personages as bishops with equanimity.

Enid Marcourt's father had been tucked out of sight in a village of one of the western counties. He was not a believer in your modern Ritualistic propaganda, therefore for him was little, if any, chance of promotion in the Church of England.

He brought up his family, with the village incidentally helping in minor ways. Life pursued its quiet routine. Then, one day, the squire with a friend strolled out of his big house on the adjacent rise, and passed, as the squire had passed many times, the old church and its vicarage.

The squire stopped to chat for a few moments. Marcourt, more interested in prospective shooting than in country vicars, was a little impatient. They were talking of cabbages, too. Marcourt felt a distinct aversion from the topic. Unwillingly he had followed the well-fed squire and the worn-looking parson with the bent shoulders around the house to the cabbage patch.

And there and then, suddenly and inexplicably, George William Marcourt began to take an interest in cabbages, and the bent-shouldered vicar, and all pertaining thereto.

A long-legged girl, in a shabby brown skirt and a faded sports jacket, and with hair that was quite red in the sun, was at work with a shovel between the rows of the cabbages.

What it was George William Marcourt was never afterwards quite sure. Even though he zealously came for several days in succession and talked of nothing but cabbages, and why one grew so many.

The impressions he carried away with him that first day were rather jumbled. There was a scholarly parson with stooped shoulders, a library full of ancient books, and a garden full of cabbages, *plus* a tired-looking wife. Whenever any door in that vicarage opened a crowd of small children fell out. There were so many that they appeared to bulge out from the windows. And they had an annoying habit of getting under one's feet when one went out to talk about cabbages to the girl with the red-tinted hair and the shabby brown skirt.

But something had happened to Marcourt on that first walk of his through the village of Weaslehurst that was without precedent in his career. He fell in love, and being a man of methodical instincts and settled, if few, ideas on a subject, he soon weighed the pros and cons of the matter, and decided that life without the girl in the rusty brown skirt would be a very poor business for him.

For Enid, the girl herself, eldest of all the vicar's human collection, there could be only one answer. True, she had dreams like other girls, but in a crowded vicarage with poverty staring one desperately in the face, reality must of very necessity oust dreams. She had sighed a little and cried a little over that proposal of George Marcourt's, but never when the little mother with the weary eyes, or the uncomplaining father with the care-stooped shoulders, was in sight.

It is these brave little mothers and uncomplaining fathers who have, after all, made the Church of England ministry the power it is. The incense, and the gorgeous vestments, and the procession of white-robed acolytes form a very pretty if not soul-satisfying picture, but it is the old school of village ministers that has done more to keep Anglicanism together than any other factor.

Enid Marcourt, then, came straight from a village vicarage to Marcourt Place and incidentally one or two more houses in Great Britain.

For a girl on her wedding-day her thoughts were perhaps not so romantic as one would have expected. On the long drive from Weaslehurst to London, when Marcourt with a lover's natural anxiety asked her of what she was thinking, she answered:

"Kilcattle and Bunman and the others who were paid this morning."

And when Marcourt had looked at his wife in amaze she added earnestly:

"Oh! I forgot in the sheer joy of it to tell you, we paid *all* the tradesmen. All of them! You should have seen their dear faces! Poor things, they've been waiting such a long while."

And as Marcourt was still wrapped in astonishment, she said timidly:

"Oh! I hope you didn't mind my using part of the money you would insist on settling on me. You see I would rather have spent it that way than on clothes. I really would, Mr. Mar—I mean—George," she pronounced it very timidly.

She leaned towards him. "It was like this. We were going to pay, of course, as the children grew up. It takes such a lot to keep children. There are twelve of them and——"

"Only twelve!" Marcourt gasped. At a rough guess he would have said it would take at least half a hundred to sprawl all over the house and the garden, and hang on fences and climb trees. He seemed overcome at his want of calculation.

Anniversary

"Only twelve!" said Enid happily. "The dear things! But children take so long to grow up, you know, and such a lot to keep on a small stipend."

She was little more than a child herself, this girl who had twisted her long plaits into a tight ball at the back of her head for the first time on her wedding-day.

"When they grew up we were going to pay off the bills. I couldn't go out into the world to work because there was so much to do in the house and garden. And often mother was ill. We used to save a bit by growing our own greens. I know all about planting vegetables, so if we had a garden in London——"

"Good heavens!" said Marcourt very low. He mopped his brow as if he found the weather suddenly above the normal. A vision came to him of his wife, George William Marcourt's wife, digging up praties or setting cabbages in the small but exclusive plot of lawn on which dukes and duchesses had been pleased to dine on summer nights when one's butler discovered that such surroundings were fashionable. One's butler, even if one be a duke or duchess, always knows better than oneself what is most fashionable!

Marcourt's face looked quite grave for a moment. A fashionable sister-in-law of his whom he had hitherto left out of the programme would have to be given charge of the social orchestra, if the matrimonial intermezzo was to be well and duly performed.

He could see the horrified glance from Lady Emma's eyes when they rested on his bride's travelling costume—a veritable triumph of the village dressmaker's heart,—yet even Paquin might have dressed the bride had it not been for that butcher chap, What-was-his-name, and Thingmebob the baker, and all the rest of them.

"Are—you—angry?" whispered a voice near him and he turned quickly. There were tears and something of fear in the eyes watching him. The little freckled hands, still holding the unstretched kid-gloves, were hot and trembling. He held them fast, protesting. Words tumbled over one another.

"My dear one . . . no—no. Why should you think that? . . . Don't cry, dearie! It's all right. Only I'm going to make you so happy, you're going to forget all about everything else. And there'll be no more bills for the people at Weaslehurst vicarage. It is really too terrible." He mopped his brow again.

She sobbed a little. He bent his head, his good-natured, loving face near hers, trying to hear what she was whispering over and over again.

"What is it, little one?"

And at last he heard.

"I—I want to go back. . . . I want to—go home."

"But, Enid darling—you are married now. You belong to me."

"I don't want to be married. . . . I—I feel lonely. If they had all come with us——"

Marcourt thanked heaven piously that "all that tribe," as he designated them, had not. He was thankful also that he had decided on the long drive in the motor-car. He prayed devoutly that his young bride's eyes would be less red and her face less white when they reached London.

He was very much in love with his wife, and he was, above all, an honest English gentleman in every sense of the word. Otherwise life might have spelt wreckage for them both at the very outset. If he were a little elderly, he was kind and forbearing. Youth might have been less considerate, more impetuous. But Youth, on the other hand, might have answered to youth!

But if Enid Marcourt had, then and there, registered her impressions of that first step in her honeymoon, she would have said with characteristic frankness, and unaware of all that was in the admission, that she felt very sad and vaguely afraid of something unknown, but looming ever nearer; of a long journey, with the kind elderly gentleman who was a friend of the squire's fussing over her, and wanting her to eat something or drink something at almost every inn they passed.

Because she was very tired of the preparations for her wedding—in the baking and cooking for the village feast she had played no small part—she had fallen asleep on that journey. It was growing dark then, for they had left Weaslehurst late in the afternoon. Marcourt had not the interior of the car lit. He sat very still while his young bride, with her face against his shoulder, slept in the sheer exhaustion following on a week's hard work.

Unknown to Marcourt she had been up until two that morning even, doing some necessary mending and darning for some of the twelve, because the little mother had been utterly worn out by the bustle and unexpected preparations of an early wedding.

So the girl-bride slept, her face against her bridegroom's shoulder, his arm about her. Now and again it tightened and he stared straight before him at the square of window-glass in front, at the chauffeur's head outlined blackly and stiffly against the car-lights!

The car-top was open and the wind fluttered the girl's hair gently, stirring the childish curls about her face. A lump came to George Marcourt's throat.

"God deal with me as I deal with her!" he prayed silently.

They came to a London gay with lights, full of strange, hoarse cries; jostling human beings, like black ants, surging backwards and forwards in different directions; whistles shrieked with unnecessary shrillness, motors hooted hoarsely, buses thundered by.

The noise woke her with a start. The glare, the flashing signs, something in the volatile atmosphere caught her! She gazed in awed silence as they drove by, swept out at last by the winding river with its yellow stars flickering along the shadowed banks and glimmering in the water. It was all so different from Weaslehurst.

So they came home, George Marcourt and his girl-bride—she walking shyly beside him up the great stairs, on either side of the hall the waiting, simpering, curious servants. In all that house she knew only one soul. All else was strange, wonderful but alien. To him she had turned instinctively, vaguely afraid of him in a sense, but more afraid of the new and unknown future without him. . . .

Now, here in the smoking-den, on this day seven years afterwards, George Marcourt sat and thought of those days. The cigar grew cold in his fingers. He had not heard the light tap of heels on the polished floor of the hall. Between it and his den a great rug sprawled, deadening the sound of footsteps. Mrs. Marcourt came to the door, looked in, then stood stock-still.

"Why—*George!*" she half whispered. She leaned against the door, staring at him as if she were not sure whether he were a vision conjured up out of her thoughts.

She was all in blue, a deep warm tone of blue, simply made, clinging to her figure in soft lines. She had a light cloak on, a little pill-box hat tilted high at one side with a single red rose.

"George!" she said. The rose trembled on its wire stalk.

He sat up at once and jumped to his feet when he saw her.

"Why—my dear!" he said, "I believe I have been dreaming."

He came towards her, drew her, unresisting, into the room, looked at her and smiled happily.

"How charming you look, little wife, even in this half-light! I must switch them all on so that I may take a good look at you——"

Gaily he talked on and led her back to the chair.

"Sit down, Enid, while I light up."

"Don't—switch on the lights—yet," she said, and

then: "George, why were you sitting here, all alone? Has—has anything happened? Are you ill?"

He patted her hand reassuringly, coming back to her at the first sound of her voice.

"No, dear, nothing has happened. And I am not ill." He laughed heartily. "It is unusual for me to come home at this hour, I know. But then this is a most momentous day, dear, as you will admit."

He seated himself on the arm of the chair, passing his arm lightly about her shoulders.

"The—most momentous day!" she repeated. A sharp note came into her voice.

"Do you mean to say you have forgotten, Enid? And after my telling myself that you would remember and would scold me if I were late for dinner. And you were singing when I came in."

"Yes, I was singing," she said. She quivered suddenly in his embrace.

He tweaked her ear playfully. "So you did remember after all and were only teasing me, Puss, were you? Of course, I might have known that no woman ever forgets the anniversary of her wedding-day."

"The—anniversary—of—her wedding-day," she said dully. Then suddenly she began to laugh, fighting hard against hysteria. "Of course, George! And so you came home—like an old-fashioned husband in a book——" She began to laugh again, a little shrilly. "Like in a book—the eleventh hour——"

He looked at her anxiously. Something was wrong, but what was it? Good-natured, blundering George Marcourt, burdened with more heart than perception, had a sudden sense of chill. It passed as swiftly as it came.

"Don't you know," Mrs. Marcourt was saying, still shrilly, still laughing, "that no husband, nowadays, ever is so much in love with his own wife that he comes home expressly to tell her so? Modern husbands should not be in love with their wives at all——" She stopped suddenly, running down like an unwound clock. But against him her shoulders shook with suppressed emotion; whether laughter or tears, one could not guess. George thought she was teasing him.

"I am one of an old-fashioned type, then," he said cheerfully and proudly. He patted in that characteristic way of his the hand, clenched a little, that rested on her lap. "And you, I know, are only echoing Emma's claptrap sentiments. Dear, terrible Emma! which reminds me when I came in I saw some roses in the hall from her, which shows that she hasn't forgotten us either. By the way, I suppose she will follow in person directly. What is the time?" He had taken out his watch, but was unable to see clearly in the fast-fading light.

Mrs. Marcourt stirred suddenly and spoke. "It is—almost seven," she said, and then, speaking in a curious jerky way, "Why do you—think that—Emma—will be here?"

He put his arm again with its air of possessive affection about her shoulders. He felt her tremble. "Oh! she rang me up on the telephone at the club, and said she was coming. Confound her!" he said easily. "Of course, I told her this was an evening when one didn't want inquisitive sisters-in-law poking round. But you know old Emma! She said she knew you would not refuse and that I must tell you she was coming." He laughed. "Which reminds me that she sent you another message. One of those fashionable tomfool messages that only Emma and her special coterie consider mystical and smart."

Somewhere in the half-darkness a clock ticked steadily.

"And—the message, George?" She spoke very quietly, but her hands lay tightly closed in her lap.

Marcourt scratched his head. "Dash it! If I haven't nearly forgotten it. But it was something about the Park——"

"*The Park!*" The words, formed soundlessly, caught back at the very instant of utterance. She sat up suddenly, very straightly.

George yawned. "Let me see now. Oh! this is it, one of those problem-things, you know, that are considered epigrammatic. Emma wants you to solve it. Says she couldn't wait until to-morrow."

"Well?" Her heart was pounding fast; and in the shadows the clock ticked on and on, flinging the seconds madly aside as things of no account.

"The problem was how many women in London suffer from myopic sight through watching the Spring in the Park?" He began to laugh. "Did you ever hear of such a thing? What a subject for a discussion! And what Society woman goes to the Park to look at the Spring?" He pinched her cold cheek. "She goes to Bond Street instead."

He chuckled at his own wit, got up and began

to wander about the room, dilating, as was his way, on the subject.

In the chair Mrs. Marcourt sat, very rigid, staring straight before her.

"And that is what Emma wants to know? To-night?"

He chuckled anew. "Cunning old thing, Emma! Isn't she? She comes here, gets you to solve the problem for her whatever it is. For the life of me, I can't see it! And then she will go off and proclaim it triumphantly as *her* find."

His wife, still sitting in the chair, shivered. Dear, terrible old Emma! How those chance words of Marcourt's described her!

Old Emma, otherwise known to the world and his wife as Lady Beckendon, could be dear or terrible, according to her mood. She smashed her way, like a kicking colt, through all the barriers you might raise. Emma came straight to the point; indeed, she came down on it with a crash that also brought down all one's prettily-painted wall-plaques, on which one's thoughts were beautifully mottoed for the view of the public.

What you laid out for the inspection of the public did not matter a tuppenny toss to Emma—the simile itself is Emma's, and characteristic. Emma wanted to know what you had stored away in the cupboard under the stairs. She had a veritable genius for discovering that you had such a cupboard. Other people were content to walk up your well carpeted stairs, and smile and bow over your hand at the top. But not Emma! She looked in the cupboard first to see what your family skeleton was like, and whether it might well be so old that it had practically crumbled to dust. Incidentally, she had been known to remark that the old family variety was of small moment. It was whether you went in personally for collecting skeletons nowadays that mattered most to Emma!

So while George Marcourt chuckled, and looked forward to Emma's visit in spite of the preference that he would rather have had dinner alone, Mrs. Marcourt sat amid the growing shadows of the room and peopled it with visions. But the dear vision that had held her all day had vanished. She knew then, what she told herself bitterly she should have known before, that this thing might not be. And Emma, somehow, knew!

Oh! mad and glad, and bad and sweet, it could not be! The river of her destiny flowed on, passing those high banks on which the flowers of her dreams still bloomed. . . .

Oh! she would have gone whatever came. If only Emma did not come! But Emma had razed her castles to the dust. She put her hand to her head in a dazed way. What was it George was saying? How far away his voice seemed! It mingled with the peremptory jangling bell that announced a visitor.

In the hall a queer old figure, which at a distance looked as if she had donned the heterogeneous collection of a secondhand clothes shop, was scolding the footman soundly for delay in opening the door.

She resembled nothing so much as a beflustered turkey, with her small bright eyes, the gobbler-like pouches under them, and with her general air of ruffled plumage, wisps of hair escaping from its net and cheeks flushed with rouge.

Emma Lady Beckendon could afford to dress in this weird fashion, because one of her ancestors came over with the Normans. People who knew Emma well decided that he probably came out of curiosity!

And last, but not least, in the worldly world in which she moved, this style of dress was considered eccentric. Eccentricity, by some queer conclusion, masquerades nowadays as intellect and notoriety passes for fame.

As George and his wife came to the door the haranguing in the hall ceased. The queer, turkey-gobbler figure fluttered forwards, neck outstretched, talking volubly.

"My *dear* people——" it began shrilly.

Dear, terrible old Emma had arrived!

CHAPTER VII

La Dame Terrible

LADY EMMA BECKENDON gave her hand to George and pecked Enid on the cheek at one and the same moment.

"Were you going out?" she asked, an enigmatic light flashing into her shrewd eyes. "I see Enid is dressed in walking garb."

George broke in cheerfully. "No, no, not at all, I assure you. No—Emma—really, not a scrap of bother! My fault entirely! I have just told Enid, as a matter of fact. You're nice and early anyway, Emma, so that gives us time to tumble into something."

Emma had lifted her gold lorgnette. She gazed at him and then at Enid grimly. She looked somewhat disappointed. Had she been mistaken, after all?

"Of course, if dear Enid was *not* going out——"

Dear Enid, George assured her on the brilliant inspiration of the moment and with a desire not to offend, was not going, but—but—er—just coming in.

Lady Beckendon's gobbler eyes blinked at that. She appeared to be thinking with amazing rapidity.

"Is that so! Well—how stupid of me, to be sure! But I thought Enid looked as if she were going out to dine quietly. You were not thinking of that, were you, because, after all——"

"Oh! I assure you we weren't thinking of that at all," Marcourt answered her. "On the contrary, to tell you the truth, Emma"—they were following Enid, who was leading the way into the small, cosy room that opened off the drawing-room—"to tell you the truth, I have been asleep."

"Um!" Emma gave a snort. "I often wonder, George, if you are ever properly awake."

Marcourt threw back his head and laughed. Emma delighted, he knew, in saying rude things. It was considered very smart.

"You scored there," he agreed amicably.

She was looking past him at his wife. "Yes, I can score," she replied significantly.

She sank into a chair. In another minute she would follow Enid upstairs and take off her cloak, and get Enid's maid to pin up some of the stray wisps of hair that would persist in tumbling down. For the moment it would be interesting, as well as cool, to sit in this softly-shaded room.

Enid was wandering round in restless fashion. Now she, too, sat down for a few seconds. The gobbler eyes, noting that she chose a seat as far away from the light as possible, blinked thoughtfully, the lips pursed.

"Now tell me just what you thought you were dreaming about, George Marcourt?" said Lady Emma. "Of your wife, of course?"

"Of course!" He laughed happily and bent forward. In a way he was fond of old Emma, and old Emma in her gruff way was fond of him.

"Umph! It's nowadays the fashion to think of

someone else's wife, George. Not that I would ever expect that of you, all the same. Were you dreaming that Enid was still a little country-girl, with more knowledge of cabbages than life?"

Enid spoke suddenly. "Ah, no! He could not think that." She tried to smile as usual. "You see, Lady Emma, you turned me into quite a worldly person and gave me worldly ideas. The credit of the complete metamorphosis belongs to you and you only."

This was certainly a bomb flung right into the enemy's camp.

Lady Emma snorted and frowned thoughtfully.

"Did I? Well, well"—she looked at Enid—"I'm wondering whether I've made too good a job of it."

Marcourt said lazily, "She certainly is as stylish and as up-to-date as any of them." He drew out his watch. "Well, if you people are thinking of dining——"

Lady Emma rose and prepared to follow Enid.

"I'll come in with you, if you don't mind," she said pleasantly enough, "and talk to you while you are changing your frock. I thought we might go on to something or other afterwards at one of the theatres—that is," and she shot her a quick glance, "if you have no other appointment."

For a moment the last tapering flame of hope leaped up in the heart of Enid Marcourt. She knew it was not right, but the thought and the hope persisted. If she just might for one moment, even, say good-bye! Oh! it was cruel, cruel, that Fate should have chosen to-night, should have herded her like a sheep into a pen from which there was no escape. If she could only go to the telephone and send some word through! Then she thought of the restaurant, of Philip in mufti, sitting there. If she telephoned and gave a message his name would be cried out amid that gathering. He would be in mufti she knew.

"Captain Territt! Is Captain Philip Territt here? A lady wants him at the 'phone."

Captain Territt! She could see the curious, interested faces, hear the eager whispers. Territt! Why, yes, it was *the* Territt, you remember. Got his V.C. in South Africa, you've heard the story, bravest thing of its kind, and there was that affair at Banshari—and so on.

How could she speak over the 'phone? What could she find to say? For the same reason he would wait on and on. From the restaurant or from a near-by booth he would not 'phone lest she, detained until then by some chance, should come in his absence. She saw the passing moments turn into hours. Still he would wait until knowledge came that waiting was in vain.

She went up the stairs slowly, answering Lady Emma at random. As they went into her boudoir Lady Beckendon said casually:

"Enid, get rid of your maid. I'll fix your hooks and buttons for you"; and then, "I want to talk to you."

When the maid had been dismissed, Enid shut the door, stood there, slim and tall, for a moment. She looked straight at Lady Emma Beckendon.

"Is it about the problem?"

Lady Emma laughed as she sat down on the divan.

"So George told you there was a problem."

"Yes," Enid spoke quietly. "You wished me to solve it apparently, or you would not have sent me the message."

"My dear girl, there is only you who can do so."

"Is it so complicated, then? Am I supposed to have a special gift in that direction?" Her quiet voice trembled now.

"You have many gifts," said old Lady Emma sharply, "and one of them the God-given one of a good husband, Enid. Another and, to my mind, greater, He gave you among other gifts that priceless one of an old name that has never known dishonour."

The colour flooded into Enid's face. She walked over to the mirror and began aimlessly to fumble among the ivory and gold brushes. She stared at them blindly.

"And—has this any bearing on your problem?"

"A very great deal," said Emma, still sharply. "Enid, did you see me in Hyde Park to-day?"

"No, I didn't." Her hands fluttered.

"I thought you didn't. But I saw you. Luckily nobody else did—nobody else, that is, that counts in our world. Enid, aren't you rather foolish?"

The girl said nothing. At Lady Emma's quick words, tinkling forth one on the heels of the other, she had started and the colour went out of her face.

"I believe you have too much good sense to drag the name of Marcourt into the arena of gossip and scandal. So I thought a word of advice from one older and wiser would help."

Enid went over to the wardrobe, lifted out a frock in silence, and hung it over a chair. Her face was quite white now. Her hand, removing her outdoor boots for satin shoes, trembled slightly.

"You don't want to talk about it, I see," said Lady Emma. "You think I'm an interfering old busybody. But I ain't! If I've taken you in tow in other things, and piloted you safely through smooth waters, I'm not goin' to let you drift now you are near the rocks of disaster."

The girl turned passionately round and cried to her, "Oh! cannot you be silent? Have you never lived? Have *you* never suffered?"

"Yes, Enid Marcourt, I have," and the old head nodded violently and the eyes blinked rapidly. "It isn't one's own little boat alone, remember, that smashes on the rock. It's the big stately ships that follow one that are also caught and sucked under. And when it's all too late there's nothing to do but weep and wail over misfortune and blame it on to everybody else but oneself. Weeping and wailing don't do anybody or anything any good. But when I first knew—five years ago——"

Enid caught hold of the edge of the dressing-table.

"You knew five years ago," she whispered. She stared at Lady Emma. "You—knew."

"Of course I knew. I saw it from the first moment Philip Territt looked at you. Over my table, too. Um! I didn't interfere because I knew there was nothing to interfere about. When he went suddenly away I knew you had sent him. It was the right and proper thing to do, and you did it. I felt proud of you. But now, Enid, I'm not going to beat about the bush. For one thing there isn't time before dinner, and I hate to have to talk about unpleasant things after a meal."

She swung open there and then the door, as it were, of the cupboard under the stairs, dragged out the skeleton peremptorily, and rattled its bones victoriously.

"Enid," she said, "why did you meet Territt, if you were going to meet him at all, in a public place like Hyde Park?"

"Our meeting was quite accidental." Enid was fumbling with her gown, glad of the occupation, for the opportunity to turn from those searching eyes.

What was the avail of anger, of resentment? What did any of these things matter, in face of the fact that she and Philip Territt had once and for all said good-bye to each other?

"I believe you," said Lady Emma, "and I believe, also, that you must be feeling things very deeply when you could forget that other people besides yourself and Philip Territt existed. You forgot even that you held your husband's honour in your hands."

The girl swung round. She looked at Lady Emma. "I was—as you term it—feeling things deeply. I am not ashamed to say that. Oh! I feel I could go to George and tell him so as well. I will go this minute——"

"You'll do nothin' of the sort," declared Lady Emma, rising in her wrath. "Would you go and wreck at one blow all the happiness of about the only good man I know? Out upon you! No, you'll do the only thing left to you to do. You'll go on livin' and playin' the game, lest you bring trouble and sorrow to others; and you *will* play the game. You'll do as I did in similar circumstances."

"As *you* did!" Enid exclaimed. Suddenly she threw herself face down on the couch near and broke into repressed sobbing. Until then it had seemed incredible that Emma had ever been young.

Lady Emma walked up and down the room for a moment, her old head nodding, her mouth set very tight. Presently she came to a pause by the girl's recumbent figure.

"Yes, as I did," she said. "Do you think you are the only woman to suffer in that way? By no means! This is the commercial age when the heart and the hand go but seldom together. But it's a sportin' age, too, and therefore the game is played for the most part in a fair spirit. Do you think that either you or Philip Territt could bring happiness to yourselves without inflicting sorrow on others?"

"What am I to do? Oh, what am I to do?" Enid was whispering to herself. "I can't go on living."

"You'll go on livin' right enough," remarked Lady Emma stoutly. "You can't wrest things from life, or death, or Nature itself, without havin' to pay the price, and a terrible price at that. The laws that govern this world are, after all, not earthly laws, when one comes down to bedrock facts."

She bent over the girl and touched her up-flung arm with unexpected gentleness.

"Come, Enid!" she said in a softer tone. "It is your call. In a little while the curtain will go up and the play begin. There's a great many of us know just how hard it is, and how the glare of the footlights hurts the eyes. Remember, for all my gruffness, I've gone through it. And I'm an old, old woman, and it's a long time since it happened. But I can tell you that weepin' doesn't mend matters. Come! Powder your eyes and rouge your cheeks. We are late."

She had half lifted, half dragged the girl, bundled her somehow into her frock, talking volubly all the time. One began to know why the world used the prefix "dear" as well as that of "terrible."

"Enid, my dear, this is the hardest part of all, the first step into the glare of reality. But it has to be done. When you get through this evenin' you will have gone over the worst strip of all the road to come. And that's why I'm here to help you over it."

The last button was done as the first bell ran for dinner.

"A little more powder," suggested Lady Emma. As the girl turned, the reflection stared back at her in the mirror—a slim, pale reflection, wide-eyed, tragical, wistful-mouthed. "*And* some colour!"

Lady Emma frowned as she hunted for rouge and herself applied it. Enid's eyes haunted her.

"One of the lessons of life," she announced, "is

this, that if you have suffering, you have no right to inflict it on others who, but for you, might otherwise escape it. The world has far too much of suffering as it is. There ought to be a special purgatory for people who go bansheeing through the world. A dog gets into his kennel, a beast into some quiet corner of the field, and each suffers mutely. So should we!"

Enid shivered, but said no word.

Lady Emma went to the door and opened it.

"Let us go down," she said. "After dinner we might go to a comedy——"

"Oh, no, no!" said Enid quickly, but Lady Emma nodded her head sharply.

"I know what is best for you, Enid. Even if I went now, as you are wishing I would, would it not be more terrible for you to be left alone with George? Heaven only knows what you might do! You might even tell the unfortunate man, and if I can prevent that I will, because it can serve no good end. Why should you break his heart? The knowledge would kill him."

Enid looked at her, her mouth twisted piteously.

"Oh, child! Don't look like that! Nothin' in life is worth it, I tell you. *Nothing!*" She bent forward suddenly, kissed the girl fiercely, and pushed her away quickly. "You've got to come somewhere to-night, Enid. You and I and George. We will go where there is music. Not to a comedy, after all, for you would not laugh when others did. Your eyes would give you away."

As she neared the door, she turned back to ask a question.

"When does—Captain Territt sail?"

She spoke twice before Enid whispered the answer.

"About ten o'clock!"

Lady Emma nodded. "Ah, well! you have two hours or more in which you must not let yourself think of anything outside your own domestic *ménage*."

"And—afterwards?" Enid said suddenly, and her eyes stared at Lady Emma and beyond her.

"There is no afterwards. When a thing is inevitable, when it has come to pass and the hour has struck, then one realises that everything else but submission to fate is in vain. And then you will find a certain measure of rest that I know seems impossible now."

They went down the wide stairs. At the landing Lady Emma paused and glanced at the slim figure beside her. Then she made one of those totally unexpected remarks that had gained for her the *sobriquet* of "terrible."

She said bluntly, "Why don't you have babies, Enid? There's nothing like one's own children in all the world! They fill up all the blank places in life."

And Enid went pink under her rouge, for she was still a country girl for all her eight years of city life and city ways.

She stammered, "Oh!" and then, "I love babies. But I—I, oh, I don't know——"

"Well, then, you ought!" said Lady Emma with

her characteristic bluntness, and later that night, after the dinner was over—and throughout it Lady Emma gabbled at an amazing rate about everybody and everything and nothing in particular—she fired the same question at George Marcourt.

They were standing alone, waiting for Enid, who had gone upstairs for something or other. She took a very long time to get it.

"Probably she is praying!" thought terrible old Emma contemptuously to herself, and then sighed.

George Marcourt had looked somewhat disturbed at Emma's question. Really, dash it all, Emma was just a bit over the mark.

"I know quite well what you're thinking," said Emma. She waved her fan at him as if she consigned him and his thoughts to oblivion. "What I want to know is, are *you thinking* of Enid?"

Marcourt said with dignity, "I would lay down my life for Enid, but I don't want her to lay down her life for me."

There followed a short pause.

"Um! A great deal of that sort of thing is stuff and nonsense, of course. What makes you say that?"

Marcourt interrupted her. "When Enid was very ill once, after that riding accident the year of our marriage, I had a chat with the doctor."

They were skating over thin ice, and George Marcourt tried to perform his evolutions as delicately and gracefully as possible. Emma, on the contrary, might flounder into deep water at any moment and drag one under.

"And the doctor?"

"He said that an operation would have to be performed, that it might not be satisfactory, and that in any case it would be serious. She was much more badly hurt in that fall during the hunting than I knew at the time."

She nodded. "It's a pity." She spoke as if to herself.

He said with sudden passion, "As far as I am concerned, I do not care. I love my wife. She is more to me than any child, much as I perhaps once would have cared for one, could ever be. She, in fact, is my child to me as well as my wife. Once, Emma"—and he turned to her with dignity—"once, you remember, you told me I was too old for her."

"Yes, I remember," she said sourly. "I was always a wise woman."

"Well, time has proved you wrong. No two people could be honestly happier than we are. Look at Enid! I never see her flirting around, like many another young married woman of our acquaintance. There are no poodle-men hanging about *my* home, thank God! Here we are, eight years married to-night, and not even the shadow of unhappiness lies between us. Enid and I are all in all to each other."

And then Enid came down the stairs, with her wistful mouth trying to smile, and the rouge flush bright on her cheeks; and Lady Emma turned her head abruptly away and cleared her throat.

"By the way," said Marcourt later as they filed into the waiting motor, "did Enid solve the problem for you?"

"Oh, yes!" said Lady Emma carelessly. "Quite well! We have decided that hypermetropic sight is the solution."

Marcourt laughed.

"And what in the name of all good fortune is that?"

"I'm not sure if it isn't misfortune, George. Anyway, hypermetropic sight is what the oculists call long sight—the power, you know, of seeing things at long range, but inability to discern those close at hand."

"Oh! I know what you mean now," he laughed, as he followed them into Lady Emma's car. "I once had a dog who suffered from it. It sounds very involved, and what it has to do with your problem I can't see; I've forgotten it anyway; but it—the complaint, I mean—is pretty common, isn't it?"

"*Very!*" said Lady Emma caustically.

CHAPTER VIII

The End of the Night

THE play was ending; the curtain would soon ring down; the last bars of the music were drifting towards triumphant close. In the stalls and the circle people were searching furtively for the usual mislaid scarf or handkerchief.

Everybody in the theatre knew that everybody on the stage in another second or two would troop before the footlights, holding each other's hands and bowing and smiling in the same old way. Lady Emma yawned and leaned forward, resting her marvellously beringed hand on the velvet ledge of the box.

"Everything fizzles out so just before the end," she complained. "Even the elocutionary outbursts of the hero fall flat then, because he is thinking more of his supper than of the audience. Well, the profession would rise up and call me cursed if they heard I said that. They would write columns about it in the paper denouncing me and pointing to the lofty heights of drama. They would speak of the food of the soul."

She looked at Enid, who was white under her rouge.

"Which reminds me, dear people," went on Lady Emma, "that I know of a dinky place for supper. Just a little—well—out of the usual. But I don't see why you shouldn't go. One had better be dead than not up to date, you know, and the ideal of smart Society at present appears to be to ape the demi-monde as much as possible."

Marcourt protested. But Enid said nothing. She was still looking at the stage, where someone or other was giving the cue for the final move. She seemed very interested, but Lady Emma Beckendon knew that Enid Marcourt had not heard a word.

"You are an old fool, George," Lady Emma was saying complacently. "The only time you see life is when I put you on a lead and drag you there."

George Marcourt chuckled.

"Did you hear that, Enid? Well, well, one never knows! To think of you, Emma, at your age!"

The band burst forth in a blare of sound. Everybody on the stage crowded towards the footlights, wearing that thin, rather weary smile, and offering up a silent pæan of thanks that the performance was over for the night.

Under cover of the music and the medley of voices in the final chorus Lady Emma said to Enid:

"Come! If it is only for half an hour."

"But I am so tired." Her eyes were piteous. Save for the pink patches of rouge her face was white.

"But not tired enough. Stay until you are too tired to think, to move even. Then go home and go straight to bed. There's nothing in life that is worth the wrinkling of one's face."

The old eyes looked strangely kind, peering at the girl. Enid gave a sigh. To George's astonishment it was she, after all, who seemed most eager they should go to the restaurant of which Emma spoke.

George looked puzzled, a trifle discontented with the new order. He had hoped Enid and he might go home and sit and chat together. But he did not oppose. If Enid wished it, well, there you were! So they went. From the darkness of the streets with their hooded lights they came to a blaze of brightness in a garish, heavily-perfumed room, tables crowded with flowers, beautiful and shining gowns of every hue, and a whirl of ragtime music.

They found a table in a corner. On the strip of carpet dividing one side of the room from another a barefooted couple, clad in some queer garb, were dancing.

Laughter and chatter of many voices and the clink of glasses rose about them. The haze of smoke grew thick, wreathing its way towards the decorated ceiling.

"This is life," said Lady Emma in her grim way, "of which we read in the evening papers. You get a far better impression of the wickedness of London and its gaiety from the evening papers than one ever gets from the real thing. I always think those reporters must dip their pens deep into the well of imagination."

"It all seems very dull to me," George Marcourt remarked. "Women and men eating, and eating very poor food at that, and another man and woman dancing a Russian dance, or a French dance, or an Italian dance. What is their nationality, anyway?"

"Oh! you can only tell that by the costumes they

wear. The nationality changes with the garb, you see. Probably they are all Cockneys. Yes, it's all very dull. It always *is* dull. But the reporter-man must give a hint about wickedness or no one would come at all!"

George grunted and attacked the microscopic portion of food which the generous proprietor of the restaurant doled out to his customers. What it lost in quantity was made up apparently in name, a many-lettered and puzzling combination which might be Russian—and might not.

The dancers had danced themselves out of the red-carpeted aisle. From another corner of the room, near the piano, a young girl in an Italian costume and an unmistakable Yorkshire accent began to warble of how she longed to be in Dixie.

"And them's my sentiments, too!" quoted Lady Emma as she listened critically. "I wonder whether the supper is to help us forget the singer, or the singer is to help us forget the supper."

Enid Marcourt sat apparently listening. Her face was towards the singer and when the song ended her eyes rested on the far end of the room. There was an empty table by the orchestra. Enid peopled it with two, herself and one other. The glare of the room, the glitter of silver, the chiming of laughter like bells a little out of tune, a little harsh and hard here and there, all this passed her by. And Lady Emma chattered on like an irrepressible magpie. She dragged Marcourt after her, whether he would or no, in her excursions of thought.

Once over Enid Marcourt's face came a queer,

pinched look. Her face took on a greyish hue. The purple shadows under her eyes showed plainly. She was staring at the clock on the wall with its gold cupids, its rose-wreathed motto underneath in gilt letters:

"Gather the roses while ye may, Old Time is still a-flying."

Lady Emma glanced hurriedly at George, but he was engrossed in the whitebait. George was very fond of whitebait.

She thought Enid was about to become hysterical, or faint. But Enid, turning her grey face to her, smiled wanly. Then her eyes went back to the clock again, and Lady Emma saw that the hands stood at the hour when from the Docks a big ship would slip quietly from its moorings.

And here laughter and mirth rioted, gathering the rose of the flying hour, a rose wilting, its stem secretly rotten, but passing fair in the glare of artificial light. Mirth masqueraded, its mouth twisted into smiles, its painted face alluring and mocking. It danced on the very edge of death for a good many of the men here that night. But they lifted the glass to their lips and quaffed the sparkling draught.

The music swung on into a mad revel and carried them all for the instant with it. Faster and faster it pulsed and beat as the night began to die away. What was the use of remembering? cried the music. Live for the moment and the moment only! And like a minor chord a question crept into it. What of the morrow and the after-reckoning? But the band drowned the answer. Life was but a revel, a battle of flowers, and the mind was but for idle thoughts. Why think of the morrow? it cried, forgetting that the morrow was almost here.

Lady Emma leaned over and touched Enid lightly on the shoulder with her plumed fan.

"You are not eating anything," she said, "and the proverbial penny is yours for the taking."

Enid roused herself with a start from her absorption, turned her eyes towards her, and then for a moment her eyes rested on her husband's face with a curious, steady gaze.

"I was thinking—just then—of home, of the vicarage"; and then to her husband, "George, I think I should like to go there to-morrow—to Weaslehurst. May I?"

"To-morrow," said Lady Emma, "is almost here." But neither heard.

"Why, of course you shall, Enid." He looked at her, puzzled. "I thought you were enjoying yourself listening and watching the crowd. Are you tired, dear? Shall we go?" He half rose.

"Directly," she said. "No, not just now! I have a fancy to wait until midnight."

It lacked but twenty minutes to the hour. The band was beginning to play a dreamy, haunting waltz. Enid sat very still, her face turned towards it, listening. George sat back in his chair and told himself that they really had good whitebait here, the only decent thing on the menu, and he hummed the tune the band played as an outward expression of his inward satisfaction.

Lady Emma leaned forward with her elbows on

the table—one's ancestor's coming over with the Normans makes all the difference in one's doing or not doing this—and beat time with many noddings of her head. Every time she nodded the tall black osprey with its single diamond nodded, too.

Into the room, to that table at the far end, ushered by an obsequious waiter, came a small party of people. Lady Emma lifted her gold lorgnette at once.

"It's the War Horse and her daughter," she announced, "the last remaining one, that is. What's-her-name? Beatrice? Oh, yes, that's it!"

It was, indeed, the Byndhams and a couple of well known folk—a notoriety-seeking Duchess and a girl friend, and two staff officers, relations home from the vicinity of the staff headquarters.

"That girl Beatrice," observed Lady Emma, "really looks very well. She is quite pretty." She turned to Enid. "Is she engaged to anybody, to anybody that is anybody, that is?"

"No!" A spasm of pain passed for a fleeting second over Enid Marcourt's face, and Lady Emma's shrewd eyes noticed it.

"And this is her second season! Humph!" She looked again at the vivacious party. They all seemed happy and very gay indeed.

George broke idly across her comments. He held his cigarette-case across to her as he spoke. "I believe there is an understanding between her and Territt," he said, "Philip Territt, you know. Awfully straight sort of chap; good sport. You used to be interested in him, Emma."

Lady Emma was looking very attentively at the

cigarette-case with its array of different brands that Marcourt carried for just such occasions. She selected one very carefully, looked at its purple silk critically, and then answered:

"I still am. What makes you think there is anything between him and this Byndham girl?"

He nodded his head in the direction of Mrs. Byndham's flat white back with its almost superfluous bodice.

"She told me so herself."

"Beatrice—or the War Horse?" asked Lady Emma casually.

"Mrs. Byndham. She said they met in India. That nothing was definitely arranged, of course."

"And possibly never would be," interrupted Emma. "'Distance makes for safety,' as the cat said to the monkey. Well?"

"That's all there is about it, I think," George remarked heavily. "Enid! Would you care for a cigarette? Try one of those silk-topped thingmebobs. You don't care for any? All right!" pressing the hand nearest to him. "Just as you like, of course, dear. We will have a smoke when we go home. What was that you were saying, Emma?"

"Is that all you know about it?"

George laughed. "Do you think I'm a matrimonial agent, my dear Emma? Of course, I said I hoped it would soon be publicly announced so that we might offer our congratulations, that he was a fine fellow—as he undoubtedly is—and that I knew the Territt family well. Old family, plenty of money, and all that sort of thing! She seemed very interested."

"She would be," said Emma drily.

"But I think the girl is genuinely in love with him. Really I do, and I'm rather glad of it. You know those Byndhams are the very deuce if they take the bit between their teeth."

"Yes, I know." Lady Emma rose. "Well, dear people——"

George rose, too, but when you got George interested in one particular topic you couldn't easily shake him off.

"Now this girl Beatrice, I like her," he said earnestly; "but still there's the Byndham strain in her, too, and sooner or later it will come out."

He was hunting round, finding their wraps, gathering up the paraphernalia of vanity-bags and fans and the apparently useless trifles women burden themselves with. "And I wish, Emma, you'd take the girl up. I know you wouldn't come to that little dinner the other night because Mrs. Byndham was coming."

"I don't like the War Horse. I never did," said Lady Emma bluntly, "and life is too short and your dining-table too narrow to be bothered with people one doesn't like."

George laughed and then grew serious again.

"Well, honestly, I'd like to see the affair through. Apart from what Mrs. Byndham told me, Tom confided in me before he died." His honest, well-meaning face turned to Emma. He knew that if Emma had ever really cared for anyone that person had been Tom Byndham.

Lady Emma sighed. "People always do confide

so in you, George. I wish they wouldn't, for all your relations have to suffer for it. What was the particular nature of this particular confidence, George?"

"He said it would break Beatrice's heart if anything came between her and Territt."

"People's hearts don't break so easily. I shouldn't think a Byndham heart was a brittle affair," she said impatiently and coldly.

The waiter, with a platter and a deferential air of having discovered who his guests were, was returning, bowing low, and fluttering around expectantly.

"It isn't. And that is why a Byndham is likely to run amok. I'd be sorry to see it in this case for poor Tom Byndham's sake. He was very fond of his youngest girl. I always liked him."

"Is there anybody you don't like?" asked Lady Emma in exasperation. She turned to Enid, who had been listening but had taken no part in the conversation, "Come, child, we must go!"

They went out of the restaurant, passing the group at the table. They looked up and nodded, and Lady Emma spoke to the Duchess a moment. The Duchess remarked conversationally, and with the air of one who knows, that things were very bright in the military zone at present. Lady Emma replied briefly that it looked like it. She also kindly asked one of the staff officers whether he had been within sound of the guns yet.

"Old cat!" said the Duchess when they had gone. She laughed uncomfortably and then shrugged her shoulders. "How sharp her claws are!"

"I thought," said one of the men, ignoring the subject of Lady Emma, "that Mrs. Marcourt looked a bit off colour to-night. Pretty woman, don't you think, but rather sad?"

"Anyone," declared the Duchess, "who sat between George and Emma would be sad. What do you say, Mrs. Byndham?"

Mrs. Byndham said that she agreed. But Mrs. Byndham always did agree with a Duchess.

During the drive homewards Emma did most of the talking. She was to drop them at the door. She rattled on in her grim, amusing way on almost every topic under the sun. George frankly dozed. Enid sat up very straight, answering only in monosyllables.

As the car drew up at the porticoed entrance Enid said briefly:

"Emma is coming in for just a second, George. I want to speak to her alone."

"About the problem?" asked Marcourt. "Or are you going to quarrel?" he chuckled. "Well, call me if you want any help, Enid."

He went upstairs and left them in the hall together.

"You can tell Marie I shall not require her, Trevor," said Mrs. Marcourt to the footman. He vanished. The two women faced each other, the girl tense and very white under her rouge, the older woman watching her with beady, enigmatic eyes.

In her white gown with the cluster of pale pink roses at her breast, her long azure, white-furred coat half slipping from her shoulders, Enid looked very lovely. But the childlike look had left her face. She was older, more resolute. Her eyes held a strange bitterness.

"The night is past," said Emma quietly.

Enid looked straight into her eyes. Her hands at her side clenched.

"There is one thing I want to tell you," she said, "and then we shall never speak of it again. Nor shall you speak of it to me. But"—and she drew her slim figure up to its proud height and she spoke very, very slowly—"only for you, only for you I would have gone away to-night somewhere. I would not have cared for the world—for anything—for anybody—for honour, or home, or king, or country. You didn't think that of me, did you? If he had asked me I should have gone away."

Lady Emma faced her. Her head was high too. Her voice rang like steel.

"It was because I knew that," she said, "that I came."

And then she went out into the night, where the car with its shrouded lights and its sleepy chauffeur winked. She held her head high as she stepped into the luxurious roomy comfort of the tonneau. All the way home to Grosvenor Square she held her old head high, but the tears dropped on her wrinkled hands.

"She hates me now," she said, "and she will hate me for a long, long time. But I have done the only thing I could do. I have done that which no other woman I know would have had the courage to do.

But I have saved the Marcourt name! In the morning she will thank me."

But the letter of thanks never came. Instead there arrived a note, brief but to the point, written from a heart that was undisciplined and surcharged with suffering, and in a moment when nothing else in life seemed to matter. It was indiscreet, but dreadfully in earnest.

"That night, had I gone to Soho," it said, "and had Philip asked me to go away with him, I would have gone."

Lady Emma shook her head as she put aside the note safely under lock and key. "It would be mean and wicked to show it to George."

She had hesitated whether she should burn it. But some impulse stayed her hand.

CHAPTER IX

Ashes

The footman came back into the hall, yawning. He saw Mrs. Marcourt's cloak lying on the floor where she had left it, and he picked it up and yawned again. He heard a slight sound behind him and turned hastily.

The wide door of the picture gallery opened on to the hall. The door was open. Two lights burned in their golden sconces above one of the pictures. And before the picture Mrs. Marcourt stood, looking fixedly at it.

Then her hand reached out. The switch clicked and the room was in darkness again. Mrs. Marcourt came into the hall walking slowly like one in sleep. The footman stepped quietly forward with the cloak, but Mrs. Marcourt apparently did not see him. When he spoke she did not hear him.

She went on up the stairs walking with incredible slowness, as if each step were an effort almost beyond her strength. As she went she whispered to herself just one word over and over:

"Ashes!" she said. "*Ashes!*"

And so she went up the stairs and came at last into her room. She began to take down her hair wearily. Its weight pained her, pressed against her brain. One idea was in her mind—rest and the quiet darkness, the quiet darkness and rest. She tried to hurry, but her fingers fumbled. She was still fumbling at some stubborn hooks on her bodice when the door between the rooms opened and George came in.

He was in silk-striped pyjamas of atrocious purple. George was very fond of purple. The heelless slippers made him shorter, the stripes seemed to accentuate his stoutness. His bald head glistened in the light. Mrs. Marcourt turned her head and looked at him as if she had never seen him before. Suddenly she sat down in the chair and began to shake with silent, soul-tearing sobs of suppressed laughter or tears. George hurried over in alarm. His fussy kindness tortured her almost beyond endurance.

"What is it, my darling? Darling, tell me. . . .. Tell George all about it. There . . . there .... there," with many pats he emphasised his words.

Then all at once his wife began to laugh instead of weeping. She laughed and laughed until the tears ran down her cheeks, and then as suddenly and without reason she began to sob, to sob and laugh and sob again.

George was genuinely distressed. He thought of ringing the bell, of sending for all the doctors he knew; his kind, slow-moving brain tried perplexedly to arrive at some decision as to what was best to be done. He hated scenes. He had never before known Enid to be hysterical. And then all at once Mrs. Marcourt stopped. She gave a great shuddering sigh and passed her hand over her eyes.

George looked at her with the kind, vaguely-tortured eyes of a sheep that dully knows it faces slaughter in some way. He knelt beside her.

"What is it, darling? What is it? Tell George all about it."

She did not push him away or answer. She just looked at him with her eyes so bright, almost hard, the tears trembling on the long dark lashes.

"Darling, can I get you anything? Shall I ring for Marie?"

She shook her head wearily. "No, I only want to sleep—to be in the cool, quiet darkness." She spoke very dully. "I want to be alone for a little while."

"So you shall, dearest," George said soothingly. "You shall. Rest here until I get you something—a glass of wine perhaps."

All sorts of odd rhymes were running mad races through her brain. One after another they leaped over hurdles, or filed through the gap of nothingness, like the sheep of dreams, searching vainly for the road of sleep.

"Yes—a glass of wine," she repeated mechanically, in answer to his anxious importunacy.

Then George left her, for he had elected to go himself instead of rousing the servants.

Enid Marcourt rose in his absence and wandered aimlessly, feverishly round the room. The rhymes still raced on in maddening, never-ending procession, round and round, in circles within circles. She lifted the blind and looked out into the night. It loomed black against the pane. Far below, by the river, the merest glimmer showed, the bandaged eyes of the lamps peering shortsightedly into the water.

What was it Emma had said about hypermetropic sight? Oh, what did it matter what anyone said! Nothing mattered, nothing would ever matter again. So her mind raged, fevered with the ceaseless treadmill of thought.

The rhyming lines found the way at last to her lips. Mechanically, walking up and down the room, she voiced them as they came:

"Oh! that we two were sleeping
On the sward of some sheep-trimmed down,
Watching the white mist veiling
River and mead and town."

Like an Irishwoman grieving, she rocked to and fro for a moment, and then a very passion of longing shook her. If she could be alone! But she could never be alone again. "In marriage one is never alone, never really alone," she said to herself.

And the rhyme ran on, and on:

"Oh! that we two were lying
At rest on the greening sod,
With our limbs at rest
On the quiet earth's breast
And our souls at home with God."

Out of the chaos of suffering the last line resolved itself, dully and incoherently at first, then hammering its reiterated way into her brain. The words and their meaning began to flame before her, very clearly and as something etched in lines of fire against a black, storm-riven sky. It seemed that hands reached out to hers, not the hands of angels, but warm, clinging hands of mother and father and children. A longing for them swept over her, a rush of emotion that drove her to her knees.

God and the little ivy-clad vicarage—how near they once had seemed! The two always inseparable in those days of happy youth. For God was in all the rooms of that old house, in the garden, in the trees and the shrubs and the ever-recurring wonder of the flowers. He walked with the bent figure of the vicar. He stood beside the careworn mother, sat in the sick-room, and made the burdens of their house less heavy. The children echoed the simple belief of father and mother as they prattled, "God will take care of all of us."

There came to Enid Marcourt, out of the years, that never-to-be-forgotten night before her wedding, when at the hour of prayer they had all knelt, while the vicar thanked God that the love of a good man had been granted to one at least of his children. He had thanked God that at last in His own way He had shown them His wondrous mercy and grace, had lifted from shoulders, that had striven meekly to bear them, burdens that had oft seemed too heavy almost to be borne. But Faith and Trust had been well and truly answered.

She heard her father's voice, out of the years, quite clear and distinct, saying that, and saying also:

"But Thou hast stood beside us. Thou wilt be with us, each and every one of us, and Thou shalt guide us. With Thy help we cannot fall. Thou, O God, art my staff, my help in the day of battle. . . ."

And it seemed to her now, in this hour of almost intolerable anguish, when the road of her life had come to a dead end, when she could *not* go on, that, one by one, they came trooping into the room and knelt around her—father and mother, and the little children. God came with them, too. And the kind eyes of God looked down at her, wise and tender, all-understanding. And it seemed to her that in that room a Voice spoke and said:

"Sacrifice is My crucible," and again, "Sacrifice is My crucible."

The foolish rhymes ran from her brain then, left it for a moment empty—terribly empty—and cold, like a cellar damp and chill. Oh! that some thought might beat in its place that would still the pain of that emptiness. She clasped her hands and cried on the God of Believing Hearts to help her.

As if in answer there came to her words that her father oft had spoken in the pulpit, words that lingered in the brain, words that at all times can make our poor human troubles less:

"'*For God so loved the world that He gave His only begotten son*' . . ."

And in the silence the Voice spoke again and said, "Sacrifice is My crucible," and again, "Sacrifice is My crucible."

George Marcourt came in at the door to find his wife kneeling by her bed in her white nightgown, her face buried in her hands.

He stood still, and the hand holding the wine shook violently. A great lump came into his throat. His mind went back to the first days of their marriage, when Enid had knelt just like that and said her simple prayers like a child.

Previously he had looked on the vicar and his views in a way as rather obsolete and unworldly. Such men did not get on. For promotion in the Church nowadays is the promotion of the world. To succeed you must have a fashionable following. You must deck yourself up in pagan garb, you must burn tapers and scented charcoal. And you must cultivate a Roman, clean-shaved appearance, and write secretly and vaguely once in a while to the Pope on the subject of reunion.

The vicar had done none of these things. He walked the way of Christ instead of the way of the Ritualistic clergy. For the vicar George Marcourt had perhaps something of the contempt which many successful business men have for those others who do not succeed, who do not advertise, nor put sand in the sugar, or "ginger" into the business, because of old-fashioned ideas about honour.

But it came to George Marcourt then that such men walked nearer God than he or any loftier, self-constituted critic.

Between him and his wife for a moment there rose a barrier over which he might not pass. The space beyond was holy ground.

He went quietly, closing the door gently behind him. For an hour he waited, but no sound came. There was chill in the air. Had she fallen asleep, to catch cold? When he could bear it no longer, he peered in at the door, and saw her half-kneeling, half-lying against the bed.

He went in quickly, lifted her up in his strong arms; her head fell back against his shoulder. Her eyes opened. They looked at him and beyond him. She muttered something, her voice hoarse and far away, as if heavy with cold. She tried to tell him something.

He put her into bed, folded the warm eiderdown close in about her, because she shivered suddenly. Then he drew up a chair and sat down beside the bed, his arm thrown across the coverlet. So through the hours he waited. She muttered words feverishly now and again, and he bent his head and whispered:

"Sleep, dear. Try to sleep. Sleep . . . *sleep*. . . ."

She was his child in that moment as well as his wife—a little child, feverish, fretted, worn out. He thought of all the causes that had led up to this—work among the poor in the East End and Red Cross work all the rest of the time. She had thrown herself impetuously into these things for years, more especially since the war.

"Oh! damn the war and everything connected with it!" said George to himself irritably. For one of the most patriotic men in the whole of Britain and a prospective member of that august body, the Coalition Government, it was certainly unexpected, to say the least.

His wife spoke suddenly, hoarsely. She turned her face towards him, her eyes, bright with fever, stared at him.

"George!" and when he bent, "have you ever had words elude you, rhymes running through your head, of which you have forgotten half the lines?"

"I generally remember all of it, dear. You know I have a good memory. What is it? Perhaps I can help you and then you will sleep."

"It is about sleep—and—ships sailing out——" her voice broke suddenly. She began to speak in a sobbing way, then as if to herself: "I can only remember that the ships are sailing—and regret." And then: "Say it all, George. Give me something to make me sleep, anything. I am so tired."

He had brought her something in a glass and made her drink it. She swallowed it feverishly, shuddered a little, leaned back against her pillows.

"Don't rest your arm on the eiderdown, George. Just let me lie here, by myself, quite alone," and then as he moved: "No, don't go quite away. Stay somewhere near. I am afraid. What was that about sleep, the words you know?"

She was a little weary child in that moment, fretful, half sobbing, lying there on her white pillows, her hair streaming out unbound over them—a very weary child, in a dim world of grief and unspeakable suffering.

George sat in the armchair by the bed and began to speak softly. Over and over again he said the words:

"'Sleep! Sleep and forget!
 The harbours are closed of regret,
And the ships are sailing out to the west!
 Sleep! Sleep, dear,
 And keep, dear,
Only that which is true and all that is best.
 With the freight of Peace glide
 On the flow of the tide
Out to the crooning seas of rest.'"

The low, soothing tones of his voice died away into silence. He laid his arm along the pillow. Her eyes half-opened, looked at him, drowsy with the drug he had given, then closed.

"'The crooning seas of rest' . . ." she whispered. Then her head fell heavily against his arm, rested there. And at last she slept.

CHAPTER X

Sleep and Tears

People who spoke about Mrs. Marcourt afterwards always dated the change in her from that month she spent in Weaslehurst.

Lady Emma, who had the astonishing gift in these modern days of prophecy before the event instead of after it, had foretold the result. She had happened, quite casually of course, to call in at Marcourt Place early on the morning of Enid's departure. She had called to see whether she had left her gloves there, she said. As she never liked losing anything, perhaps it was true.

She looked hard at George when he told her that Enid was then and there going down to Weaslehurst for a few weeks. In the hall were two or three trunks packed. She blinked thoughtfully.

"Umph !" said Lady Emma. "Do you know that August is the stated month for the country, not May? Likely a wet May at that. The new moon came in with rain."

"Enid is not well. She has a cold. She was almost delirious last night. I had to give her something to make her sleep—she is really worn out with this war work, I can see. She only wants to be alone, to go away alone—"

Lady Emma looked sharply at his anxious face.

Her eyes blinked rapidly in their peculiar way once or twice.

"—and she says she will be quite all right. Just a little change. Really, I think it is a good idea myself, Emma."

Emma considered. "Do you know that those old, spider-bitten, ivy-suffocated parsonages are all the same, damp and draughty?"

"Weaslehurst Vicarage is really comfortable in a way. And they'll look after her."

"God knows," said old Lady Emma bluntly, "there's enough of them to do it. Forty-seven children wasn't it, or something like that?"

"No, only twelve," he smiled at her exaggeration.

"Only twelve!" Lady Emma threw up her hands in horror. "What do these parsons want with more than one on that stipend? You once told me how much it was, I remember. Why, my head butler gets nearly as much. Twelve! Why, they'll worry the child to death."

George Marcourt looked troubled. "That's the queer part of it. She seems to miss them. Can't understand it myself, but Enid says when you're one of thirteen you're always thinking of the other twelve. She seems better this morning. Will you wait and see her, Emma? She'll be coming down in a moment."

"No, I won't wait. Just give her my love, not merely my regards, mind you, George. Tell her I couldn't wait. Anyhow she doesn't want folk bothering her at this time of the morning."

She prepared to go down the steps. "Twelve

children," she said again. "Dear me, I really must mention that, most interestin'. You're not sure if there are any more?"

"There may be one or two more," he admitted. "I always lost count."

"Good heavens!" said Lady Emma, "how long will this go on?"

"Till the Day of Judgment, I suppose," said George solemnly.

Lady Emma burst out laughing then, and turned abruptly on the lowest step in much better humour.

"Are you going down with her?"

"I wanted to. But Enid says I must not bother, and there's that election going to be rushed through at any moment, you know. Really, I don't know what to do."

He was obviously more worried about his wife than he would say.

"You'd be only in the way," Lady Emma told him candidly. "Let her go back to her own folk for a while. The change will do her good. The dullness will send her fleeing back to London. And—oh! tell her, George, that when she comes back, and she must come back bright and well, I'm going to give her quite a gay time. We're getting good news everywhere, and I don't see why we shouldn't celebrate it. There's nothing like dances, and good music, and parties for young folk. All work and no play makes war-workers very dull folk, you know. I really think we martyrs to duty could relax a little now."

George handed her into her carriage. She leaned out of the window.

"Of course *all* the news isn't quite good. George, tell me quite frankly, what do you think of this Kut business?"

"We are not allowed to be frank, you know," he reminded her with a smile.

She shrugged her shoulders. "Stuff and nonsense! Who is it that blabs if it is not members of the Government? I tell you that there's some restaurants in London that would make a fortune if they issued a daily paper, and published in it all they overhear. One does not have to be an eavesdropper either."

"That doesn't hring us nearer to the questions at issue," he said goodnaturedly.

"No, nor the relief force nearer poor Townshend," she flashed. "Will we ever get there? Is the whole thing over already, and the political parrot crying out too late?"

His face became grave. "You know as much as I."

"I know more," said old Lady Emma in her grim way. "But I wanted to see whether you knew it. Well, I suppose I can't blame you for holding your tongue about it."

"The newspapers are optimistic, Emma. Our newspapers, I mean."

The laughter crackled. "The newspapers! They know as well as you or I. They've known for weeks. George, when you get into Parliament, tell them that this suppression of news is a poor thing, that it serves no good purpose. I wish I were there in your place. I'd tell them that the country is beginning to have as much faith in the Coalition Government as an atheist has in the story of Jonah and the whale."

Then she drove off triumphantly, her old-fashioned hat quaking and shaking, and dipping violently when she passed anyone she knew. Against her excessively shabby dress, for everyone who was anyone was supposed to be wearing old clothes nowadays, her three-hundred-guinea Pomeranian nestled.

"I suppose I am a terrible old woman," she said to herself as she drove slowly through the Park in the blaze of brilliant sunshine, with the Walk under the trees by Park Lane dotted with dainty, costly gowns, an elegant note of defiance to the latest poster. "I suppose I am a very terrible old woman. And because I'm one, I can say this to myself quite frankly that if Enid died now, or went into rapid consumption through that spider-bitten parsonage, it wouldn't perhaps be such a hard fate as people think."

She sighed and tweaked the ear of the Pomeranian at her side. "You, you snappy, snarly thing," she apostrophised it, "are all that old age can depend on in these days. And your love is but cupboard love."

She sighed again. "Dear, stupid George!" A mist came across the hard beadiness of her eyes for a moment and she blinked angrily. "Well, I'm getting an old fool," she concluded.

What the rest of her thoughts were on the subject of the Marcourts she kept to herself. A Cabinet Minister's wife went by, extravagantly dressed, and Lady Emma began to calculate which was the worse, the Government's poster on dress, or the gowns on the Government's wives.

The Gates of Kut

Late that afternoon the Marcourt motor made its appearance in Weaslehurst, and the chauffeur picked his way slowly through the straggling street, for stray dogs, hawkers' carts, and crowds of small children littered the road always.

He slowed up at the vicarage and, at the sound of the horn, the door opened precipitately and the children, freshly washed and dressed and combed and kept indoors until the moment of arrival so that they should not obscure that impression, rushed out with a shrill chorus of greeting.

A confusion of arms and legs and a regular pandemonium of sound greeted Enid. They swarmed round her like bees, as the chauffeur said afterwards, with the exception of one or two who, when the excitement of the first greeting was over, surreptitiously investigated the tyres of the motor and wondered audibly if they stuck a hatpin in whether it would burst. The chauffeur vanished before they tried the experiment.

Enid's father and mother greeted her at the door, eager and affectionate, trying to make their voices heard above the clamour of the children. It was a day when parental authority went by the board in the gladness of that reunion. Her mother had cried a little and held her daughter very tight.

"The cabbudges has got the slugs," announced one of the twelve solemnly.

"And the kittie has turned her into a cat," said another, "and she scratches like anyfing." He rubbed his small chubby arm reminiscently.

He was the youngest but one, and Enid caught

him up and covered him with kisses. He was so little and round and fat.

"And Willie and I play soldiers!"

"Yes, and me! and me too!" said a shrill chorus, "and we take turn in being deaders."

"And at being Germans."

"I like being a German," piped a small voice, and the vicar, who was nothing if not English, looked really distressed at the latter information.

"Children! Children!" he implored. But Enid laughed happily.

They all went into the dining-room together, that old, oak-panelled sixteenth-century dining-room, low-raftered, with its brass flower-pots, and gleam of yellow primroses, and its faded red carpet.

For a while all thought but that she was home again swept past her. How good it was to be back again, to think of those few weeks that lay before her, her very own, and town, and all that town meant, far away!

Hitherto, a few days now and again, and George always coming down with her, had been her portion. The children stood rather in awe of George. They had never felt they had her to themselves as now, and she had never been quite alone with them. Even a chat with her mother had been interrupted good-naturedly by George. As he had said that day long ago, "she belonged now to him."

But now she was alone. She was back again among them all. Everything seemed unchanged. The mother looked a little less weary, for she had daily help now from the village, the vicar a little less careworn, for though he had refused help from George, his debts were a thing of the past.

He had some visits to pay in the village, someone sick or needy, poorer even than he and his had been in the darkest days, and Enid went into the kitchen while her mother and he arranged a parcel of food. The vicar in his poorest times always brought food for the corporal body as well as the spiritual.

You could see him almost any day in Weaslehurst, riding his old, rusty bicycle, with his shabby suit curiously pathetic, a Bible in one pocket, a parcel of food in the other, and a smile and a word for everybody.

The squire was a big, bluff, hearty, self-made man, who did little for his tenants except build a spectacular front on the cottages facing the main road of the village, through which he and his London visitors drove up to the imposing edifice on the hill where George Marcourt had been a guest seven years before.

A propos of Marcourt's marriage the squire had said to the vicar in his patronising way: "Ah! now things will be *much* better for you. I am really glad to hear it."

The vicar had a sense of humour which helped him to assimilate this piece of conversation and he had faith for the rest. So life went on.

The vicar and his wife, when all the rest of the household was or was supposed to be asleep, talked in whispers about Enid that night. The mother sobbed a little.

"I suppose we must expect that," he answered,

but he said it a trifle uneasily. The eyes of love are not always blind, even those of a very unworldly pastor.

"She is older-looking."

"We must expect that, too. She is not a child now, dear. It is eight years since she married, Mary, remember!"

"I wonder—is she quite happy?"

The vicar looked surprised. "Happy? Why, yes! What else could she be? Just think, Mary, Marcourt surrounds her with happiness and love. I think she is overtired."

His wife said no more on the subject then. But late that night, ere she sought her own room, she crept into that of her eldest daughter, where Enid had elected to share a room with the youngest child.

The little thing had crept into her sister's bed and prattled until it fell asleep. The exhaustion of the night before, or the quiet peace of the vicarage, had had their effect on Enid also. When her mother tiptoed across the room she saw that both were asleep, the child's curly head lay pillowed on the girl's shoulder, and her other arm was thrown protectingly over it.

Her mother stood and looked at her for a long moment. Her heart yearned over them both. Because of the wet patch of pillow that told of tears the mother crept out of the room without a sound, nor did she call her husband in to see the picture the girl and the child made. Only she knew that Enid had cried herself that night to sleep.

CHAPTER XI

A Little Child

THE sweetest and truest nurse that one may ever know is Spring. In her tender understanding hands are the rare unguents of healing for the sorest heart. The rustling trees, the very flowers, speak their message of life born anew. On a day when the sun shone down softly, filling the green world about Weaslehurst with yellow radiance, Enid and her mother spoke of these things.

"The Spring," said her mother dreamily, "is the message God writes on the earth that men may read. Nothing dies but shall live again."

She pointed to the gap in the woods near by where a fire had been in the autumn.

"The scarred places shall be healed," she said, "and the crooked paths made straight."

Enid's eyes filled with threatening of tears that were not far off. They were walking on a well-remembered path, full of child-memories. It led by the beech woods, the trees clad in new tremulous green.

The children, all but the youngest, who clung to Enid's hand, were running ahead to where a blaze of gold denoted a bank of primroses, their shrill shouts of joy floating back, instinct with childish joy of life. Here and there the coppices still showed the passing russet and red of autumn leaves that still clung tenaciously to the fast-greening branches, old age and youth together. The woods were clamorous with the chatter of birds. The low green hills undulated before them—the incomparable glory of Spring in an English countryside.

"Mother," said Enid suddenly, "in your life you must have passed through many emotions, through many moods. I have known you physically weary, but never mentally so. Even when you were most tired you laughed, when you were ill you managed to smile. Yet had you never moods that you kept to yourself? Moments of rebellion? Railings against fate because it had not cast your life in a care-free world? Desire for things unattainable?"

Her mother pondered the question.

"Yes, I believe I had. It is such a long while ago," and she gave a little laugh at that, "and so many things have happened since. But I never had that feeling after the greatest event, the greatest joy, that can enter a woman's life. When I looked at you last night when you were asleep"—her hand crept out for a moment to that of her eldest daughter—"I lived through it again."

Enid turned quickly. Her eyes wavered and she looked at her mother.

"The—greatest event?" she questioned. "The greatest joy?"

Her mother nodded.

"My first baby," she said simply. "Then all the things that worry and fret one crumpled up like a dead leaf and were whirled out of sight. A new world opened, in which one's ego was dwarfed, almost non-existent."

She picked up the little child which was looking at them both with its loving, wondering blue eyes, its fair, curling hair gold in the sunshine.

"O Baby!" said its mother, "wait until Enid has a little thing like you, all her very own." She turned her flushed, happy face to her daughter. "O Enid, the love of a little child! How it fills one's life! You don't know what you have missed or how empty life can be for people without children. Life can be very empty."

"I—am beginning to know how empty," said Enid, and she clenched her hands tightly until the nails cut into the palms. She had flushed scarlet when her mother first spoke, but now the colour slowly receded, leaving her very pale.

Her mother's eyes were troubled then. She felt she had stumbled against something that was hurting Enid intensely. She put her arm through her daughter's and pressed it in sympathy.

"Forgive me, dear."

They walked in silence for a moment, then Enid spoke, her eyes on the hills beyond. "The love of a little child, and the love for a little child! Is it, then, the sweetest thing in life?" Her eyes looked over the hills.

"It is everything," said her mother. "Toil and troubles and cares, sorrow that wrings the heart, these must be; but the touch of a little child's lips against your face can lift these things from you as nothing else on earth can." She turned her face, flushed and youthful in that moment, and laughed. "And behold it is the mother of many children who speaks!"

"But you have worked so hard, like a slave," Enid began involuntarily.

"It was sweet slavery," said her mother. "And I have always had the serene peace of the knowledge that God stood by us, that He watched over us and ours." She added: "Your father is a good man, Enid, his trust and faith are unbounded. With faith, you know, one can remove mountains."

"Yes," said Enid, "I know. And you are the best of women, mother. Oh! I never knew how good until I went to London, where one meets so many different types of people. Sometimes it seemed that only you and father—and, of course, George—were the only true people in the world. So many people in my London world wear a mask and hide their real thoughts."

Her mother nodded. "There is a great deal of sin and insincerity in London. That is inevitable. England is an open gateway for any who care to enter, and naturally all kinds of people drift through. One does not notice any difference perhaps at first, but in time the varied influences begin to tell. I have always said, when people have maintained that London is a wicked place, that it is not the English themselves who have made that charge possible."

They stopped by a stile, rested there a minute, and Mrs. Whiteway resumed: "One can't talk about those things publicly at this juncture, but different nationalities have brought their different traits into the country. They are easily distinguishable. Love of money and serving Mammon instead of God, that is a distinct characteristic of one nation; love of evil-living, the pursuit of the brilliant bubble of the passing moment, that is another; atheism, scorn of old-fashioned, nation-making ideals—oh! all these things may be traced as distinct characteristics of the different nations that are represented in London. Men have grown to look on the religion of our fathers as something to be sneered at. They ignore the lesson that Time has written in ineffaceable characters on the blackboard of history, especially the history of England."

"And that lesson?" Enid had turned her young, weary face towards her mother.

"That a country which turns its back on true religion falls, as fell Babylon. Idol-worshipping creeds, too, have brought many a great nation into the dust. It is written that men shall not bow down to the graven image, nor idols of wood or stone. Disobedience of that law has brought once-great nations to the dust. I do not think England will come to that pass. But it was very near."

Enid said then, hesitating, "And yet some of our greatest preachers in the Anglican Church are taking up the cult of idolatry, delving into the region of superstition? They call it an artistic portrayal, a linking with the ages gone by."

"Our greatest preachers? Ah no! Such men get into the papers, that is all. They are generally seeking for notoriety, or posing as mystics, or preaching sermons on something calculated to turn the limelight of public opinion on them. Not the *greatest*, child! But—the *least* of these! Christ, Who was the greatest of all preachers, walked a different road from that of these men. They are but moths, following the flickering taper-lights of a moment's fame."

They sat down on the warm green earth for a space, watching the fresh glory of the trees. Before them, in undulating waves, the countryside stretched away—here a clump of trees, there a red water-tower lifting its coned head on the slope, and the green lanes of England beyond winding in and over the brow of the distant hill. Life seemed worth while in that hour, that quiet hour far from the feverish fret of cities.

"I—would love to have a little child," said Enid suddenly. "How it would fill up all the—all the blank places as you said!" She turned to her mother. "You heard what the doctor said, that time I was very ill, you remember, when my horse came to grief at hunting and threw me?"

"I remember," said her mother, and her lips trembled. Her hand stole out and touched her daughter's, clung close there for a long moment.

"Is it—quite impossible, then?"

"No, dear! But it might mean a dangerous illness."

"You mean—an operation."

"Yes, dear."

Enid was looking at the children laughing happily, tumbling over and over in the long soft grass. The little child that had clung to her hand was toddling towards the others on fat and unsteady legs. It tumbled over and rolled like a ball, and when the children ran laughing and calling petting words to it, the little thing laughed, too, lying there and kicking its wee fat legs. The children almost smothered it with kisses. Then it toddled off contentedly after them.

"But—a woman goes into the valley of the shadow anyhow," said Mrs. Whiteway. "She goes down to the very gates of Death. And one finds God there even if one never knew Him before, and the greatest gift of God is a little child."

"Is it not worth all the suffering?" Enid said in a low voice. And because she spoke her thoughts aloud her mother kept silence. She saw the girl's lifted face, the spasm of some pain that shook it for a fleeting second. She saw also that her daughter's eyes looked away at the hills, and over the hills, and how her hands clenched tight.

"Dear," said her mother in a low voice, "you are unhappy over something."

"Yes, mother," and then gently, "but it is nothing in which you could help me, dear. Neither you nor father. But—had I a child——" She stopped as suddenly as she had begun.

And then there came to the mother the knowledge that comes sooner or later to many mothers, and brings always with it a pang of almost unendurable anguish, the knowledge that Suffering raises a barrier between itself and the most dearly loved, where even angels might well fear to tread. For Suffering asks of itself only a dim corner where it may lie undisturbed in its travail, like a dumb, tortured beast that lies silent, staring impotently up at an unanswering sky.

Mrs. Whiteway suffered, too, as all mothers suffer, in that moment of realisation. Even Mary of the Cross, Mother of all mothers, was not spared the shut door, outside which one must stand.

To her daughter, Mary Whiteway said no word that day, or for many days afterwards. But outside that shut gate her loving heart crouched, and suffered with her daughter's suffering, though to her the nature of that daughter's suffering was at the time a dim, incomprehensible thing.

But she strove to fill Enid's days so that there would be little time for thinking. She knew of sleepless nights when Enid lay, hands clenched; there was nothing to do at such times but be silent.

The days went on their way, and Enid went out with the children alone a great deal. Mary Whiteway did not go, partly because she believed Enid would be forced to romp with the children were she not present, and partly because she felt she could not bear the suffering that was leaving its impress plainly on that thin young face.

So the days passed. For Enid they were a dim procession amid which she moved as in a dream, a shadow-play in which she was a puppet. For the most part she lay on the grass staring up at the sky. The children were somewhat astonished at her demeanour. She joined no longer as of old in their romps and games, but a tactful mother had whispered that sister was ill and must not be bothered. But the little child always went with her, came back to her for comfort and petting if it fell, and slept against her shoulder when it grew weary with playing.

Enid was growing slimmer. Her cheeks were losing even their faint tinge of colour, and her eyes seemed larger than ever. The vicar, busy as he was, noticed it and spoke of it at times to his wife.

"Something is the matter with Enid, Mary. She doesn't seem to me to be improving." He looked at his wife anxiously. "Have you any idea what is wrong with her?"

Mrs. Whiteway, who was doing some sewing and mending at the time, bent her head lower over her work. "George wrote and said she had been overdoing things, working hard at Red Cross depots. She is run down. I—I think all we can do is to leave her alone, really."

He studied her bent head, in which the grey was very noticeable of late.

"But—is that all, Mary?"

"I don't know," said his wife wistfully. "But this I do know, John, that neither you nor I can help by asking questions. Whatever it is I am sure it will pass." Then she told him of that day among the woods.

"When is George coming down?" he said.

His wife shook her head. "He is very busy. The election is at hand and it seems almost impossible for him to get away. He would have motored down, however, once or twice just for an hour or two. But I know Enid has told him not to come, and that she will go back when the election is over. But in a few days one of her city girl-friends, Beatrice Byndham, is coming down."

He brightened at that. "That's good news. It will cheer her up."

"I hope so, dear." But she sighed a little.

In a few days Beatrice Byndham came. She was plainly shocked at the change in Enid and said so. She herself looked so bright and gay, radiating happiness. She went about humming bits of happy songs with an air of some wonderful mystery clinging to her. She romped with the children, too, although in secret she deplored the ruin of her delicate gowns, unsuitable for the country.

Mrs. Whiteway went out with the two girls for a while. There were teas and parties in the neighbourhood for the purpose of helping the soldiers at the Front, and Enid was drawn into them. The vicarage garden even took on a festive air, with an impromptu marquee erected between the more imposing flower-beds and the mundane but important cabbage-patch.

Enid found herself seldom alone, but at the end of the ten days Beatrice had allotted to herself as a country holiday, the latter linked her arm within Enid's and announced their intention of going for a walk.

"For a heart-to-heart talk," she said; and when Enid asked her mother whether she would care to come, Mrs. Whiteway shook her head. "There is ever so much to do," she explained. The children, too, were needed, it appeared, all but the little tot who clung to Enid's hand.

"I'm just dying to have a chat alone with you,

Enid," said Beatrice as they went out of the gate. She called Mrs. Marcourt by her Christian name now. "The dear kids—they are dear, aren't they?—but one can't talk much with them about, can one? Of course, I love children and all that, but had I a fourth of that number myself, I should suffer from brain-storms."

They went their way alone, save for the little child, past the old ivy-towered church with its clock that would never keep the correct time, through the churchyard with its grey, weather-mottled tombs and its pollarded, bushy-headed willows, down the village street with its ancient leaning shops, its sunken roofs, and its tiny out-jutting windows filled with odds and ends. Old women wearing quaint mutches were standing here and there at the doors, and along the cobbled road two farmers, in smocks, leaning on their sticks, talked over past market-days and more to come.

They passed through fields where the sheep cropped the green herbage, where the lambs scampered about playfully.

One of Katharine Tynan's beautiful poems came to Enid as they went, with all its haunting, wistful sweetness:

> All in the summer evening
> I thought on the Lamb of God.

She began to repeat it aloud, half unconsciously.

"You know it, Beatrice?"

Beatrice shook her head. "I confess I don't read poetry. Omar Khayyám, of course, when there was a craze for him. But one outgrows him, don't you think? and Swinburne and Browning made my head ache, trying to find out what they meant. I thought they never seemed quite sure about it themselves. But women—I have always been told that women do not write good verse."

Enid laughed. "Don't they? Ah! you must read Marie Pitt and Katharine Tynan, real poetesses, half the world away from one another in distance, as well as in some phases of thought. But each will haunt you. Katharine Tynan sings in the valley of tender, haunting things, and Marie Pitt, an Australian poetess, stands on the hills and flings out her woven, wonderful ribbons of thought to the winds of the world. And long afterwards we who pass on the lower road are haunted by both melodies."

They went on in silence.

"Let us sit here," said Beatrice suddenly, and perhaps it was Fate that made her choose a spot already made almost unendurable to Enid and her mother by suffering.

CHAPTER XII

The Woman Bids

It was the first time since that day that Enid had returned to this part of the woods. Always the children had dragged her off on some fresh exploration, doubtless engineered beforehand by the mother.

Perhaps it was that recognition or a mood of prescience which brought a rush of pain to Enid Marcourt, a desire to be up and away, to fly into the farthest reaches of the wood and, cowering among the dead leaves, shut her ears.

"Delightful spot!" said Beatrice. She waved her hand to the hills, winding roads, and the gleam of water between the far distant willows. "Rather dinky, isn't it? And a change from town! Really, Hyde Park will look quite dusty in comparison when one gets back, and Kensington Gardens like the estate of a *nouveau riche*."

She spread her skirts carefully, placed her parasol so that her delicate roseleaf skin should not be freckled or her eyes unnecessarily wrinkled by the glow of the sun.

"Hadn't you better sit over here, Enid, in the shadow a little? You'll get so burnt, dear."

"No, I love the sun and I'm already freckled." She lay back on the grass, shielding her eyes, however, with one of her hands. "Now, tell me all about it."

Beatrice burst into laughter. "How did you guess I had anything to tell? Why, I thought I was keeping it the hugest secret."

Enid Marcourt moved a little. "Oh! I knew from the very first day that something special had happened, or was going to happen—I wasn't sure which. But your laughter bubbled over with it. You looked so—happy," and then her voice dropped suddenly into silence.

Beatrice, intent on herself and her own feelings, did not notice. Wrapped up in her own thoughts, her own visions of happiness, she fluttered contentedly around her own compound, without looking over into that of her neighbour.

"Well—I did it," she said, and turned her glowing face to Enid. "Alone I did it," and laughed. "Quite unashamedly, too. No beating about the bush, I assure you. A sort of take it or leave it proposition."

"You did—what?" asked Mrs. Marcourt. For one instant she lifted her hand that was shading her eyes from the sun, and looked at Beatrice, and then away again.

"*Enid!*" reproachfully and incredulously. "You don't surely mean to say that you really have forgotten?"

It seemed incredible that a thing that filled her own life should not have also obsessed the thoughts of another.

"Don't you recollect," she went on in an injured

tone, "that last day in the Park when we rode together?"

"*Ah!*" said Mrs. Marcourt suddenly. The sun was glowing into her eyes and she covered them. Her lips twitched. Then she said, "You—told him."

"Told him? I proposed to him, neither more nor less."

Mrs. Marcourt started to laugh weakly. "Beatrice, you're joking. When did you do it?"

"The night he left for Mesopotamia."

"The night he left for Mesopotamia!" Enid thought that the cry had leapt loudly from her lips, that like a haunted thing it fled before her over the hills, that echoed and re-echoed it over and over again.

But Beatrice apparently had not noticed anything unusual in her tone, beyond natural surprise.

"Yes, that very night," and she laughed happily. "It all happened like a story out of a book; but it was deliciously real."

"Tell me," begged Mrs. Marcourt in a low voice.

Beatrice lay back, her hands pillowed behind her head, and gazing up ecstatically at the pale pink lining of her parasol.

"You remember the night he was going away. I had thought of nothing else all day, hoping against hope he would come and see me. Only that little Captain Spane came, however, and proposed. And of course I wouldn't think of it in the circumstances."

"No, of course not," said Enid. She spoke in a very low voice.

"But the hours passed by and no one came. No one, that is, that counted; and at night there was an invitation from the Duchess—you saw us at the Driftwood—that mother simply would not miss."

"Yes!" What did it matter how long Beatrice took to tell her story? Was it not already told? Let Beatrice wander on in her own way; had not she, Enid, already raced ahead to the end of the road!

"Just after dinner—we had dinner at home that night, and mother was so quiet and worried, too, over something—I slipped into the hall. I felt I simply must say good-bye. I rang up on the telephone to his club to ask him whether he would have time to call and say good-bye."

Mrs. Marcourt said nothing. She was quite unusually still, as a matter of fact.

"But he was not there——"

Mrs. Marcourt moved then and spoke. "What time was that?"

"About nine o'clock—and the boat left at midnight."

Enid turned her head quickly. "No, at ten, Beatrice. It was timed for ten o'clock."

Beatrice shook her head. "Originally it was timed for ten. But there was a line also in the papers that you must have seen, saying that owing to mines in the Channel all sailings would be postponed until further notice. Did you not see it in the morning paper? Naturally transports would not cross until the mines had been swept away."

"No," said Enid, and then, "I did not read the papers that day. I remember now. Then—you met him accidentally, I suppose? Where did you meet him?"

"At your house."

"At—my—house!" Enid half sat up in a sitting posture, then sank slowly down again. She repeated, "At my house!"

"Yes. Didn't Jevons tell you he had called? We met on your doorstep. Quite dramatic, wasn't it? I was going up, and he was coming down. He had called to see George, I suppose, and tell him that the date of sailing had after all not been altered, only the hour."

"And—we were out."

"You were both out. You had gone out for a real jolly time, dinner and the theatre and supper. Lady Emma, it appeared, had told Jevons that you would not be home until after midnight. She told him to tell any callers that."

"She—Lady Emma told Jevons that," and then, "I see."

But Beatrice was not concerned with the Lady Emmas or Jevonses of the world.

"I asked him whether he would not come back and spend at least an hour before he went away. He was very busy, it appeared, that evening. And then, somehow—how it happened I cannot quite remember, Enid—but when he was saying that his boat sailed at midnight, I said to him, 'Don't go, Philip.'"

She turned to Enid. "You'll never tell anyone I told you this, Enid."

"Never," said Mrs. Marcourt. Her lips were white. Her eyes stared out over the valley.

"We were still standing on your steps all this time, Jevons in the background politely holding the door open and as expressionless as if proposals on that particular doorstep were everyday happenings."

She gurgled reminiscently for a second or two.

"But of course he, Jevons, couldn't hear, and at first I thought Philip didn't, for he stared at me in such a queer way, and his face was quite white. And he looked so haggard, just as when he was ill in India. And I—I really couldn't bear it, Enid. I just put my hand in his, and said straight out, 'Philip, don't look like that, dear. Don't you know I love you? I have always loved you, and I don't care if Jevons hears me, or the whole world either.' Imagine it, Enid."

"I am imagining it," said Mrs. Marcourt, her face still hidden. She shook violently. Beatrice turned reproachfully.

"Now, I believe you're laughing, Enid, aren't you?"

"No, I'm not laughing, Beatrice."

"Really, dear?"

"Very really." She turned her face then. Though her lips smiled, there was no laughter in her eyes.

"Well, to make a long story short, Philip was so queer at first; but then, I suppose, any man who really cared for a girl and hadn't the courage to say so would be queer when she took matters out of his dilatory hands."

"And Ph—Captain Territt? What did he say? You are on the steps at present, please remember, all this time. And Jevons looking like a stuffed owl at everywhere but you two people." Mrs. Marcourt laughed a little shrilly then. "To shut the door, of course, would imply he had listened and knew, so he had to stand there and be the automaton whose mechanism would only start to revolve when you walked off.'

Which was all very amusing if a trifle complicated, and she began to laugh a good deal over it, as if she saw humour in it, especially in the picture of the embarrassed Jevons.

Beatrice laughed too.

"Oh! when you were in love," she declared, "you would know just how it felt. And you wouldn't have cared either."

"No, I think now that, as you say, I would not. What does it matter, after all, to anyone else?" She spoke with sudden fierceness. "If two people love each other they should care enough to face everything, to sacrifice everything."

"That is what Philip said," said Beatrice frankly. And suddenly there fell a silence.

"Philip—Territt said that?" repeated Mrs. Marcourt after a while.

"Yes. And still on your doorstep." Beatrice dimpled again. "I told you how queer he looked, and he spoke as queerly. He said in a strange, breathless way, 'Beatrice, if you loved a man and he was going away perhaps for ever, would you go off to a theatre and forget all about him?'"

Mrs. Marcourt's hands clenched. Her eyes closed very tight. Beatrice's young voice rose, ringing now.

"And I—I said, 'Philip, a woman who would do that could not have loved you.'"

"You—said that?" said Mrs. Marcourt, and her eyes opened and shut tight again. And this time she kept them closed for a long time.

"I knew, you see, Enid, that he was referring to somebody he once had cared for. . . . You know I told you I wondered whether there had been anybody whom years ago he had cared for. She must have done just this very thing once, and I suppose he was young and it hurt, for he had believed he loved her. Oh! I can picture what sort of a woman she would be, loving life and gaiety, and putting trivialities before love. I love life, too, but I would not put the best things it holds before Philip," and a deep, sincere note came into the girl's young voice. "But I suppose *she* didn't care enough. Don't you think she would have given up everything—everything, Enid?"

"I don't know," Mrs. Marcourt answered after a pause. "I suppose she would not know that until she—had lost him, and then, of course, it would be too late."

"Anyhow, it's too late now," declared Beatrice triumphantly. "Philip took me home in a taxi, but he could not stay a moment. It was barely a moment. But mother was awfully pleased. You see, she guessed as soon as we came in, though she did say that Philip appeared to take the Chinese view of marriage, if one were to judge by the lugubrious expression on his face. The Chinese weep at weddings, you know, and laugh at funerals. But any man going back to the Front straight away would look like that. So I—we kissed each other, and away Philip went, and that's all there is of it. But it's a big all." And then, to her mind there came the thought of the other woman, as it does to women who know they have not been first in a man's heart. "Anyhow," she concluded with a note of victory, "it's too late now. She has passed out of Philip's life. He will never think of her once we are married, I am sure."

The little child, tired of playing, came toddling towards Enid. She took it up and held it close to her heart, her face bent over it. Beatrice rattled on, talking of the plans for the future. Long afterwards, when she knew the truth, she remembered how quiet Enid Marcourt had been that day.

CHAPTER XIII

News from the Tigris

TOWARDS the end of the month Mrs. Marcourt went back to town. It was just at the time that the rumours about Kut-el-Amara grew, and whispers began to pass from one to another. But the Government, as voiced by the Premier, was as usual optimistic. It went on being optimistic, while the whispers grew in volume and intensity. After all, one's Government should surely know better than the Man in the Street, whose jaw was beginning to set sternly when he spoke of Kut-el-Amara.

Mrs. Marcourt went back to town and rode in the Row, and danced at the little dances, which one *had* to give on account of the officers coming back from the trenches. One didn't want them to think one was dull, or depressed, or anything like that, you know. And really time as well as one's daughters did hang on one's hands nowadays, and was likely to do so if one were to listen to the ravings of the pessimist. For fashionable mothers who intended to look as young as their daughters this was truly a most dreadful prospect. Even the cheerful optimist did not help matters much on this point by declaring that every man would, of course, be allowed by law to have four wives when the war was over. It was reported that some of the married men, hearing this rumour, had openly decided not to come home at all.

George Marcourt was rather astonished at the way Enid went about, and the endless succession of invitations she accepted. People liked her because she was so bright, and always said such witty things. They began to speak of Mrs. Marcourt as brilliant. George was apt to blame Emma for the change which puzzled him. But Emma, truth to tell, was more than astonished herself, and, incidentally, her young relative-by-marriage's reputation for brilliancy and wit was putting her, Emma, rather in the shade.

"It won't last," predicted Emma to herself. "She'll snap like a broken string one of these days."

But Emma had prophesied also in the past that when Enid Marcourt went down to the vicarage she would die of three parts ennui and one part consumption, and this had not yet happened, nor seemed likely to happen. Mrs. Marcourt went on enjoying herself. She grew slimmer and perhaps paler, but one could not tell that very well, for she used very good rouge and a great deal of it. Even George did not know that it was rouge. He thought Enid had a very charming colour and that frivolity suited her.

His wife held his heart in the hollow of her hand. He loved her, if anything, more than ever. But now that he was in Parliament he had little time at home, or to go about as much as before with his wife.

It was really a most momentous time in the history of England, because it was whispered that some of the members were actually earning their salaries—an unprecedented thing. It does not seem possible that such a rumour could be true; but then, when there is a war on many unlikely things do happen.

Anyhow George went a great deal to Westminster, and when Lady Emma once asked him how he liked it, he said, quite sincerely, they had very good meals there indeed.

If the truth be known, he slept as soundly as the other members during the long prosy speeches, and, obeying the Coalition commandments, put his trust in the Premier. What else, then, was to be done but eat and sleep in his appointed place? Now that George was ensconced in a very safe seat, Lady Emma Beckendon was growing quite optimistic about the war. It was she who told everybody, with a significant nod of the head, that the eye of the Premier was on George. Possibly it was, for Marcourt snored horribly when he fell asleep.

Then that rumour about Kut-el-Amara started again, and this time it did not stop at whispers. People got into a habit of descending upon you at your breakfast-table, or dragging you into a mysterious little group of people, who eventually went off and made other groups of their own, more mysterious than the first. But the Premier went away for his week-ends just the same, and the Government newspapers positively beamed with complacency, which showed that the Government was still optimistic.

Mrs. Marcourt heard the rumours, too, but she never discussed them. She seemed to have no interest in Kut and its doings. She still rode and drove, and danced and went about with the ultra-smart set, who had apparently long ago forgotten there was a war at all. Incidentally, of course, the ultra-smart set could not help remembering it on occasions, small things like flag days and sympathy teas and private theatricals, with just as few outsiders and as many reporters as one could get together. In such cases to be patriotic meant garbing yourself as a Welsh leek, or a shamrock, or a Belgian flower-girl, or a Parisian midinette-*plus*-Marie-Antoinette, and there you were. Then the ha'penny picture papers the next morning were the cause of an admiring world's coffee going cold, or the bacon despondent! Such is fame in the ultra-smart world.

Not that young Mrs. Marcourt did much of this sort of thing. She stopped short of it, but she stopped short of very little else.

It was on one of these days that Beatrice, with the dinkiest frilled apron in the world and a huge waitress bow that would have sent Lyons, Limited, into hysterics, tumbled out of somebody or other's brougham and came to breakfast at Marcourt Place. Beatrice was to be one of the Society-beauty-waitresses at a big soldiers' tea that day; hence the white apron and the patriotic etceteras, which included, among other things, silk hose and high-heeled shoes with turquoises and diamonds in the heels.

Lady Emma came almost immediately afterwards. She also was to be a waitress, but her conception was a little different from that of Beatrice. Lady Emma looked like a fat, shabby, shrewd charwoman who had purloined her mistress's clothes for the occasion. Wishing to be true to nature, she had, indeed, borrowed a charwoman's best Sunday gear, *plus* the apron the latter used on first visits to new patrons.

George, devouring eggs and bacon and his morning newspaper at the same time, looked up in some alarm, wondering whether Emma had lost her head or her fortune.

"Is it Socialism or charing?" he had asked.

"Neither," said Lady Emma, with a withering look. "It's for the soldiers."

"What those poor beggars," remarked George sympathetically, helping himself to more bacon, "have to suffer is almost beyond my comprehension."

"A great many things," said Lady Emma acidly, "are beyond your comprehension, my dear George."

Beatrice laughed. "Don't take any notice of him. He has been saying all that sort of thing to me, because I'm stopping him from reading the papers. Politicians are not supposed to read papers, anyway. They always tell us they do not."

Enid came in at that moment. She wore a morning robe of white, embroidered, arabesque-fashion, in silver. Her hair was brushed back simply from her forehead. It gave her a curiously young appearance. She looked also very frail. Under the rouge she was very pale. Lady Emma watched her searchingly.

"You look tired, Enid," she remarked. Her glance went from Enid's face to George with the newspaper, then back to Enid again.

"I am rather," she said, as she moved over to the bell and rang it.

"Of course, you people will have breakfast with me. You've had it? Well, coffee, then——"

She gave the order and came back to the table. When she lifted her arms, now and again, the big, loose sleeves fell back, and Lady Emma compressed her lips. Was George blind that he did not see how thin his wife's arms were, how delicate she looked? But George saw only the pretty colour in his wife's cheeks. They sat down together. Enid, with one of those laughs that came so often to her lips of late, had reached over and taken the paper from George.

"You always say there's nothing in any of the papers worth reading," she accused, "and here you are, mentally chewing every inch of it."

"I've only just started it, as a matter of fact," he protested. He was folding up his napkin, and now he came around to his wife and kissed her gently. "Well, dear, I must be off. I leave you in good company," and he vanished.

"The funny thing about George," said Enid with a gay laugh and still holding the paper, "is that he seems to study every bit of the newspaper, and yet often misses things that I see at a glance."

"Is there anything about Kut in it?" said Beatrice. She blushed. "I have not had a letter from Philip for ever so long. I meant to look at the paper this morning, but it had not come. When one lives in a block of flats papers never are up to time."

"Does the mail from Mesopotamia come in regularly?" Lady Emma asked her politely. Enid took up the paper, compressing her lips at the question. Her eyes glanced unseeingly over the large black type.

News from the Tigris

"As a matter of fact," Beatrice was saying, "I have had only one letter, and that just a page or two about the trip, ever since Philip left London. Luckily he is not near Kut-el-Amara yet, and if rumour be true I can't help feeling glad."

"I suppose you would feel like that," said Lady Emma. She asked the next question idly. "Where is he, then?"

"At a village of deserted mud huts. Likely to be there for months, he said, because it was in the loop of a tributary of the Tigris and floods were coming down. He was bitter because he could not get into the actual fighting." She sipped her coffee and put the cup down again. "And Captain Spane sent me the sweetest Pomeranian. I called it after the village, El-Amara," she said.

At that a cry escaped Enid, who had been staring intently at one of the columns in the morning paper.

Beatrice's eyes as well as Lady Emma's flashed straight to her.

The rouge stood out on Mrs. Marcourt's face in two distinct patches of vivid red. The rest of her face was dead white. She sat quite still, her eyes fixed on the paper. Her lips moved, but made no sound.

"*Enid!*" cried Beatrice anxiously.

"Enid!" said Lady Emma, and she got up quickly and crossed over to her. Beatrice got up, too, but Lady Emma made a peremptory autocratic gesture for silence, and the girl sat down again, but her own face went a little white. Her lips trembled, and her eyes went to the paper that rustled in Enid Marcourt's hands.

"What—is it?" she whispered.

Lady Emma answered with a harsh laugh that was like a croak. She put one hand, somewhat heavily, upon Enid's shoulder, as if forcing her down; with the other she took the paper.

She began to read aloud quickly:

"'Measles in Weaslehurst'——"

"*Oh!*" said Beatrice, and she drew a deep breath of relief, half giggling. "Me—measles?"

"'Measles in Weaslehurst,'" repeated Lady Emma. And Enid suddenly laughed that hysterical laugh that was never far off nowadays, while Lady Emma went on reading, still standing, her hand on Enid Marcourt's shoulder.

"'Measles in Weaslehurst,'" read out Lady Emma, "'is perhaps to be expected. None of the cases is serious. The vicar and his wife and family have entirely escaped. Measles at this time of the year is—er—just measles.'"

"Why—wh-what a funny thing to put into the paper!" gasped Beatrice, giggling audibly now. "To—to put it like that, I mean." She began to laugh with the sheer relief of the moment, and all the while old Lady Beckendon's eyes were following the words under the big headline, that, among so many others, George had in some way missed:

CAPTURE OF EL-AMARA.

REPORTED MASSACRE OF CAPTAIN TERRITT AND TROOPS.

Lady Emma, still holding the paper, looked

over at Beatrice. Her grim eyes were quite kind, Beatrice remembered afterwards. Emma began to gabble like a parrot.

"They do put funny things in the papers nowadays. You see, measles at this time of the year—well, it's hardly the season for them, is it? They don't usually sprout until September, or is it November?"

Lady Emma was talking nonsense and knew it. But Beatrice did not know it, and for a while at least it was imperative she must not. Also Beatrice must be got away. Enid sat motionless, not speaking at all. Beatrice impulsively went round to her and kissed her. Enid moved, shuddering almost perceptibly.

"Enid dear," coaxed Beatrice, "don't think about it. You see they are all right, your father and mother, and the—all the others. As long as you have them I—I don't think I'd worry about anyone else, dear. They—they come before everyone else, don't they?"

"I believe you are right," said Enid, and she got up then. She turned to Lady Emma and looked from one face to the other, her own still desperately white. "If you will excuse me——"

"Of course we will excuse you," said Lady Emma cheerfully. "Go and lie down, Enid, and rest. And I'll just run off with Beatrice in my car. I want to see your mother very particularly, Beatrice, this morning."

She began to gather her wraps together vivaciously, chattering away.

"But we will be late for the soldiers' morning tea," began Beatrice.

"No, we won't," said Lady Emma. "And if we are—well, I can make that all right. Come with me now, Beatrice. Your mother *is* home, of course."

Beatrice looked perplexed. Lady Emma was not guilty of inflicting her company on the Byndham flat. It was strange, too, that Lady Emma, who always prided herself on her memory, should have forgotten all about their important engagement. Her eyes, seeking Lady Emma's, were full of questions.

"Yes, but——"

But Lady Emma swept her away there and then. At the door she turned. Enid had come back to the table and was standing looking down at the paper, which still lay where Lady Emma had left it. Lady Emma looked at her, and her eyes blinked.

"I'll be back very soon, Enid." Then she whirled Beatrice down to the waiting car, and from there on to the flat near the Marble Arch. But when Lady Emma reached the door and inquired whether Mrs. Byndham were in and had received an answer in the affirmative, she did that which to Beatrice was then an inexplicable thing. She did not come in, after all, but took Beatrice to the door and followed her into the tiny hall.

"Go in to your mother, Beatrice,' she said, pushing the girl forward; and when Beatrice looked at her with puzzled eyes, vaguely afraid, Lady Emma added harshly: "There are more troubles in the world and more news in the paper than measles in Weaslehurst,

Beatrice. Take off your apron and your cap. You won't need them to-day. There is bad news."

She hurried back to the car, with the air of an escaping charwoman who has smashed her mistress's best china. Beatrice, after one unbelievable minute in which it seemed she could not move hand or foot, rushed upstairs sobbing, with the truth stabbing her heart at every step.

Lady Emma, in accordance with her own instructions, was whirled back to Marcourt Place at a terrific pace. The look on Enid's face haunted her all that journey. She never once thought of Beatrice Byndham after she had handed her in at the door and disposed of her. She would go back to Marcourt Place and talk sensibly about things being for the best, and religiously about Providence and about Fate's being too strong for everybody.

But when Lady Emma reached Marcourt Place and went up to Enid's room she found the door shut and bolted. And perhaps on this old woman in that moment there fell, too, something of the agony that Mrs. Whiteway had borne, for Lady Emma had grown to love Enid Marcourt more than anything else in her world.

She tapped at the door, her voice husky. "Enid! Enid! It is only me, *dear*."

After a long while Enid's voice answered, fiercely, intense with passion, close to the door, as if she pressed her lips to it, so that her words might carry in all their force.

"Go away!" it said. "Go away! I hate you! I never want to see you again!"

CHAPTER XIV

The Key of Kut

NIGHT lay black as pitch over El-Amara. On the left bank of the swollen Tigris, Suewada Marsh, a dark sea of mud, stretched on in infinite distance.

Here and there, from the mud huts by Es Sinn, lights twinkled or flitted like fireflies. Ghouls in flittering ghost-like garments pattered among the dead for loot. Hundreds of Turks lay stiff and cold by the edge of El-Amara swamp, sightless eyes turned to the black ominous sky. And British soldiers lay there also on the narrow strip of higher land between the river and the marsh, their names writ by a shadowy Finger on that ever-lengthening scroll of honour. For them the wars of nations were for ever ended.

Far over the marshes and the desert beyond there came the low, threatening muttering of thunder. A storm was brewing. The Buddoos hurried with the task of looting and pilfering from the pockets of those who lay so stiff and still, finished with all earthly possessions.

And back at Sanna-i-Yat, too, men heard the thunder and whispered to one another, and turned their faces often towards the brooding darkness of the marsh of El-Amara.

Beyond, long miles beyond, lay Kut, in a loop of

the swollen, muddy Tigris. But in between Kut-el-Amara and Sanna-i-Yat, what?

Dark, brooding silence hung over Sanna-i-Yat, broken only by the muttering of approaching thunder, the soft padding of camels' feet, and the whispers of men. Behind the first line of the British, a group of officers sat outside one of the mud huts and talked in low voices. They smoked in short, troubled puffs, and once when one of the men lit a match it showed his face drawn and anxious with the strain, and in his eyes the curious, fixed light of men who have fought grim battles and walked side by side with death. It was young Spane, Territt's friend.

"If one could only know!" he was saying. "To stay here like this—and not be sure."

"One can be sure of nothing in Mesopotamia, Spane. And as for Territt and the reconnoitring party, one can but hope for the best. It was a brave act, but a mad act for all its daring at a time like this. How could he hope to do that which, with all our forces, we have not yet been able to accomplish? Could he break through where others have failed?"

"It was because of that," said Spane, "that he did it. Territt always maintained that for success in this particular position the fewer men one took the better. If any man could do a thing single-handed that man is Philip Territt."

"He's daring enough, I admit, Spane. Recklessly so. I've known him do things in India that seemed, at the time, impossible"—the older man was evidently someone in authority—"so I let him go. It's a hellish business altogether, and he knew he carried his life in his hands."

"I hope no harm has come to him," said Spane uneasily. For himself Spane had no fear. He did not shrink from that which was always to be faced. He had seen death many times and in many guises. But his heart went out into the grim darkness beyond Sanna-i-Yat and followed his friend, Philip Territt.

He had been away at Falahiyah when Territt had gone, riding out into the grey dawn, two days ago, towards Dujailah.

"He was to be back this morning at the latest."

"To-day—and to-night we were to follow. In any case we are to attack as soon as the thunderstorm bursts in all its force. It is our only hope."

They talked in whispers then. Who knew but here in that place of ruined mud huts, of crumbling houses like rabbit warrens, and narrow, winding alleys, an Arab spy might lurk in some hidden place? The spies they had found and shot had an amazing knowledge of languages; they all spoke English well.

Spane sat in the darkness and waited, speaking little. His thoughts went often to his friend, and as often, too, they travelled across the land and the sea to far-away England—England, where men sat in the House of Commons and said plausible things about Kut, and where newspapers for the most part told the world that, whatever one did, one must not think for one moment any other thought than that the relief of Kut was immediately at hand.

But these three men, crouching there while night, like a buzzard, winged its slow, uneasy way across the world, these men knew. True, Hope, that last invisible staff, still lingered, but it was dogged, unconquerable British determination that drove them on. The road was there, winding its way between sunbaked mud and marsh and desert—the road of madness, of terrible things, perchance; but they were British, and, if they piled the road with dead, if their own bodies formed the last barrier, to the last man, to the last bullet, they would take that road, for it led towards Townshend and his desperately beleaguered army.

Far away, in England, politicians spoke glibly of the unconquerable spirit of these men, with small realisation of what it meant, of how it could drive men on, as Germans are said to have driven their men with machine-guns, to the triumphant or bitter end. These men knew, too, that annihilation might be their portion. Territt, who had gone ahead with his sowars, reconnoitring, had not returned.

The British need no machine-guns to enforce obedience. Nelson's undying words were enough, flaming in letters of fire across the red skies of war: "*England expects that every officer and man will do his duty this day.*"

At Sanna-i-Yat that night the thoughts of all the men there turned to their own country. English, Irish and Scot, and an Australian who had led his troops in the fiercest of fighting on Gallipoli Peninsula in the great battle of Chunuk Bair, under the shadow of that grim mountain rising from the Anzac beach—these men crouched now outside the low mud huts of Sanna-i-Yat and waited for the word of command.

The Gates of Kut

The word came towards the dawn when the great artillery of the storm-guns of God rattled over Sanna-i-Yat, the thunder that roared and volleyed from the mountains beyond Bedrai. The lightning twisted and crackled like a thing in pain, lighting the dark world below with its swift-vanishing fire.

The world knows now how Beit Eissa Outwork was taken on that stormy dawn; how men waded waist-deep in water after bivouacking in mud, gaining ground, flung backward, and gaining ground again, a handful against a host; how at last they took the Outwork at Beit Eissa. The world knows and speaks about it now and will speak of it for many years to come. Only the few men left who fought there will not care to speak of it.

When the morrow's sun flung its level rays across the great marshes and the flood-swollen Tigris, the British held wearily but firmly a line within four miles of Es Sinn, that Turkish position which, with its strong defences astride the river, was the strategical key to Kut.

Thousands of Turks lay piled in motionless heaps. When the roll-call of the depleted British was read out that day, the name of Captain Douglas Spane was among the missing. They found him towards noon, his sword broken, and five Turkish dead around him. They found one other thing, too, later, and this they buried with him, a newspaper photograph of Beatrice Byndham.

But of Captain Territt, who, with his sowars and a handful of soldiers, rode out on his dangerous quest three mornings ago, there came no tidings. The

Turkish prisoners vowed they had heard neither word nor sign of that reconnoitring party.

That he had passed beyond the grim, strongly defended barrier of the Bridge of Boats was-unthought of. Somewhere, probably in the old river-bed of Dujailah, the little reconnoitring party had come suddenly and for all time to the end of the journey. In the far loop of the Tigris, surrounded by the enemy, Townshend and his army, starved of the very necessaries of life, held on with fierce determination, though they knew well that help might never come.

The news of Beit Eissa redoubt flashed through to England and, well adulterated with the honey of optimism, began to trickle into the papers. The Coalition Government was on the brink of disaster, the man in the street crying out for a Business Government, and the troublesome section of Ireland becoming more troublesome. One did not know what might happen. Therefore, when one's political reputation was at stake, it was decidedly not the time to issue pessimistic views about Kut-el-Amara. So the magnificent work of the iron 13th Division, already covered with glory in the epic struggle of the Dardanelles, filled the papers instead.

The world read of deeds of daring, of magnificent fighting, of how men died in the ranks where they stood, and hope and pride of race beat high in the hearts of the waiting nation, but of other things happening in Mesopotamia there was no word.

"Things were going well with Kut." Most of the newspapers flaunted jubilant posters. . . .

But over Kut hung a silence as deep as the grave.

CHAPTER XV

Territt and the Turk

THE wind was idly fluttering the leaves of the tamarinds and the liquorice trees by the Tigris. It stirred the robes of the silent Turks and Arabs and the sowars who lay so still on the sun-baked earth; it touched with cool, and tenderer fingers than the looting Buddoos', the quiet faces and forms of the British by the old dry river bed of the Dujailah Bank.

Morning came and passed, and grew to noon with a sun that blazed hotly down. In the cool of the evening or, perchance, the next dawn, the Arabs and the Turks would bury their dead. But wind or rain, or burning heat, mattered not to those who lay so still.

In the meantime the thieving Bedouins gathered together and clattered shrilly of the Outwork beyond Beit Eissa and the need of Turkish reinforcements. By three o'clock they made their way in that direction, and Dujailah Bank was practically deserted of the living.

A few camels padded by. A whir of wings and harsh cries broke the stillness, a flight of mallard and teal and white geese sailed overhead. A flutter of dirty white robes and faint, distant, weird cries, and Arabs and Bedouins swept by at intervals, circling out from the horizon and sweeping in again. Then silence once more.

But, towards sunset, all at once it was broken. The ring of horses' hoofs sounded distinctly on the hardened path of mud in the narrow strip of higher land between the marsh and the river. A Turkish horseman came into sight, riding slowly, thinking of nothing in particular apparently, and leading a pack-horse. From the Outwork of Beit Eissa onwards to the Turkish line of investment what had he to fear? A handful of hard-pressed British behind him, the Turkish investments before, and, in between, the silent dead.

As he rode on, a flock of sand-grouse rose before him and fluttered away like drifted smoke. Their disturbed cries, not unmusical, rose and fell for a space and died away again. But among those stark forms on the Dujailah Bank something moved suddenly at the sound and began to mutter hoarsely.

It began to speak of spring, of irises and Mary lilies, of yellow primroses and green trees waving in a cooling breeze, of yellowhammers singing by an English garden.

It was a strange thing to hear in that deserted place. For in Mesopotamia spring brings none of these things. Neither irises, nor Mary lilies, nor flowers of any kind bloom in Mesopotamia. Spring touches with but fleeting fingers the prickly bushes and wiry tussocks.

But the voice rose again and spoke hoarsely and insistently of these things, as if they were there, at hand, and as if the eyes of the speaker saw them.

"Violets!" it said now, and even through the delirium pain rang through the quiet air. "Violets!" *All* that spring meant to her, he said and *he* knew. "Faded violets—and ashes." . . . He knew, you see. . . . There are things that cannot be hid. . . .

The Turkish horseman had stopped abruptly at the first sound, slipped from his horse, his rifle to his shoulder. His eye, glinting along the shining barrel, flashed warily around. All that could be seen in that desolate place was a scraggy group of tamarind trees and the deserted dead.

But the voice rose again and went on, a little querulously now, rising and falling. The Turk began to move slowly forward, behind the barrier of the horse, still holding the rifle ready for immediate action. The voice had ceased as suddenly as it began. The keen eyes of the Turk swept the scene before and behind him. No danger lurked there apparently. But among the huddled heaps of dead at his feet a voice had spoken.

He began to search, stooping and turning. About the Buddoos he bothered, seemingly, not at all, and one or two in passing he kicked contemptuously with his foot. "Thieves and robbers!" he called them. "Treacherous dogs!"

Investigation showed him that the bodies had already been looted and he gave a sigh of resignation. These Bedouin pigs, of course, would have been hovering around like vultures and taken flight long ere this, and so an honest, Allah-fearing Turk could find little or nothing for his pains.

Then the voice spoke again, almost under his feet.

"Water!" it said, and again even more faintly, "water! . . . water! . . ."

The Arab turned and looked down into the face of a man in the uniform of a British officer. The eyes stared up at him, faintly filmed. The dry tongue showed in the parched mouth.

"Water!" it whispered again.

The Turk looked at the wounded man, at his own half-empty *zamshych,* or water-bottle, and then towards the west. He appeared to be calculating the distance thoughtfully.

The wounded man tried to speak again and failed. His tongue clicked and his lips moved, but no words came.

The Turk stood there for what seemed an unconscionably long time, debating the point mentally. True, this was a British officer and his enemy. But true also that at Gallipoli the British had been good to many a wounded Turk. What had his brother, who was wounded at Gallipoli, said of them—"that the Germans and the way of the Germans he would follow no longer, but the British would he serve gladly and faithfully."

The Turk who had escaped had spoken of these things to all of his brethren. This Turk, remembering them, bent over the wounded man and held the water-gourd to the parched lips. The water gurgled and spilled. With a half impatient movement he knelt down, and lifted the wounded man's head on his knee, while he tilted the water-bottle.

"Drink!" he said in Turkish.

The wounded man drank copiously, though pain

racked and tortured him with every movement, and even to swallow was agony.

"And now," said the Turk in his own language, "what is to be done? Thou canst but lie here, and I must go on my way and to-night they will bury thee." He shrugged his shoulders with the fatalism of the East. "It is better that thou diest before then."

The sick man, lying on the ground, opened his eyes. He spoke drowsily, still deliriously, but in broken Turkish.

"Kut!" he said. "To Kut!"

The Turk shrugged, shaking his head. "Thou speakest Turkish? Then, listen! I also face towards Kut. But thee I may not take, lest worse still befall thee than lieth here."

He knelt down again and lifted the *zamshych* once more to the parched lips, then stood up with an air of finality.

The sick man opened his eyes. He stared up at the Turk, who was preparing to pass on his way. Some dim idea of what it meant came to the wounded officer. He struggled into a sitting posture, his face white and grim with pain.

"Worse would befall thee," said the Turk. "Thou wouldst but take the road in vain. For Kut hath fallen."

"Thou liest!" cried the sick man aloud in sudden passion. "Thou liest!"

The Turk shrugged his shoulders philosophically and turned to his horse.

"'Tis not I but thou and thine that lie," he declared. "Kut hath fallen." He shrugged again. "How could it be otherwise? A handful of sand amid the desert, what would you? Only Allah worketh miracles. I say to you that Kut hath surrendered."

"Thou liest," the man cried again, this time in English, but he spoke weakly, slipped inertly to the earth, exhausted with the outburst. He lay very still, his hands clenched.

The Turk looked down at him and spoke in that calm, detached way that carries conviction.

"Kut hath fallen. They have surrendered. What else would happen? Men cannot live as the birds of the air. Even if thou mightst go to Kut, thou wouldst find nothing there. They would make thee a prisoner."

The man answered nothing, but his nails dug deep into the palm. His lips were distorted with pain. The Turk's voice rang true. For a few moments consciousness, terrible in its impotence, came to the sick man. He would lie there while the sun beat down hotter and hotter. The Turk would go his way. Later would come the treacherous and cruel Arabs!

Against his chest, pinned to his shirt and soaked with blood, were papers and notes containing valuable information. If the reconnoitring party had ridden into danger, risking its life for the sake of that loved country far away, it had at least not gone in vain.

But when he died, as he must in a few hours, if left there untended, the prowling Arabs would come at nightfall and, undisturbed by the Turkish infantry, as in the morning, search his lifeless body thoroughly. They would find the papers, would sell them, perhaps, to a Turkish patrol, or send one of their number ahead to parley at the German headquarters. The Arabs, as well as the Turks, knew the value set by Germany on all papers found on officers—and also on British uniforms. Even of that would he be denuded.

The sea of delirium was beating about him again. He heard its threatening murmur and mutter, steadily drawing nearer. A wave breaking over him receded again. It was a moment of terrible clearness, a moment that told him that, whatever he did, his weak, fluttering fingers must not clutch at the papers, or turn in their direction, lest the Turk suspect.

In that moment memory spoke to him, irrelevantly it seemed, of Gallipoli, of the unsuspected faithfulness of the captured Turks, of how, after their wounds were bound, they had followed at heel like faithful dogs. One could not have got rid of some of those Turks even if one wished.

How the British had laughed, back in Gallipoli, when one night Spane had announced solemnly that the Australian Government had been stricken with dismay at an official announcement from Constantinople.

"Four-fifths of the population of Constantinople," Spane had solemnly averred, "were evacuating that city and, consequent on the treatment accorded to them by the Anzacs, were setting sail for Australia, there to take up residence for life in a land where free bully beef and cigarettes and other luxuries were to be permanent features."

How they had laughed at that skit on the good-natured Australian who sabred his enemy one minute and the next was binding up his wounds and lighting him a cigarette to ease the pain!

Little hope had the sick man, lying there by the dry bed of the Dujailah Bank, he would ever see those comrades again. But if only the papers could be brought back! If someone could be found to carry them! Yet who was there in this desolate world about him, save only this Turk, his foe, who was already mounting his horse and preparing to proceed on his way?

At that thought the man cried out sharply. He asked the Turk whether he had fought at Gallipoli. He fired question after question at him.

The Turk answered stolidly he had not been to Gallipoli, but his brother and many friends had fought there. His brother, he added, politely and without any sarcasm whatever, had been one of the friendly Turks who helped to push the boats off when Gallipoli was evacuated.

Had the English Excellency been at Gallipoli? he asked without interest. But when the English Excellency answered in the affirmative a change came over the Turk. He slipped from his horse and bent low, lest even the dead should hear.

"Then thou, perhaps, art he who saved my brother. How can I know? Thou wert there and that is enough." He bent still lower and put his lips to the sick man's ear. "Because of a life saved, thine shall be saved. Where dost thou turn thy face?" And then, "Kut hath fallen and all therein have surrendered. Turn thy face from Kut!"

The sick man moved a little. How the sea of delirium enveloped him! The waves buffeted him now, hurting him cruelly, tossing him against jagged rocks that tore and twisted him with pain. But wavering a little as if in the wind, he seemed to see a small taper burning, a pin-prick of light, clear and cold. It came to him that this was his brain. How strange it seemed, burning like that so coldly, afar off so that he must fight towards it, swim towards it, though the sea of delirium roared by him and the sound of it was in his ears!

While the taper gave its faint, pale light he managed to speak—"To Falahiyeh!"

If he could but hold out until he reached there, until he handed over that package of papers.

The Turk answered still in that unemotional voice, and as if it were no great matter, "There is no need for the English Excellency to go to Falahiyeh. Four miles from Beit Eissa are thy friends."

"Beit Eissa!"

"From Beit Eissa!" the Turk repeated with the calmness of inherent fatalism. "The Outwork was captured last night."

The eyes of the sick man closed again. The lids lay heavy, waxen-pale on the tanned cheeks. Now they opened again and he cried in a suddenly loud voice.

"Take me there, and anything thou desirest that I or they can give thee is thine." His voice trailed away. He was swept out on a wave of weakness. The pin-prick of light flickered.

And the Turk answered, "Thou hast already given one gift to me and mine. It is mine to repay. I will take thee. But the way I take thee may be dangerous. Listen! If thou art ill, and should cry aloud in the English tongue, my life also, as thine, shall pay the purchase. And now I take thee. Thou art as my wounded brother. When men ask questions thou shalt keep silence, or speak but in Turkish. Prepare!"

CHAPTER XVI

One Man Returns

ON the day that the newsboys in London cried aloud the news shrilly, and the posters in big, black type announced those three tragic words,

FALL OF KUT,

young Mrs. Marcourt went slowly up the steps of an imposing building in Wimpole Street and, pausing for a moment to look for one name among the shining brass plates, pressed the button beneath.

The door opened quietly. A neat maid in starched apron and cap, stiffly frilled, volunteered the information that the doctor expected Mrs. Marcourt. He had been waiting some time.

Then the door closed again behind Mrs. Marcourt as quietly and unobtrusively as it had opened.

Outside, in the Marcourt car the chauffeur yawned and unfolded the paper. He read aloud those words, printed in great staring headlines, "Fall of Kut."

To the chauffeur they conveyed little or nothing. He would perhaps have told you, had you troubled to ask him, that the papers always were printing something or other in big, black headlines like that.

Last week it was the Irish trouble, now it was Kut, and next week it would be something else. Kut was a far-away place, a collection of mud huts and factories, in a loop of a river called the Tigris. The Tigris was somewhere in Mesopotamia. The chauffeur, wearing an armlet, was more interested in France, where, if the war were not over by the time he was ready, he would take his share in the fighting.

There were some graceful, pretty theories about Kut in the paper he was reading. Only yesterday this very same paper had stated that Kut would never fall! It had vigorously belaboured all other papers for pessimism. Kut was impregnable, it had asserted. Prospects had never been rosier. *Kut* fall! Unthinkable!

To-day it as glibly stated that the fall of Kut was not unexpected; that it did not matter, anyhow. Kut had never been of the slightest strategic importance, as everyone knew!

In the House a worried Minister, interrupted in his flood of eloquence on the fall of Kut, was reminded by someone stormily that he had maintained that Kut was practically impregnable, its prospects brighter than ever. He had snapped in answer:

"And so it *was*."

The chauffeur yawned as he read on, wondering vaguely perhaps why so many lives are lost for "places of no strategic importance whatsoever" and whether people who fight in the House mightn't find a better sphere for their activities on the field of battle.

The news of the Irish rebellion was also most cheering! Only a few hundred people had been killed, as well as a good many of the military, well-trained soldiers and officers among them. With a simply wonderful grip of the affair, considering they were so far off, some Irish prelates in Australia had cabled instantly on receipt of the news of the rebellion that "Home Rule was the *only* solution." The chauffeur had been in Australia, and he wondered whether these were the same prelates who had persistently refused to recognise Empire Day.

There were a great many people besides the chauffeur that morning who felt that Redmond's patriotism would urge him to cable back at once: "Conscription, not Home Rule, needed first."

Up to this issue of the paper, the cablegram had not yet been sent. But probably, as it is written that the wise men came from the East, the prelates, who lived in a land where no one else thought of being disloyal to Empire or King, were wiser in their subtle reasoning and its deduction. The said deduction, apparently, being this, that when you have proved you are utterly incapable of ruling yourself, and when you have nearly killed the other fellow, let the reins of Home Rule be given into your hands entirely, so that this time you can quite kill him.

Meanwhile, out in Mesopotamia men fought a succession of battles and thought not of warring creeds, nor puzzled their brains over the exemption of the Irish from conscription. Thwarted almost at every step by intrigues, surrounded with the treachery of the Arabs, fighting the by-no-means-to-be-despised Turks (with German organisation in the background), that mere handful of men struggled on.

It was a succession of small but deadly grim battles, creeping fights, gains of a few yards only in some cases. But the bulldog breed of soldiers hung on, with Death snarling at their haunches. So the days came and passed for them, each taking its toll of human lives. But the men at the Outwork sang to themselves in the weariest, darkest hour. They sang songs of the old country to the last. Parched lips that set tight, lest a cry of pain escape, yet opened to sing those words:

"They may build their ships, my lad!
They think they know the game,
But—they can't build boys of the bulldog breed
Who made old England's name."

And again, through the roar of guns and the black flame-lit hell of battle, the words rolled forth—

"Rule Britannia! Britannia rule the waves!
Britons never, never, *never* will be slaves!"

And sometimes words broke abruptly, caught in the throat of one who could sing no more, but the song went on, flung out on the alien marshes, with a fierceness and a passion of desire and overwhelming love for England, Ireland, and Scotland, lying warm and green under a June sun, safe and sound because such men as these made it possible.

Oh! the story of Mesopotamia that might be written! the things that men did! the things that men endured, and shall endure as long as Britain is Britain, and honour is honour, and both are one!

By that far Outwork beyond Beit Eissa men were counting the hours before they should launch the great night offensive which was to carry all—or lose all. Grimly they faced the alternative. An hour ago, passing overhead, an enemy aeroplane had dropped a message. It read:

"Kut has fallen! Surrender! We will be kind to you!"

A great oath had risen then, a hoarse volume of sound. Men spat the word "Liar!" into the sky, where the wheeling, shimmering plane-bird darted and circled.

Kut fallen? Who would believe it? Not they! And even *if* Kut had fallen, what then? *They* would not give in. Surrender! No! Not while one man was left to man a gun or shoulder a rifle!

The sun was dipping over the great marshes, the world slowly darkening. In the west the red, ragged flare of the sunset, like a blaze vomited from a huge gun, was flaming and beginning to fade.

Soon darkness would come upon the earth and upon the troops. Soon the sun would step over the rim of the world, the marshes blacken, and the last light die away.

Men talked in throaty whispers as they waited for nightfall. In the officers' quarters they spoke briefly of the night attack, the "carrying on" a step farther along the road of war. There were only two men left of the five that had launched the previous night attack. They spoke, too, of Territt in that last hour ere the sunset died.

"Word would have come in by now, if all were well."

"Yesterday," said one, "one of the friendly water-carriers in the village told of a rumour that men in British uniforms lay dead on Dujailah Bank."

"They may have been Germans, and Territt met them and saw through their disguise. For we have one special way of recognition that they could not know. But—if it were Territt and his sowars——" Dretton paused then. He was a hard-headed Scotsman, but his lips set tight.

A low voice said, "You think it is all up then with them," and a nod was the only answer.

The flare of the sunset burned slowly in the west. Its last glow, as of dying coals in the brazier of a grey sky, was fading, when two Arabs, riding slowly, came out on the road from Orah.

Their fluttering garments of dirty white were easily distinguishable even at that distance. One was hunched forward on his camel in a huddled, curious way, and it was this that brought the glasses of the officers levelled on them.

Dretton, the senior officer, peered at them, watching each step they took. Wandering Arabs and friendly, perchance? But in that country one could trust an Arab only so long as one held him in power.

Along the road that led from Orah they came, the camels' feet padding softly, the hunched-up Arab jolting with every step.

"The first chap looks ill. They come apparently from Orah," remarked an officer.

"I wonder! There are many ways of taking the Orah road. They may be spies from beyond Sanna-i-Yat." Dretton had his glasses still levelled to his eyes. "They will no doubt swing out by the road beyond Umm-el-Brahm."

They watched the two figures intently. The

Arabs came on, apparently unconcerned or unconscious of their danger. The minutes went by. The turn in the road brought them steadily nearer. The Arabs would undoubtedly swing now away from the distant British camp.

Then one of the officers gave a low exclamation, for the Arabs came on to the road that led to the Outwork at Beit Eissa.

What did it portend? Who could trust a Buddoo? A low order ran through the camp. The guards stepped into place, rifle to shoulder, heads just showing above the parapet of mud.

The Arabs paused now. A path led directly to the camp. One of the Arabs slipped from his camel and came for a moment to the other who was hunched up in that curious way.

He turned his face once towards the Outwork. If he saw the last light gleaming on the barrels above the parapet, or the keen watching eyes, he gave no sign. He stepped to his companion's side, stayed there a second as if talking. Then he walked back in dignified fashion, mounted his camel, and suddenly, with a loud cry, loped away, back on the road to Orah.

A warning bullet sang after him, but he paid no heed; and then an officer's voice rang out, and the sound of firing ceased as suddenly as it began.

For a strange thing had happened. A rag that had once been white, like a man's dirty handkerchief, fluttered from the camel that was slowly and unconcernedly padding its way towards the Outwork.

In its peculiar, mincing way, the camel came on, its head nodding, its long neck swinging rhythmically.

One Man Returns

The huddled figure of the second Arab still lay like a bundle flung loosely across the camel. When it came nearer, Dretton's eyes, searching through the field-glasses, saw it was strapped. A murmur, questioning and suspicious, went through the camp.

"A wounded Arab!"

Under the grim guard of those shining barrels, waiting the order to fire, the camel came on, the human bundle on its back jolting with every movement.

The officer in command, his glasses still levelled at his eyes, watched intently. Then all at once he flung down his glasses with a great cry. He leaped on the parapet and over it, and for a moment men wondered whether the suns of Mesopotamia had turned his brain.

But at his swift command a dozen men leaped after him, following. They ran forward, unstrapped and lifted the Arab from the camel's back, and laid the dirty bundle of rags on the ground. Dretton, who, in a moment of intuition, had leaped the parapet, knelt down beside that bundle and lifted the burnous back from a white man's face.

A gaunt face, worn with pain and sleepless nights, stared back at him, out of hollow eyes. A thin hand fluttered to a blood-stained breast, clutched there at something that rustled, then dropped lifelessly.

"*Territt!*" said Dretton.

Philip Territt, in the garb of an Arab, had come back, after all.

CHAPTER XVII

The Charity Bazaar

THE news trickled through on the day of the great Charity Bazaar in London.

All the papers were full of that bazaar, its galaxy-to-be of beauty. All the known-to-the-world-through-the-picture-papers women in Society were to be there in full force, arrayed specially for the occasion, and presiding over wonderfully arranged stalls or parading up and down the great hall. Specially selected Duchesses, bland Bishops, who were considered most fashionable at the moment, wealthy *nouveaux riches* who had practically stocked the bazaar, poets who would recite their own verses, stars of the chorus world, everybody who was anybody, and incidentally the outside public at a guinea a head, all these were there, crowding the hall to its utmost capacity.

In weird, wonderful creations of the costumière's art, Society and stage beauties fluttered up and down in gorgeous raiment, dangling artistic and inartistic things for sale.

Outside in the night, the hooded lights of London blinked tired eyes at the Economy posters, but from the hall a flood of music eddied and swirled merrily into the darkness. The band played, and someone sang, and everybody talked at one and the same time.

The Charity Bazaar

For weeks beforehand the bazaar had been talked of. It was to be for three days and three nights, and the first day and the first night were to be most exclusive and mostly for one's friends or wealthy *protégées*, and those in the swim, or in the proud position of just donning the social bathing suit, and being allowed to dog-paddle in the sacred stream on account of the size of one's donation. The next night the Duchesses and the pet poets and the majority of beauties would melt away like snow in May, but the place made hallowed by their footsteps and voices would still be packed to the uttermost.

It was on that first night which had crowded the columns of the newspapers with a long list of the great folk and the lions on a lead who were to be there, that news trickled through from Kut, a few terse lines which informed those who cared to read that:

"The first wounded and disabled from Kut have been transferred and exchanged with the Turkish and other prisoners. A complete list will be published in a later issue."

Beatrice Byndham, who had never quite lost hope, noticed that paragraph as she was starting out for the Charity Bazaar. She stood in the quaint, square hall of their small flat, and read and re-read it. Just those words stared up at her and no more.

Beatrice was waiting for Lady Emma Beckendon, who was to chaperon her that night. Her mother was down with a sharp attack of influenza, and bemoaning a fate whose cruel and unromantic emissary had seized upon her at the last moment.

The Gates of Kut

Beatrice stood in the hall, in her lovely apricot-pink gown, with the touch of black velvet she always wore lately, and said to herself: "A list will be published later; a *completed* list."

Trouble came into her voice. For a moment doubt shook her. If his name were not there, in that list! Then she cried out, "No, I will not think so, I will not."

She read it again as if she would force from those few lines all that she would know, and then her eyes, lifting slowly, saw one other thing. The paper she held in her hand was an early afternoon edition, and the words stood out from the column: "A complete list will be published in a later issue."

How long had she to wait ere news trickled through—an hour, two hours? It seemed eternity. She stood there, her hands clenched, her eyes troubled, uneasy. Never, in spite of that news from El-Amara, would she believe that Philip Territt was dead. Though all others believed it she had refused to do so. Many who had been believed dead had come back to those who had mourned. Some day, she said, Philip would come back to her also.

Impulsively she acted on a thought of the moment, searched in a telephone book, and then rang up the leading newspaper office.

The attendant at the other end of the wire said he was not sure whether it were possible to answer the question she had asked; he believed the list would be in their possession.

Beatrice said, in a voice that trembled, "Can you tell me whether Captain Territt—Captain Philip Territt—is among the wounded?" The trouble in her young voice crept across the wire. She added simply: "My name is Beatrice Byndham; Captain Territt and I are engaged."

She was asked to wait a moment. For a moment that seemed like an hour she did so. Then the voice came through.

"The Editor," it said courteously, "had much pleasure in informing Miss Byndham that Captain Territt, recommended for the D.S.O., is the first to head the list. Captain Territt had been sent to the base hospital ahead of the Kut wounded. It was reported, though this at the moment could not be given as certain, that Captain Territt was included among the number of officers who had left in a hospital ship for England. If that were so he might be expected any day after to-morrow."

So, to Beatrice Byndham, the news came in such strange and almost incredible fashion. Was it any wonder that she sank down on a chair and wept happy tears, punctuated with bursts of laughter? She flew rather than ran up the stairs to her mother's room.

When Lady Emma Beckendon, looking more like a ruffled turkey-cock than ever, sailed majestically into that small flat, she found an almost incoherently happy young person and Mrs. Byndham with a red nose and hysteria.

Beatrice told Lady Emma the news without delay, and Lady Emma Beckendon blinked several times in her peculiar way as she heard it. She stared at the girl, at Mrs. Byndham, and at Beatrice again.

She seemed as if she hardly knew what to say, which was rather strange for Lady Emma Beckendon.

"Such a romance!" Mrs. Byndham said ecstatically. She had a romantic soul. "Dear Lady Emma, if only I had not this influenza how I would have loved to go with Beatrice! For I should have so enjoyed letting people know that dear Philip is *safe*."

"I am sure you would," said Lady Emma. She turned to Beatrice. "Is this going to keep you at home, Beatrice, or do you still intend to go on to the bazaar?"

"I am coming now," said Beatrice. "Of course, I'll come. I shall just dance for sheer joy. And I'll tell everybody, whether they know me, or Philip, or neither of us," and she vanished into the room adjoining for a wrap.

"I'm so pleased about it," Mrs. Byndham reiterated for about the tenth time to Lady Emma, who sat very stiff and still. In spite of her unexpected interest in Beatrice's career, she was always very formal with Mrs. Byndham. "The *dear* child! I'm in an ecstasy of happiness about it."

"I am sure you must be," Lady Emma agreed politely. Beatrice came out of her room, ready for the bazaar, dressed as a Czech, and they whirled away.

There they soon separated, Beatrice to flutter about like a lovely iridescent butterfly, radiating happiness and disseminating her news. She had never looked so lovely. Excitement had brought a flush to her cheeks, a light to her eyes that had been missing since that morning weeks ago, years it had seemed, when the news came to London.

The band was playing haunting, wonderful music. The crowd grew thicker until it seemed one could hardly move. But Lady Beckendon went persistently in and out among the guests as if she searched for someone.

Though it appeared as if everybody she knew and had ever known was there, the face for which she searched was missing.

George Marcourt, she knew, was at the House, for there was to be a late sitting that night. Enid, whom she had not seen so often lately, at different entertainments and friends' houses, would most surely be at the bazaar.

But Enid was not there. It was nearly an hour before, in that constantly-moving mass of people, Lady Emma Beckendon, with her short sight and grim determination to hold her tongue as to the purpose of her quest, could be sure Enid had not come.

Since the night when young Mrs. Marcourt had flung those passionate words through the closed door of her room, Lady Emma had resolutely stayed away from Marcourt Place.

George, used to her constant visits, had naturally noticed her absence. He asked his wife the reason on one occasion, and she had said simply :

"I cannot tell you. I think she is offended with me because, when she last came, I refused to see her. She wanted to—to interfere in my life in—in a way that I could not allow——"

She had ceased speaking abruptly. She hastened

to turn her face away from her husband's kind, honest eyes, a little perplexed now.

If only George were not so kind, so trusting, how much easier it would be to tell him everything. She had tried so many times, and always the vision of his utterly destroyed happiness and peace rose before her.

She tried to tell him now as suddenly she clung to him. The tears filled her eyes. "George——" she began.

But he put his arm tenderly about her. She had grown so fragile, so thin and pale, and the change in her wrung his heart. He would not let her go on.

"Don't think about it, dear," he begged; and then, so kindly and stupidly in his misunderstanding: "She won't stay away for ever. She is growing old and touchy, very easily offended. She will come back some day soon, and unexpectedly."

But though Lady Emma did not come soon, as he had anticipated, she did come at last and unexpectedly. Because she stayed away so long, however, much that was happening in the meantime was unknown to her. Perhaps George was more hurt than he showed at her silence. He had fumed over it more than once in secret, but because mention of it seemed to make his wife unhappy, he did not speak of it again to her.

The weeks had grown into months. Lady Emma had been away for most of them. She had come from her country house to town specially for the famous bazaar and to chaperon Beatrice. She began to search for her now, and found her in the centre of a group as excited as herself.

"Beatrice!" said Lady Emma. "I am going to

call back for you. I have to go on somewhere else for about an hour."

Beatrice, still flushed with happiness and excitement, walked as far as the door with her, talking all the time, Lady Emma listening without hearing. They were stopped in that progress down the room every now and again. Beatrice was being overwhelmed with congratulations.

There came a little space, however, for which Lady Emma had manœuvred and waited. Carelessly she said:

"I notice Enid is not here to-night?"

The carelessness did not deceive Beatrice. She knew, without knowing the reason, of the breach between Lady Emma and Marcourt Place. She had wondered at what she termed Lady Emma's heartlessness. She hesitated and then, remorse overcoming everything else, added reproachfully:

"Oh! I should have gone to Enid to-night before I came here. I should have told her the good news. But also, in any case, I should have gone. Because of to-morrow."

She ended hastily, looking at Lady Emma. Some of the gladness went out of her young face.

"Oh! Lady Emma," she cried, "I forgot you did not know. Enid would not come because—to-morrow is the day of her operation."

Lady Emma stood still and stared at Beatrice.

"Operation?—then—Enid is ill?" She spoke very slowly.

"Enid has not been well for months. You have been away lately, so you would not know," Beatrice answered. "But the last few weeks she seems to have grown worse. And to-morrow she is to undergo an operation. I don't know why, or whether it will be severe, but she did tell me that the doctor says she would be quite well afterwards, and that it is going to mean just everything to her."

She looked at Lady Emma, who was staring at her in a queer way, blinking fast. Beatrice said:

"I must go and see her, too. Would you take me with you?"

Lady Emma gave a queer, empty laugh. So the child knew she was going to Marcourt Place. Was her face, a mask for all these years, so easy now to read?

She said to Beatrice, "Not now; I want to go alone. I will send the carriage back for you and drop you there on my way home."

She left Beatrice in the big lighted hall, with its gorgeous flowers and gowns and shaded lights, its wonderful string bands, and laughter and chatter.

The laughter and the music followed old Lady Emma into the night. Rain was falling. Queer caricatures of men, stooped of shoulder and twisted, mere distortions of human creatures, ambled along, attracted, like night-moths, to the light and sound of revelry. They peered, with eyes like those of some starved animal, half-wolfish, at this old, painted woman in her costly silks and glittering jewels, hurrying down the scarlet strip of carpet which an obsequious footman unrolled before her.

When they came to Marcourt Place Jevons, who answered the door, perceptibly hesitated at sight of her. He knew Lady Emma had not been to the house for a considerable period.

"I am afraid, my lady, Mrs. Marcourt is not at home to anyone to-night. She is not seeing anyone at all, my lady."

"She will see me," said Lady Emma. As she swept along the hall she turned to him, "Where is Mrs. Marcourt?"

"In her own sitting-room, my lady."

She went up and Jevons, in the hall below, watching her stately progress, metaphorically washed his hands of the whole affair.

She knocked on the door gently twice before an answer came. She trembled very much as she waited, but she held her old head high.

Enid, at her writing-desk, lifted her head and half turned her face towards the door. When she saw it was Lady Emma Beckendon her lips trembled. Then she said in a voice that shook for all its gentleness:

"Come in, Emma; I was just writing to you."

CHAPTER XVIII

God's Greatest Gift

ENID rose and went slowly across the room to greet Lady Emma, who stood quite still, watching her. All at once she swallowed abruptly.

"*Enid!*" she said, and then began suddenly to cry. Mrs. Marcourt did not speak. She drew up a chair, pressed Lady Emma gently into it, patted the shaking shoulders, then went back to her desk. She began to fold up the letter she was writing, as if waiting for the moment when Emma should care to speak.

It was borne in on Lady Emma that it was best not to speak at all, at that moment at any rate. In the first glance at Enid she saw the startling change the weeks had brought. She saw it the more clearly because from the night that Enid had shut her door against her Lady Emma Beckendon had not been at that house, and had arranged her engagements so that even at friends' houses they should not meet.

Emma had been deeply wounded, and anger had followed closely on the heels of hurt. She had brooded as only women of her age and disposition would brood. Beatrice's words in the gay bazaar had thrown a flood of light on the screen where hitherto the stereopticon of her mind had flung but brooding shadows of resentment.

If Lady Emma had not been sure before, she knew

now that in all her selfish existence she had never loved anything as she loved Enid Marcourt. All the love she might have given a child had been hoarded up in her withered heart for many years, centreing almost unconsciously about this young, delicate wife of George Marcourt.

She looked at Enid, and all the shadows that had been conjured up during their misunderstanding vanished. That lift of the brown head, the light in the eyes, told her that if she had come any time before this night, even an hour after that never forgotten morning, Enid would have greeted her as now, with the old kind gentleness. But Lady Emma had been too proud to call.

There came to her now the knowledge that there must be the one hour that a suffering soul demands, one terrible hour in which one *must* be alone; and Emma, for all the kind thought behind the impulse, had blundered into that hour when, that night when Philip Territt's death was announced in the papers, she found herself outside a barred door.

"I am sorry," said old Emma, her voice shaking and the moulted-looking osprey on her grey head trembling exceedingly; "I—I should not have come —then."

"Don't let us speak of it, dear," Enid said gently.

She had risen, and in passing the queer old figure put her hand on its shoulder again, this time with tender, understanding pressure. "It is all over and ended. It is I who should ask your forgiveness." And she bent and kissed Lady Emma's curiously-working face. She spoke casually of other things. "You have been to the bazaar, of course, Emma? And how did Beatrice look?"

"Very pretty and—animated." She almost made the slip of saying radiantly happy. "She went as a Czech, or what Madame Celeste decided was a Czech."

Emma wiped her old eyes as she spoke, and fought for her old proud calmness. Enid laughed as she turned her face.

"Well, I don't suppose anyone there would be any the wiser. The critical folk don't appear until the second night as a rule. So Beatrice was enjoying herself." She paused a moment, and then said wistfully, "I am glad. Poor Beatrice!"

For a moment silence fell between them. Enid had gone to the mantelshelf and was rearranging some beauty-roses in the tall-stemmed crystal vase. In her pale blue velvet gown, with its loose-falling lines and its border of heavy white fur, she shone out of the quiet greys of the room as a delicate piece of porcelain or illuminated alabaster.

The change in her, almost imperceptible to those who saw her constantly, was very distinct and clear to the eyes of Lady Emma Beckendon. Enid Marcourt was very thin, wasted almost. The purple shadows beneath her eyes were very noticeable and her eyes seemed too large for the small face. The mouth was pinched but firm, as if sorrow and it had fought a tough battle. She was old, immeasurably altered in some inexplicable way, but with it all was a still peace, a sureness of something, that diffused about her a pale aura of happiness. Its still shining was in her eyes that looked away and beyond the moment.

It was as if the glory of a forbidden sun shone on her through a separating screen of glass—the dim light that falls softly through old, stained windows.

But this was not the only change in Enid. Though Lady Emma sat so silent at first, and then began to plunge into descriptions of the bazaar and all who were there, her heart contracted with grief. Was George blind not to see the change in his wife? What was he doing there, in the House of Commons, listening to, or nodding over, prosy, meaningless speeches, when his place was at home?

There came to her in that moment the memory of that problem she had once set Enid. It had answered itself, or rather, George Marcourt had answered it. He was not the only husband in the world who suffered from hypermetropia or long sight. The world was full of men, Lady Emma told herself bitterly, who were so content at seeing a long way ahead that the things right under their eyes were hidden from them.

It was not that Enid, on a surface impression, had changed. Colour glowed in her cheeks, her lips were red. She spoke in her old voice and without a thought of anger or remembrance, apparently. On the surface it would seem, as she said, it was all over and ended.

But the old eyes of Emma Beckendon were keen. She, too, had trodden the road when one rouged and painted one's lips, and smiled and laughed, and walked the while with the shadow of things that had been or could not be. Enid had suffered.

So she was in no way deceived as Enid spoke

lightly of the bazaar, of the people they knew, of the receipts that should mean so much for charity. Neither of them as yet had spoken of that morrow.

"You did not go to the bazaar," Lady Emma said.

Enid shook her head. "No, I didn't feel like going. I am down in the East End a great deal nowadays, you know. There is so much to be done there. War has brought prosperity to some quarters, to others but greater poverty. Prices are so high now, and many of these people find it easier to die than to live. Death is the only thing they have not to purchase."

She was looking at the roses as she spoke; her arm lay along the mantelshelf. In the grate a low fire, for the night had been unexpectedly chilly, burned. Her foot in its small, pointed shoe rested on the fender. She went on speaking in that gentle voice that was so strangely at variance with the bright rouge on her cheeks, the vermilion on her lips.

"They grow to look on death, these very poor people, as a friend; and they view life with an almost Eastern fatalism. I am not sure that they are not wiser than we, after all. We expect far too much out of life. What it is ordained we must not have, we are fain to wring from life."

"And when one comes to the end," said Lady Emma with a sigh, "one knows that the things which seemed impossible to live without, counted little in the scheme of real things, or in what constitutes happiness. One often thinks that, I know. Sometimes I, and I am a selfish old woman, have felt it myself.

But I have never felt it so strongly that I became a Socialist, and divided my estate and all I had."

Enid smiled and spoke to the roses. "I wonder," she said meditatively, "who was the anonymous giver of a thousand pounds to that East End mission lately?"

Lady Emma grunted. "One must do something. Once I did slumming, too. I used to start out with a bundle of tracts and come home with a family of fleas. So I gave it up."

Enid laughed suddenly then—a ghost of her old laughter, perhaps, but still laughter. Then they spoke of the bazaar again, skirting all other topics but that which memory had undoubtedly brought to both their minds. Enid chatted on, sitting now in the chair by her desk. She talked brightly. It was difficult, but in the last few weeks she had overcome many difficulties.

She spoke of the vicarage, and her mother and father, and the children. The squire of Weaslehurst's house and lands were in the market, it appeared, and George thought of buying them. He had plans, if that came to pass, of rebuilding the village on more sanitary lines.

"You would like to live there?"

"I should love it, Emma." She turned her eyes to the older woman. A flush that was not rouge warmed her cheeks. "How much one could do for the poor there! And we shall not want the whole of the Manor House for ourselves. Only a wing. The rest of it, and a new wing which shall be built as well, is to be for children from the East End. How they will romp in the woods! You know the woods, Emma, the tall beech trees, like the haunt of fairies, and the carpet of russet and gold, and the blue hollows of wild hyacinths. Why," she added breathlessly, "it will be a glimpse of heaven to those poor little souls."

"It will mean a lot of worry for you," Lady Emma began. Enid shook her head.

"Ah, no! It will give me happiness to give them happiness. They are so old before their time, those children of the poor. They grow wizened, and many of them never know the meaning of youth. Fancy catching them up and setting them down again in those woods! My mother"—and the tender smile that always came to her lips when she spoke of her mother rested there now—"my mother always spoke of the beech woods in spring as 'the green glades of God.'"

A hush followed her words, and in the ensuing silence Enid said, very softly, "And, in the future, Emma, I, too, hope to walk there, with another little child, as well as the poor children."

Lady Emma looked at her and understood. "But—do you think you are quite wise, Enid?" Her old eyes blinked. Her voice trembled. "The—the risk and the pain——"

"I look beyond the pain, Emma," and Enid lifted her head and stared dreamily before her. "I know now that God's greatest gift is a little child. Once, my mother told me so. A little child, she said, filled up all the blank places in life." For the first time her voice faltered, ever so slightly. "There are a great many blank places, sometimes, in life, Emma. When I have a little child of my very own—— You, in other words, have told me the same, Emma."

"Yes, I know," said Emma helplessly. She, too, stared before her for a while. "But you have greater courage. For all my domineering ways—I didn't know I was domineering until a discharged butler told me so—I am really a coward at heart. I get into a panic at the crucial moment. Indeed, I fear I am one of those people who give to others the advice they are incapable of taking themselves."

Enid's smile became a laugh.

"Dear Emma!" she exclaimed. "Anyhow, no one can say you are blind."

Lady Emma smiled grimly. "No, I'm not blind."

Enid moved uneasily at that. Lady Emma took up the thread where her brief comment had suddenly snapped it.

"What does George think about it, Enid?" and then answered her own question. "What you desire, of course, is his desire."

Enid nodded. It was a subject so near to her heart and so sacred she did not care to speak about it further. And George, in the last few days, had taken to wandering about the house like a restless ghost. But Emma went blundering on in a foolish but well-meant fashion.

"Is it quite—safe?"

"Quite, Emma dear. I haven't the slightest fear. As I told you before, I look beyond the moment."

There came a knock on the door and a servant told

her that Beatrice Byndham was waiting. Lady Emma gave a start.

"Bless my soul! Have I been here that long, Enid? I promised to send the carriage back for Beatrice at eleven. I told my man to go at that hour. I never thought I had been here so long."

"It has not seemed long to me either, Emma." She turned to the servant. "Show Miss Byndham up——"

But Lady Emma gave a sudden exclamation and put out her hand.

"Not yet, Enid. Tell him to ask her to wait for a few minutes. I want to speak to you before Beatrice comes."

Enid obeyed, but her face went pale under the rouge. She seemed to shrink for a moment, and then gather herself together as if for strength. As the door closed behind the footman Lady Emma spoke hurriedly.

"Beatrice is coming to tell you some news, Enid. Can you guess what it is?"

Enid turned to her a startled face.

"What is it?" she asked, in a voice of suspense. Then, "Oh! I suppose I should guess Beatrice has become engaged to—someone else. That would, of course, happen eventually."

"Beatrice *is* engaged, Enid. She was engaged to Philip Territt you remember, and then came the intimation of his death. It was all in the papers, the notice of his death——"

"Yes." But she wondered, drawing stabbing breaths of pain, why Emma probed the wound anew.

She sat very still, her hands clasped on the desk before her, her head bent.

The words came with a rush. "Territt did not die, Enid. As Beatrice is here to tell you so, almost incoherent with joy, it was better, perhaps, for me to tell you even if I blundered in the telling. But George will be home with the news, too, shortly. I thought you had better be prepared beforehand."

At Lady Emma's words Mrs. Marcourt's cheeks went white. The patches of rouge flared up, like bright spots of colour on her colourless face. She rose slowly from her chair and stared at Lady Emma with wide eyes. Was Emma mad? Had her brain turned with advancing age? Had she brooded over this thing, until it seemed real? Her breath came in sobbing fashion.

"It is true," said Emma quietly, "quite true. The editor of one of the evening papers told Beatrice. Later the nine o'clock edition had, in its stop-press column, the bare intimation. Philip Territt's name headed the list. He has the D.S.O. The whole story will be in the papers in the morning. You had to know—before she came."

Enid sat down heavily.

"How could they know? How could it be true?" she cried, in a kind of despair and, for a moment, as if stunned, she laid her face in her hands.

"Beatrice," Lady Emma reminded her, "is waiting downstairs. Shall I send a message and say you are too tired to see her?"

Enid shook her head. Her eyes wandered round the writing-table, at a cluster of roses in the opal bowl, at two piles of invitations, answered and unanswered, and at last came back to a picture in a silver frame, an exquisite reproduction of the Madonna and Child. She was silent a moment or two, her eyes fixed on it. She seemed to gather strength from the Mother of Sorrows, to see in the future only the little child, a little child who was to fill in all the blanks of life. The still shining came back to her eyes, poor eyes that had been so suddenly scared, so full of unbearable pain in that terrible moment of realisation. She caught her breath with a sobbing sound. Philip was no more the dear ghost, companion of her hours of solitude, walking beside her in tender counsel and understanding. He was alive. He was coming back—to Beatrice, her friend. . . . She spoke at last.

"I will see Beatrice now. Before George comes, Emma. Not here"—she had risen—"but downstairs. Come with me, Emma."

Her hand clung to the older woman's, then she straightened herself, and looked over her shoulder at the picture in its oval frame. The eyes of the Mother of all women met hers, the Little Child held out its arms to her.

She turned and went downstairs, Lady Emma following.

CHAPTER XIX

Lady Emma's Dream

"AND so," said Beatrice breathlessly, "I had to come and tell you. I simply couldn't wait until the morning. I knew how glad you would be. You were always so kind to Phil." She laughed, and her eyes shone and her cheeks flushed adorably. "Doesn't it seem wonderful, though, you know? I kept saying to myself all the time, since the first terrible news, that it wouldn't be true. God could not be so cruel." Her voice shook. "Oh, Enid, you don't know how I felt! To see him no more! It was unthinkable."

Enid was silent for a moment or two. Then she answered, "I think I can realise it, in some measure," and after another pause, "but, you see, I have never believed when a loved one dies that one loses him and that one shall not see him again. Life goes on somewhere else and goes on without limitations that are of earth. One is not fettered there, as one is here, by things which seem beyond our control but which, after all, man and not God is mainly responsible for."

"Then, if anyone you loved died," Beatrice cried, and Lady Emma moved suddenly, "you would not suffer to the same extent as other people. You would think of a future life, be content with that? You would not suffer at the thought of separation——"

"I do not know about the suffering," said Enid,

turning her head so that only her delicate profile was barely visible. "I—yes, I think I would suffer, too—but I would always have felt like that—about the future. I should never have walked quite alone."

Beatrice shook her head mutinously. "I am different. I don't want anything in any Beyond half as much as I want it in this Now. And a great many people, a very great many people, Enid, are like that. Only they will not admit it. I would rather have all I desired now than in some visionary future."

Lady Emma stirred uneasily.

"And so," Beatrice went on, "I'd rather have one year with Philip in this world than half a lifetime with the company of angels. I am sure if they were anything like the prints of the saints they would bore me anyway."

"Have you had any further news?" asked Lady Emma. She was shocked at Beatrice. Those Byndhams! One never knew what they would be saying next. She thought it time to steer the boat of conversation into other channels.

Enid lay back in her chair, delicate and lovely in her blue gown with its high collar of white fur framing softly her face, apparently listening as Beatrice rattled on.

"News is coming in galore, it appears. Some question cropped up in the House to-night, and there was ever so much more told than one hears in the ordinary way. I heard such a lot of news just before I came away."

Her pink cloak was slipping from her white shoulders. Her young face glowed. Lady Emma, who had always questioned Beatrice Byndham's beauty, grudgingly admitted it now.

"Philip was the only one left out of the reconnoitring party which he led. He was badly wounded and left for dead. It all happened on some place known as the Dujailah Bank. And a friendly Turk came along and rescued him, and brought him back to the British camp."

"Who told you this?" Lady Emma asked, rising and preparing for departure. She felt she wanted to scream to relieve the tension.

"One or two of the members who had just come from the House."

"I thought they weren't allowed to tell secrets?"

"Oh! but it isn't a secret," said Beatrice, "all the papers will have it in the morning anyhow. Enid, dear, how tired you look, and we are keeping you up! See, Lady Emma, it is nearly twelve."

"Don't go!" said Enid, as she had said more than once to Lady Emma. "Stay to supper. George will be home at any moment now——" She looked at Emma somewhat wistfully. "He has been wondering why we have not been seeing anything of you lately."

Lady Emma would not stay. "You look too tired for entertaining people. Give my love to George. I will come to-morrow. Come, Beatrice!"

Beatrice stood up, draping her cloak about her. She turned her glowing face to Enid, and lingered.

"When Philip comes back," she said, "I suppose he will suggest an early marriage. Do you think I should, Enid?"

There was hardly a pause before Enid answered.

"Yes, I think you should, Beatrice."

Lady Emma moved towards the door without speaking.

"Of course it would be terrible and all that," and Beatrice shivered, "if he came back crippled or without an arm or leg, as some men have done."

Enid looked at her in a queer way. "Would that matter to you, Beatrice?"

"It would," said Beatrice frankly. "I love Phil very much. It would nearly kill me if anything happened to him. But it would be very dreadful for me if he were crippled and broken. Wouldn't you, too, feel like that?"

By and by Enid replied quietly, "No; I don't think I should."

They heard George in the hall then. He came in breezily, kissed his wife and Lady Emma, and turned to Beatrice, listening intently as she told her news and asked him had he heard any more. He, too, was excited.

"All sorts of rumours are racing ahead," he said. "Nothing really definite, however. One does not even know when the boat will be in, whether it will come by the Biscay or whether they will berth at Marseilles and come overland. In the latter case, of course, they would be here almost any day. Perhaps to-morrow."

"To-morrow!" cried Beatrice. She radiated delight. "Then I must rush home and get my beauty sleep, and be bright and fresh in the morning. Just in case, you know!"

George laughed. "You young people!" he said. He put his arms about his wife as he stood thus and she leaned somewhat heavily against him for a moment. In the light her face looked suddenly very tired and worn. Beatrice had shaken hands with them and was dancing down the steps to the carriage, when Lady Emma rustled back.

"Oh! George, I wish you'd run down to Beatrice a moment while I talk to Enid."

George smiled. "Don't quarrel again then, you two." He vanished.

Lady Emma and Enid stood and looked at each other.

"I rather wish," said the former, with tears in her eyes, "that this had not happened."

"It will make no difference," was Enid's answer.

Beatrice's gay laugh rang outside, where the lights flung wan reflections on the damp pavement.

"You see," added Enid with difficulty, "I have mapped my life ahead. I am stepping on to a new road that will bring me, I am sure, the content I would never otherwise know. You will believe that, Emma. We—we don't want, either you or I, to speak of this again. The gates are closed, closed fast as those miserable gates of Kut, which it was written we should not open."

"We will not speak of it again," said Lady Emma. Then and there she, too, slipped out on to the new road that would hold no mention or thought of the old. "May I come and see you—in the morning?" said Lady Emma anxiously. But Enid shook her head.

"No. You would only worry yourself unnecessarily. I will be quite all right. Come and see me on Thursday, that will be the day after. Mother will be here to-morrow morning."

"I am glad of that," said Lady Emma. Her old head bent and shook, and then she said abruptly:

"Good night, dear. *Dieu vous garde!*" The tears brimmed in her eyes. She lifted her withered cheek, and Enid bent and kissed her warmly, clinging to her a moment, then Lady Emma went out of the hall and down the steps, looking old and bent and very tired.

As she stepped on to the pavement she looked back. Enid was standing there in her blue gown with its deep-bordered fur, like snow, against the soft velvet. Then she went to her carriage and George helped her in.

"I fear I am getting old," she said to him. "I get strange fancies. George, do you believe in intuition?"

"I have heard it said that a premonition is often but another name for impulse. What are you planning, Emma? Nothing wicked, I hope. Second thoughts are best."

"Are they? Ah, I wonder!" said Lady Emma, and then she leaned back, her head against the delicate grey cushions. "Good-bye, George."

"Good night," said George. He stood on the steps and looked after the carriage as it rolled away, somewhat perplexed. Emma was a queer old stick. One never knew what she meant. Probably she never knew herself.

At that he smiled and went indoors. Lady Emma closed her eyes and her head nodded as if she were asleep, and she did not answer when Beatrice offered a tentative remark.

But she woke suddenly when the carriage stopped outside the dark block of flats silhouetted against the moonless sky.

"I think I will come in for a moment, Beatrice. There might be a letter for you from Marseilles."

Beatrice was surprised. It was the first time Lady Emma Beckendon had shown any great interest in her engagement. Beatrice had, in fact, a feeling she secretly disapproved of it.

"Oh! do you think there might be a letter to-night?" cried Beatrice.

"I don't see any reason why there should not," said Lady Emma in her practical way. "If dispatches could reach the House to-day, and the nine o'clock editions be able to give us some news, it looks as if a mail might cross the Channel as well. Let us go up and see!"

As Lady Emma had said, the mail was in. Among the half-dozen letters on Mrs. Byndham's modern Jacobean hall-table was one addressed to Beatrice in Philip Territt's handwriting.

Beatrice looked as if not sure whether to laugh or cry. It had been a day of emotion and surprises. As Beatrice opened the letter, Lady Emma said:

"What time do you get the last mail here, in Chelsea?"

"About ten."

Lady Emma said to herself, "Then he didn't write to Marcourt Place. Not to Enid at any rate. For George had the letters in his hand when he came into the hall. And Enid asked him if there were any letters for her, and he said 'No.' So he wrote to Beatrice."

There came to her then, as she waited, the words Enid had spoken a few minutes ago, "It will make no difference."

Lady Emma sighed and wished she could be sure.

As she turned to Beatrice she became aware that the girl was crying silently. Her tears dropped on to the letter.

"It is very short," she said. "Would you like to read it? Do. There is really no reason why you should not. Philip is not a poet lover who sends his love impassioned verses and many pages. And you know him so well."

It was indeed, as Beatrice said, very short. But its brevity was, perhaps, explained in its very first sentence.

"Dear Beatrice," it ran, "my right arm is still pretty stiff, so excuse this scrawl. I thought you would like to know that we have just touched at Marseilles. Whether we go overland, in which case we will get to London as soon as this letter, or by the Bay, I don't know at present. Anyhow, this is just a note to say I am quite all right, really, save for a left arm in splints and a limp, which I hope to get rid of soon in order to get to France for the final *coup*. I want to have a long chat with you when I come back, so will keep all the news until then." He had signed it simply "Phil."

Lady Emma handed the letter back to Beatrice in silence.

"So he may be here in London now," she said, "this very night."

Beatrice smiled through her tears. "It seems all too wonderful to be true. I feel as if I were dreaming. I have often dreamt that just such a thing happened, and then I woke up and found myself in my room and everybody believing Phil was dead."

She was still crying softly, but her eyes shone with happiness behind the tears.

"Good night, Beatrice," said Lady Emma abruptly and went her way.

But that night in her room she thought of Philip Territt's letter again. She shook her head. Two sentences out of it came to her mind.

"'I thought you would like to know that,' and 'I want to have a long chat with you when I come back. . . .'"

"I hardly think," said Lady Emma to herself, "that if it had been Enid instead of Beatrice he would have written like that."

She shook her head again.

"Poor Beatrice! The eyes of love *are* blind. How will it all end, I wonder?"

And then, when she would have slept that night, the thoughts that beat about those four people came back again and again persistently, fluttering around her like stormy petrels, crying of the morrow and the menace of the gathering clouds.

"It's a queer world," said Lady Emma wearily, "and it's a problem of which I cannot for the life of me see any real solution. On the surface it will be solved at least. Phil will marry Beatrice, for the long chat will never come to pass, for even if it does he will find he cannot tell her the truth without breaking her heart. And breaking one heart is not likely to mend another."

She tossed sleeplessly to and fro, wishing she could purge these annoying thoughts from her mind. "What is it to me, anyway?" she said angrily, but the thought still fluttered about her. "Beatrice will marry Phil, George will get on, and probably be knighted next year if he gives any more to the Party funds. And Enid—Enid will have her baby, and go in for mothers' meetings and singing hymns, and teaching dirty little slum children to wash their faces in—in—what was it?"—she yawned, she was getting sleepy—"in—in green glades, yes, that is what she said, the green glades of God. . . ."

Her old head, guiltless now of the imposing and bejewelled front, lolled to one side and she fell asleep.

She fell asleep and dreamed. And in her dreams the words that had haunted her ever since Enid Marcourt spoke them came back to her and followed her like elusive, flitting feet.

For she dreamed that she, very tired with walking on a long and aimless road that presumably led nowhere, came at last quite suddenly to a tall forest of beech trees, slim, silver-boled trees, golden in the sun, delicate leafy green underneath. The sun filtered through in long shining spears of yellow light. The trees whispered and whispered, their branches fluttering together like dumb hands that would fain tell her something.

There was a russet-red carpet of leaves; the leaves

of the autumn, as it were, of life. And across them, under the swaying, sun-rifted branches, a path ran, shining and very straight. There were wild hyacinths beside it, a haze of blue like to the June sky reflected in a crystal pool. And she saw Enid, Enid in the warm hollow of blue hyacinths, with a little child clinging to her hand. . . .

In the dream it seemed to her that Enid turned her face and spoke. Enid said, as she had said that afternoon in the grey room at Marcourt Place:

"Life goes on. . . . Nothing dies. . . . Life goes on . . . and on . . . in the green glades of God. . . ."

CHAPTER XX

The Hospital Ship

THE boat was beating in against the sunset, her tall masts tipped with flame.

The white cliffs of Old England showed, shining in the sun—the white cliffs of Dover and the green swoop of the land that many of those broken men had thought never to see again. The hospital ship was swinging home on the tide of sunset. From her crowded decks a hoarse, throaty cheer arose, failed because of a lump in the throat, and rose again. The great dark leviathans of the sea, ploughing the dangerous deep, cheered, too, as the signal flashed from ship to ship, echoed and re-echoed from lip to lip.

"*The hospital ship from Kut!*"

The slug-bodied torpedo-boats swinging on their way, dipping to the trough of the sea, the saucy Admiralty yachts, the brave little fishing trawlers, the mine-sweepers, an old tramp rolling drunkenly, her rusted sides ducking to the blue-green sweep of waters, all cheered her, waved hands wildly, and flung words to the wind. On she came, gliding up the Channel, shining white in the sun, the Red Cross aflame. The cheers rose upon every side—men crowded the decks to have a look at her.

"*The hospital ship from Kut!* Hip-hip, hip-hip, hurray!"

The Hospital Ship

The volley of cheers rose and fell, speeding her onwards as she dipped her weather-torn flag to the Admiralty yacht, and swung proudly on her way, the sea frothing and spurling about her bows. The sunset was fast fading now. The waters rippled with reflected, ever-changing lights. To their left the coastline of England ran, curving and twisting, its lighthouses perched like painted toys on a miniature green cliff.

On the decks of the hospital ship men looked with wistful eyes at that green and white line that was England. Many clung to the railings staring out over the intervening strip of waters as if they were visualising already the back wharfs, and quays, and dear waiting faces.

"We are late," said Philip Territt, who walked with another officer along the pale yellow, freshly scrubbed deck. He limped as he walked, leaning heavily on his stick. His left arm was in a sling.

"We are a day late," said Dretton cheerfully. "And a wasted day on a short leave is like a year. But we mustn't grumble. We're here, breasting the Channel, and the old tub making for home like a greyhound, both ears well back, and her tail wagging."

He laughed joyously, glancing at his friend's pale face.

"You'll soon be as fit as a fiddle, old man. Cheero!" he said. They leaned against the rails for a moment and the sun danced by them on the gleaming brasses. "I feel like a schoolboy, and it's a regular schoolboy treat I'll have when I get home. Right turn! March—for the pantry!"

Territt laughed then, his eyes fixed on the tumbling stretch of water. He had been very quiet throughout the journey, but he was still very far from fit. As a matter of fact he should have been obeying doctor's orders at that moment, lying back in a deck chair and thinking of nothing in particular.

"Are you married, Dretton?" he asked his friend suddenly.

His friend nodded. His face lit with pride. "The best woman in the world, and three children. They'll all be at Victoria. Tons of folk for you, I expect."

Territt roused himself. "I don't know. Yes! Perhaps there will be one or two people there. The War Office would send word to them, I suppose." He explained then, "My fiancée and her mother no doubt will be at Victoria."

Dretton nodded. He thought Territt took his home-coming less rapturously than most men. Men of course said "that Dujailah business had smashed up Territt." Dretton spoke of it now.

"So the D.S.O. is yours, old chap?"

"They say so." Territt had shown extraordinarily little enthusiasm over that, too. "After all, I did no more than any other man would have done in like circumstances."

"It must have been a terrible time, Territt."

"Oh! pretty rotten while it lasted." He seemed disinclined to enter into conversation on the subject. His eyes were turned towards England, at the green line growing dimmer as the sunset died. If one could only leap over that strip of water, follow swift-footed Thought that was racing the streets of London, sweeping by the old Thames, coming more slowly but very surely to one house of all other houses, to one woman of all other women.

Dretton was talking to him about Kut, and Territt drew a deep breath and roused himself from his dreaming.

"For those three days beyond Dujailah," Dretton was saying, "it must have been hell."

"It was," Territt said simply. For awhile he was silent, then he went on. "I could never have got through but for the Turk of whom I told you. I remember nothing, after I lay on Dujailah Bank and he bent to lift me, for hours afterwards. The pain, I suppose. It—well, it was pretty bad."

"Yes." The other man shuddered. He remembered how Territt had come to Falahiyeh.

"When I became conscious it was dark, and I was bundled somehow on a camel. An Arab was beside me—my Turk friend, that is, in Arab garb. He had robbed two of the dead Arabs my sowars had killed when we got trapped at Dujailah. We were turning our faces to the marshes—a sea of dark, shining mud, with treacherous patches, where a false step meant the end to oneself and the camel as well."

"And the Turk knew that?"

"He knew that. He knew, too, of a path that might or might not be safe. The floods of rain that followed the thunderstorm might have made the path one with the morass.

"But it was the only way where safety lay, and it was the quickest."

He came to an abrupt pause. Dretton was silent.

understanding that this man was going through that journey again. He wished he had not asked the question. But presently Territt resumed:

"At midnight all at once the path ended. The Turk was ahead of me a few yards, when suddenly the camel seemed to dip and sway. There was a hideous, sucking sound, and then the Turk leapt as his feet came level with the mud, and rolled at the feet of the camel I was riding. How I did it, smashed as I was, I don't know. But I managed to grip him with my right arm. The effort pulled me off the camel. I lay there beside the Turk in the narrow strip of the path that had ended so suddenly."

He looked at the rippling water of the Channel, surging and foaming past them.

"Then we went back. I think that was the hardest part of all. To have spent the hours along that path in the black darkness, to come to that end. The Turk had been mistaken about the path. But it had been a long while since he had traversed it. Anyhow, there we were, following the road we came, two of us on one camel, I half delirious, imagining half the time that it was I, and not the camel, who was being sucked down and down, to be suffocated."

Dretton said in a low voice, "I can guess what you felt."

"Well, there was I, light-headed, and Johnny Turk sticking to me all the time, instead of tipping me off either side of the path. If he had done so, no one would have been the wiser. They are clean fighters and brave enemies, these Turks. I'll say that much for them."

He turned to Dretton, then spoke earnestly. "And, you see, I would not have cared if it had happened there. For, after all, the papers would have been safer with me in that marsh than on Dujailah Bank. That was the main thing."

Dretton nodded, clearing his throat.

"We went back to Dujailah, reaching there before dawn. I became unconscious again, though I fought hard against it. I remember the Turk's lifting me off the camel, creeping forward and placing me on the ground from which earlier in the day he had taken me. I thought that this time he was leaving me to my fate. And that was all I could remember, for I lost consciousness for a long time. Then at dawn I opened my eyes. A crowd of Turks and Arabs were there, getting ready to bury the dead."

For a moment he heard their shrill cries again, their quarrels over the spoil, the primitive casting of lots for the officer's uniform that had been transferred by the shrewd, far-thinking Turk to one of the dead sowars. The long robes of dirty white and yellow and brown fluttered about Territt; and he lay there, thinking of none of these things, not even of the apparent desertion of his Turkish friend, but of the papers against his breast, and far away a woman's face turned to him, calling him, it seemed, across the very Bridge of Death.

"They were moving about among that scattered group. They came to the sowar who was in my uniform, or what was left of it rather. They searched him thoroughly, as they had been told to search; stripped him of the uniform, as they had been told to strip

British officers. Uniforms are always of use to the Germans, who have men to fill them who can speak almost faultless English."

Dretton leaned forward, his lips tense. He seemed to see that scene as Territt went on:

"Then suddenly I became aware of two things. That I was no longer in Arab uniform, but garbed as a Turk. I think the first glimmer of light and hope of escape from living burial, or capture of myself and the dispatches, came to me then. I began to understand why the Turk had changed my uniform. I had probably been raving wildly, and, repassing Dujailah Bank, he had discovered a band of approaching Arabs."

"When he took you back he, the Turk, had done that? Then he was coming back for you, after all?"

"Precisely. It was just when that knowledge beat into a half dazed brain, incapable of thinking very clearly, that the confirmation occurred. A Turk, bewailing his dead brother, was going the rounds of the dead. He stooped over me, crying aloud that here indeed was his brother, and I looked into the face of my friend, Johnny Turk."

Territt was staring straight in front of him again, his voice quite quiet, as if he had purposely paused to reflect, and now a faint smile lightened his lips.

"He told me in Turkish I was dead, and that dead Turks closed their eyes tight, for the moment at any rate." A laugh escaped him. "So I obeyed; and what do you think at that time came into my mind, Dretton?" He turned his face to his friend.

"Your prayers," said Dretton dryly, but his eyes twinkled.

"No; a verse of that comic song, called 'Pat Malone.' You will remember the Irish used to sing it occasionally to cheer themselves up. It goes something like this:

> "And, shure, Pat Malone forgot he was dead;
> He sat up in his coffin, and swately he said,
> 'If there's a fight, begin it!
> Bedad, I must be in it!
> For I'm all aloive when crackin' somewan's head.'"

Dretton laughed and Territt threw back his head and laughed, too.

"Queer, wasn't it? How that thing haunted me, Dretton! Over and over again it cranked its way through my mind, until I wanted to burst out laughing or sing it."

He laughed again, then as suddenly became sober. "The next thing Johnny Turk had tied something over my face, which you will admit was just as well. He was wailing at a terrible rate. A few of the others joined in apparently out of sympathy, and most obligingly shouted a requiem over me as Johnny Turk bundled me on the camel."

He straightened himself a moment, fumbling for a cigarette.

"Will you light it for me, Dretton? Thanks! We might as well walk while we talk."

The two men began to pace slowly up and down the deck. One a typical Englishman, clean-shaven, quiet and expressionless, limping as he walked and leaning heavily on his cane; the other a Scot, keen-eyed, red-haired and ruddy-faced, his torn glengarry saucily atilt, its ribbon fluttering idly in the wind.

"Johnny Turk took me, his newly discovered brother, away with him then and there. I know a little Turkish, but I'm hanged if I could understand all he said to them. I should imagine, however"—and his eyes twinkled—"that it made a very pretty story."

"Ay," said Dretton, and chuckled, "like the Turkish official communiqués!"

"Exactly, and about as consistent. For he had to tell it many times on that journey back to the Outwork, and each version varied. He kept close to the river all the way, making, as you will see, a wide detour from Dujailah Bank. It would hardly do to find the dead Turk of Act 1 a live Arab in Act 2."

"I see. You'd be pretty light-headed by then, too. Raving, no doubt, as well."

"I was. That was the trouble. It meant travelling by night, hiding in isolated and deserted mud huts by day. I don't know how that Turk stuck it, but he did. He risked his own life every hour of those three days."

He smoked in silence for a second or two. Then continued:

"More than once we were nearly discovered. On one occasion a band of thieving Bedouins was encamped less than a quarter of a mile away. Johnny Turk muffled the camels' hoofs that night, I can tell you, and transformed me and himself into Arabs for the nonce. We travelled all next day in the open, making for the road to Orah presumably. There was nothing suspicious in that, if anyone were following."

"No. But it must have been hard with those dispatches to feel that you were lengthening the distance instead of shortening it between you and the camp, when every minute counted."

Territt bent his head. "It was that thought that kept me sane long enough to get out of the danger zone. When I might have raved and shouted out mad orders in English, and cost the life of Johnny Turk as well as my own, the thought of the dispatches and the camp by the Outwork held me up."

They turned in their walk and came down the deck again. The land glimmered dimly through a shore mist. The twinkling lights that once would have greeted them at this hour were darkened, but by a faint glow here and there they picked out places they knew; pleasant seaside towns, with memories of happy days, and youth and fun, ere the grim god of war strode into the careless arena of many a life.

"Of that last day on the road to Orah, Dretton, you already know. The night before we had changed into the garb of Arabs. Johnny Turk wore his Turkish garb underneath. Travelling away from the Outwork, how slowly we went when we had the road to ourselves, how quickly and as men going about our business when anyone appeared on it! Then, an hour before sunset, we turned back. The road was deserted for the moment. I think, when I saw the Outwork so near and the businesslike gleam of the barrels of English rifles, that I must have wept. The weariness I had flouted, the weakness I had held back swept over me. I just remember, as Johnny Turk spoke farewell, that he had repaid me what I, or my kind, had done for his brother, and then—he had gone."

"Ay! He fled like the wind," said Dretton. "His robes fluttered out behind him like scarecrow streamers. It was then, as I leapt over the parapet, that the first thought came to me that it might be you." His eyes twinkled. "We Scots hae the second sicht, ye ken."

Territt smiled. In the dusk the two men gripped each other's hands for a moment.

Behind them a bell rang peremptorily. Sailors began nimbly to uncoil ropes and the ship to slow down perceptibly. Excited voices rose, broken men hobbled painfully to the rails.

Out of the misty half-light ahead a fussy pilot-boat spluttered through the water towards them. The dim bulk of a torpedo-boat hovered near, watchful, ever ready for emergencies.

"*England*—and *home,*" said Territt suddenly, and all at once his voice shook. Dretton stole a glance at his face, and was silent. His own pulses were beating fast.

The pilot came clambering up the swaying ladder. He raised his hand smartly to the salute, with a proud lift of the head, when he saw the two officers. He spoke to them and the broken men, huddled by the rails, or stretched out on deck chairs or camp beds.

"Half England is on the quay," he said to them with a lilt in his voice and the sea-twinkle in his eye, "and the other half at Victoria. Ay, but you'll get a great reception."

They heard the first cheers as they swung in, ringing cheers that brought a lump to the throat of the bravest man there. They were swinging into port, home at last, following that fussy bantam of a boat, that was clanging its bell importantly and proudly flinging the news ahead as it went:

"*The hospital ship from Kut! The hospital ship from Kut!*"

The reply came all at once from the land.

The big guns in the harbour shook the earth and rattled the windows far and near with thunderous welcome. A volley of cheering followed, rising and falling, and rising again. People clustered on the pier, like black ants, packed tight. The Union Jack fluttered proudly on the breeze. Strings of flags were flying into meaning from different mastheads, shaking and bellying in the wind.

The great guns shook the world about them again, and yet again. The cheering was nearer now. One saw the waiting, watching people more clearly. How thick they were on that old wharf with the sea lapping at the piles! The Scotsman gripped the railing hard. Territt turned to him and, with shaking voice, said:

"If only Townshend were here . . . coming home with us to-night!" And both men's thoughts rushed to that brave and gallant gentleman who had held Kut as perhaps no other man on earth would have held it, and who was now in far Mesopotamia with the last of his heroic band. That others, on the black mass of the pier, thought of Townshend at that moment there was no doubt. For a voice cried aloud his name, and the sound of wild cheering followed.

"*Townshend!* Three cheers for Townshend and his gallant little army!"

And the cheers rang so loud that it seemed as if in far-away Baghdad the echo of them must surely be heard, or the very spirit of them reach there and tell the splendid fellows that England had not forgotten. The cheers drowned almost the answering roar of the guns. So the hospital ship from Kut, with its broken freight, came home to England.

CHAPTER XXI

At the War Office

THE train to London was running late. For two solid hours it had been cooped up in a tunnel. The guard flitted up and down, reassuring anxious passengers.

"Only them there Zepps," he announced contemptuously. "Killin' a fowl or two, or makin' 'oles in a field as usual, and a-knockin' off the roofs o' respectable folks' 'ouses."

"Where are they?" someone queried nervously.

"Somewhere in the Heastern Counties, lidy," he said cheerfully, and a quick burst of laughter followed the sally.

The lights were still on and the blinds drawn. People began to hunt compartments for cards and settled down for an hour or two's wait. Some fumed and fretted and wondered audibly what on earth the Government was doing. Old stagers, who had been through it all before, thought placidly of the thickness of the tunnel and went to sleep. In another compartment someone began to sing a rollicking chorus.

How far they were from London no one exactly knew. The train had been late in starting through some delay on the line ahead. It was an express and whirled by stations with a fine contempt. Faces that had cautiously peered out from between an inch of blind to look at the station lamps had seen that all was in darkness. Almost following their exclamation of surprise had come the answer across the night:

"*Boom! Boom! Boom!*"

Then a louder, more significant, soul-shaking sound:

"*Crash!*" And here and there faces blanched and trembling lips whispered:

"*Zeppelins!*"

"*Boom! Boom! Boom!*" The anti-aircraft guns were firing, making a terrific row. With a shrill whistle, a rush and a roar, the express at that instant swept into the safety of a convenient tunnel. Puffing and panting and steaming she had come to a full stop. The sound of the guns and the crash of bombs seemed suddenly muffled and far away.

For two hours the express panted in the tunnel. The engine-drivers and firemen stuck to their posts. Men congregated in the passages, recalling other raids cheerfully or lugubriously. Some of them clambered out on the footboards. Nothing could be seen but the long dark barrel of the tunnel and the flare of the engines ahead.

Territt sat in his corner, his eyes closed as if he slept. For him the guns were far too familiar for alarm. He had heard them pound over the beach at Suvla Bay in a din indescribable, he had heard them thunder in Mesopotamia.

"Them guns is worse than the Zeppelings," the conductor was remarking confidentially to one of the passengers.

Territt looked at his watch. He noticed with a start that it was nearly two o'clock.

"Goin' directly, everybody," announced a wag from the corridor, imitating the voice of the conductor. "Tike your seats and get ready for the show, lidies and gents. The Zeppelings are hoff, but Winston's little 'ornets are a-goin' hup after them in another hour or two." He began to sing cheerfully:

"Don't be frightened, little birds,
It's only a dummy gun.
Winston's 'ornet's on its nest,
A-doin' of its wery best,
And we will soon have them all on the run."

The conductor came into sight at that moment, crying, "Tike your seats, lidies and gents," and wondered why everybody laughed so heartily.

A whistle echoed along the tunnel. The wheels began to move, slowly at first, a little uncertainly. Then with a rush and a roar the train raced out of the tunnel and on its way towards London.

At the terminus the lights had all flashed up again. Porters bustled about unconcernedly. In answer to eager inquiries they said they had heard there was a raid somewhere. No one knew where or seemed to care very much. Everyone at that hour was much more interested in reaching home.

Very few people were at the terminus. Everybody had been advised to go home as soon as the raid ended, and the suburban trains started again. One never knew when the express would come in. But a few had waited.

A friendly porter confiscated Territt's bag and

another was unearthing his luggage. A third ran for a taxi. The heroes of Kut found a willing crowd of helpers.

Territt was very tired. His leg ached. He limped heavily and once he stumbled.

"Lean on me, sir," said the porter. "I've got your cab waiting."

A friendly policeman cleared the way, sweeping a passage through the little group beyond the barriers, the last of the huge crowd that had waited for hours for the express.

Beatrice was not there; he had made sure of that. Anyhow, neither she nor Mrs. Byndham would have waited until this hour.

Yet his eyes swept that crowd again as he passed. He saw Dretton meet a little bit of a woman barely up to his broad shoulder, and heard him say, his voice thick with emotion:

"*Jean!*"

Then they moved away, the little woman clinging tightly to him, sobbing.

Territt got into the cab, tipped the porter, and asked if there was an hotel left standing after the raid.

The porter chuckled. "All of them, sir," and his eyes twinkled; "you'll no doubt be surprised to hear it, but the dome of St. Paul's is still there, an' London Bridge, an' the Tower likewise, sir."

Territt langhed, too, at the allusion to the enemy's oft-told fiction on the subject of air raids. He felt suddenly lifted upon the wings of exhilaration. He was back in London again. *London!* Was there any place in the world like it, that could tug so at a man's heartstrings, that could draw him back from the very farthest reaches of the world?

London! He felt he wanted to stand up and shout and shake hands with everybody in his gladness to be back. The very cab had a Londony, homey feeling.

He pressed his face to the glass of the window as the cab began to move, looking back at that fast-melting group on the platform. The rain had blurred the glass and he let slip the window. Then suddenly he stared and looked again.

The cab rolled out of the station under the great arches. A policeman lifted his hand to the salute. Territt sat back and told himself that he must have been dreaming. He thought he had seen Lady Emma Beckendon there, among the last waiting group, a queerly-garbed, expectant figure, her face drawn and haggard.

Lady Emma! He threw back his head and laughed at the idea. Of course, it was nonsense! What should Lady Emma Beckendon be doing at a London terminus at that hour in the morning?

The woman's face he had seen, for all its momentary likeness to Lady Emma's, was stamped with the unmistakable impress of misery. He thought of Lady Emma's hard face, her shrewd, blinking eyes, the sharp tongue. Lady Emma was as little likely to allow herself to look miserable even if she felt it, as she was to be there, at that unearthly hour on a fast-emptying station platform.

He put the idea from him, dismissing the thought as a curious twist of the imagination. The cab stopped and the hotel loomed before him. Territt went up the steps into its wide, cosy entrance, with its vista of warm red carpets and tall palms and gleaming marble.

The proprietor welcomed him proudly in person. He had stayed up to do honour to Captain Philip Territt, whose fame and daring had preceded him. The supper was of the best, his bedroom and sitting-room of the cosiest. A fire burned briskly in the grate because of the chilly rain that had set in suddenly and unexpectedly, as such changes in the weather do in England.

Philip Territt ate little; already a crowd of reporters had gathered, but he sent a message that he could not see them until he had presented himself at the War Office in the morning. Then he went to his room.

The rain lashed the windows and the fire crackled, sounds that were a lullaby indeed for a tired man. But he did not sleep. He sat by the fire a long while, and listened to the rain and the wind that was rising and moaning in gusts about the building.

He thought of many things that night, of far-away Mesopotamia and Townshend, of London and all that London held, and he thought, too, of Lady Emma Beckendon and how she would laugh when he told her that he had fancied he had seen her face among the crowd at the terminus.

She would probably tell him, in her grim, smart way, that those were the hours when her face was not on view to the public, but instead undergoing a process of restoration to its original beauty.

But though he did not know it, Lady Emma

Beckendon had been there. It was her face he had seen through the rain-blurred cab-window. And though he did not know it then the thought haunted him.

That night Philip Territt slept ill.

In the morning the rain had gone as swiftly as it came, in one of those capricious visitations that swing unexpectedly into the very heart of summer.

Philip Territt came out of the hotel and found the rain-washed world fresh and sweet and sunshine flooding the earth.

He had an appointment with the War Office at ten. It was yet just a little after nine. He lifted his stick and hailed a taxi, and it was significant of much perhaps that he went first to Hyde Park instead of to Grosvenor Mansions, where his fiancée waited.

It was a morning he would remember long afterwards—how the sun shone in all its yellow radiance, clearer for the night of storm and rain that had preceded it, how the very earth smelt fresh and sweet, and the beautiful flowers glowed on the sloping beds by the iron fences.

He had gone to that part of the Park where the separating road by Kensington Gardens curved by the Powder Magazine, and where sentries, rifle to shoulder, marched up and down. To the right of him the Serpentine flowed, rippling and shining in the sun.

Under the great trees where he and Enid had sat on that never-to-be-forgotten day he paused. It seemed almost incredible that months had passed since then, months so feverishly crowded. So much had happened in them. What had they meant to her, he wondered, and had himself answered the question.

She would be working hard among the poor, the harder, perhaps, because of the memory of a night when he had sat alone and vainly in a little café in Soho and waited for someone who never came. She had never even written to say why. But he knew. He told himself passionately that when it came to the final test she had failed. She had said she loved him; but love had not been strong enough for even an hour's sacrifice. She had never even bothered to wish him good-bye.

And he laughed bitterly then. She, the woman whom he would have laid down his life for, had, in the last hour he might spend in England, chosen an evening's pleasure at a theatre in preference to his society. He had hardly believed it possible. Impulsively and not too wisely that night he had gone to the house in Marcourt Place. He had half expected to hear that she was ill. Indeed, it had been that persistent thought that sent him hotfoot out of the Soho restaurant.

And Jevons had told him that his master and mistress had gone out to dine and were doing a theatre afterwards! He believed they had gone to a musical comedy, then the rage. A musical comedy!

He laughed again bitterly. What a fool he had been! To Enid it was but a flirtation of the moment. She had probably forgotten his existence when he had gone out of the Park that day. She had probably laughed at him in secret.

But his heart cried "No," even though his lips said the words.

"But the fact is there!" he cried stubbornly to the voice of his heart, "and facts do not lie. She could have written. She might even have telephoned."

She had said she would come. And she had not come. She had believed, as he had believed that morning, that the boat sailed earlier than was afterwards arranged. While his boat was sailing out she would be in the theatre laughing happily, intent on stage tragedies or a musical comedy. "Perhaps," he said bitterly, "this incident to her had been but comedy also."

At the thought the world suddenly, for him, became a lonely thing, empty of everything he desired. He looked up at the trees with their already yellowing leaves and thought of the approaching autumn of his life. Crippled and almost useless, he cried fiercely that, with nothing really worth while left to him, life was not worth the living!

Then the thought of Beatrice came to him, as Beatrice would have come to him, perchance, over that sun-warmed grass, had she known he was sitting there alone. His hands clenched and he stared before him. How little, how terribly little, the gift of that young sweet life counted!

Yet this morning, in an hour or two, he must see Beatrice, he must dissemble.

"No," he cried aloud in that silent place, he would not dissemble. He would tell Beatrice the truth—that he cared for someone else, that he thought he would always care. He need not name the woman he loved, and so all clue to her identity would be hidden. The rest was for Beatrice to decide.

Yet the chill, as of approaching autumn, was in his bones as he limped across the grass and along the path to where the taxi waited.

In Rotten Row there were very few riders that morning. Perhaps he had half expected that Enid would be among them, sitting the chestnut mare with her easy grace, in her dark blue habit and bowler hat.

But this morning even Beatrice was not there. There came to him then the thought that in that stuffy, crowded flat of Mrs. Byndham's Beatrice would be waiting, shining like a golden daffodil out of the tawdry richness of the room—Beatrice, his fiancée.

A pang struck him. Here was he, engaged to one woman, loafing in the Park and dreaming of another woman, a woman who had scorned his love and him! Only he had been blind to that fact. Poor little Beatrice! He thought now of her troubled, loving eyes, and of the poverty that lurked behind all the brave fight for appearances Mrs. Byndham made. Perhaps it was the knowledge of that poverty that stirred him most. But never once, for all that knowledge, did he think it had actuated Beatrice in any way.

Beatrice, mercilessly frank, had spoken of that poverty in the last letter he had received from her. She had written what she knew their world would say, what it was no doubt already saying, that she was marrying for money; but Beatrice, in the glory of youth and love, flung out her challenge.

"We will show them it is not so," she had written enthusiastically, "but that I love, love, love you, Phil; if you were ever so poor it would have been the same! Have I not always been poor?"

He got into the taxi and was whirled off to the War Office. There they detained him much longer than he had anticipated. But he came out with a lighter step for all that he limped. His voice had a more cheerful note.

For the man who even then counted most in the affairs of the nation, had shaken him by the hand, had said the limp would not matter. A man who had done what Territt had done could not be spared. There was Flanders ahead, the Great Offensive. The hour to strike was almost at hand!

Territt went out from that interview with his head high, a glow in his bronzed cheek. He was not to be shelved or to stay at home and train others, handicapped by his wounds.

"We need you—*now*," they said to him when he had asked in his brief way, "When?"

"We could send you to-morrow, to-night even, Territt. But we will not. Take a rest until you are fit. You will be all the better of a rest."

"I am as fit now," he said, "as I ever will be."

"Well—next week, then. Things are beginning to move."

CHAPTER XXII

A War Wedding

THE taxi went on its way to Grosvenor Mansions. Life, for all the ache that ran through it, was brighter. He was not to be shelved! He was to be of some use!

But when he told Beatrice all about it she did not look at it in the same light. Her level brows frowned.

"Oh!" she said, and her voice broke. "Phil, I thought you would be here for months, or weeks at least, perhaps always. You're not fit to go. You—you limp quite noticeably."

"In this war," he said, "a man fights with his heart and soul, not his legs, Beatrice."

But she frowned. Of course it was very patriotic of him, and all that sort of thing! Had she not proved her patriotism, too, by all these charity things, and getting up collections for cigarettes for soldiers? But this was really too much of a good thing. She was quite hurt that he had rushed straight away to the War Office about another commission.

He was somewhat astonished at her point of view.

"My country needs me, Beatrice."

"You have given it enough, surely. There are hundreds and thousands of other men," she cried, "all in training."

"That is it, Beatrice. In *training*. But I am already trained. I am an old stager, in fact. You wouldn't have me staying at home when I can do so much. It is just a man like myself that can be of more use in Flanders at the present than at home in England."

She moved impatiently. Her voice was fretful. All her plans seemed agley.

"I'd arranged ever so many things for you," she complained. "Everybody is quite excited about it. Why, there's half a dozen big 'At homes' already fixed, and a special supper with speeches——"

His eyes were rather weary. The cigarette he had been smoking burned slowly in his fingers. He tossed it suddenly into the tray beside him.

"Good God, Beatrice!" he said, "can't you see that men who have gone through what I have don't want to be bothered with these finicking affairs?" and then, as she shrank visibly, he added more quietly, "I am sorry, Beatrice. Forgive me! Mesopotamia has stripped a great deal of the niceties of speech from me apparently, as well as desire for the things that once might have meant much to me."

Beatrice was silent. Her lip trembled. He came forward and took her hands.

"Look here, Beatrice," he said earnestly, "I'll do anything you want me to, only don't look so unhappy. I've been rather a brute to speak like that to you. Please forgive me. Won't you?"

Mrs. Byndham, who thought half an hour alone quite enough to get over the affecting greetings of reunion, tapped at the door and put her head in.

"Don't you two people want any lunch?" she asked brightly, "or do you believe in the sustaining qualities of the proverbial bread and cheese and kisses?"

"I can't stay really," Philip replied hastily. "My first day is bound to be crowded. You'll excuse me, I know——"

Mrs. Byndham came in at that and looked from one to the other decidedly perplexed, but smiling agreeably, as usual, and as if she had not noticed that something was wrong. An air of tension distinctly prevailed in the room, and she immediately sensed it. A chill touched her ambitious heart.

"Of course, dear Philip," she said in her charming, just a little too charming, manner, "if you must go, you must. But," playfully, "we will see a great deal of you every day naturally. How many months will you have now? Or is it true, as reported, that you won't be going back at all?"

"I will not be going back to Mesopotamia," he answered. "But I expect to be in Flanders in little less than a week."

"A week! Flanders!" Mrs. Byndham started and Beatrice drew a quick, short breath and said, "Oh, *Phil!*"

He nodded. "The W.O. was very decent about it. I'll probably limp all my life and they know it. But they said that they would find a niche for me somewhere in Flanders."

"But you wouldn't go," cried Mrs. Byndham shrilly. "You must have felt most indignant with them, expecting you to go so soon. It is really too bad, positively heartless of them. Really, the War Office has absolutely no consideration."

"I asked that I might go," interrupted Territt quietly.

Mrs. Byndham looked at him in unmistakable surprise. She sat down as if waiting for an explanation. Philip gave it in his frank way.

"I couldn't stick it here in England, you see, when I was wanted out at the front," he said earnestly. "Every seasoned officer is needed now. What a wretched existence it would be for me, when all my pals who hadn't gone under were out there fighting!"

"But—you would have had *Beatrice!*" said Mrs. Byndham quickly and somewhat reproachfully. Beatrice blushed adorably. Territt went quite red. He cleared his throat.

"Oh, yes! I would have had Beatrice," he said somewhat vaguely. It was clear to the keen, searching eyes of Mrs. Byndham that up to then this aspect of the case had not occurred to him. Her eyes narrowed, grey, a little angry. She had been very sure that he was in love with her daughter. What had happened?

Mrs. Byndham looked at him with apprehension. All sorts of ideas shot through her mind. Had Philip met anyone out in Mesopotamia? Had he imagined he had fallen in love with his nurse? Good gracious! one did not know what to think. Philip did not look like the stage adaptation of an eager lover, back from the trenches.

Mrs. Byndham's eyelashes fluttered uncertainly over her half-closed eyes. Then she looked up, laughed in her charming artificial way, and rose. She was a very wise woman.

"Well, here am I disturbing you two dear people," she said lightly, "when you want to talk to each other alone! How stupid of me to interrupt you!"

She turned carelessly to her daughter. "And, of course, dear, if Philip has really to go to Flanders in a week you will want to discuss all the little details of your wedding. For dear Philip will wish to be married before he goes away again."

She smiled her charming smile at Philip and shook her head roguishly at him.

"A week is such a short time," she said, "and it will mean a terrific rush. But I don't mind. Come and see us to-night, Philip. In the meantime, leave everything to me. I assure you everything will be quite ready. A hurried wedding is quite the fashion of the moment."

When she had gone Philip still stood in the centre of the room. He seemed to be listening to the tick-tacking of her high French heels on the polished corridor without. One could not tell from his face what were his thoughts.

Then he said suddenly, "Beatrice! Do you mind getting married in such a hurry?"

She looked at him and smiled shyly. "No, Philip, if you don't."

Territt straightened his shoulders.

"It is as you wish, Beatrice."

She looked at him with a feeling of alarm, a sudden chill at her heart. His voice was so grave and quiet. It had none of the eager lilt in it that she wished to hear.

"And your wish, dear?" she asked. Her voice trembled.

"Only this, Beatrice. No fuss, or as little as possible." He walked to the window and tried to laugh. "No Shakespearean or carnival processions, or Mayday effects. I don't care for that sort of thing, as you know."

She looked disappointed. "It is our one great day, Phil dear. And I did have such a perfectly ripping idea." She waited a moment, then said disconsolately, "But, of course, as you wish, dear. It is your wedding as well as mine. But it doesn't really take any longer if one has seven bridesmaids than if one has none at all. But there's all the difference in the world, really."

He seemed to have forgotten her presence. While she spoke his thoughts flowed on, uninterrupted, too far away for mere words to follow. It was only when the sound of her voice stopped that he came back to consciousness of the room and her.

"Very well, Beatrice," he said vaguely. He turned and tried to infuse more enthusiasm into his voice. Dash it all! he must not treat Beatrice like that.

But Beatrice went suddenly pale and began to breathe quickly, for she knew then that he had not heard the question she had asked him. There were laughter and the sound of approaching footsteps in the hall. She understood that visitors had arrived and would be in the room in another second. She moved quickly to the door of the smaller drawing-room beyond, opened it and beckoned Philip.

"Quickly!" she said breathlessly. He followed her into the room and she shut the door behind him, then sat down on one of the divans, moving her skirts that Philip might sit there also.

But Territt, all unnoticing, sat down in one of the easy chairs near the window. Beatrice leaned forward.

"Philip," she said in a suppressed voice, "have you anything to tell me?"

Territt started, pulling himself abruptly out of the reverie into which he had fallen again. He threw off his air of abstraction. The meaning of her words came to him; the meaning also of the tears that brimmed in her eyes.

"Have you—tired—of me, Phil?" said Beatrice. Her lip trembled, but she went on. "Do you know that you have not even yet kissed me, your fiancée? And we are to be married in less than a week. Oh! Phil, have you fallen in love with anyone since you last saw me? A nurse, or anyone like that?"

"No, Beatrice!" he said. He looked at her, drew his chair nearer, then leaned forward, facing her. He took her two hands in his. His eyes were very clear and straightforward. "The trouble is, dear, that it was before I met you."

"I—I have always felt that," she answered, and the colour came back into her cheeks. "And, of course, it didn't matter, Phil, at all—I am the last woman and I am to be your wife. Of course, I know men have love affairs, sometimes more than one," she went on eagerly, "but of course they are mostly schoolboyish affairs."

He was somewhat at a loss. Here was an excuse,

found for him by Beatrice, ready to his hand. But he shook his head.

"I must be perfectly straight with you, Beatrice," he said. "Before our marriage takes place you must know this, that it was not a schoolboyish affair, dear. I—I cannot stop myself from loving the other woman. I still care for her."

He got up then and walked abruptly over to the window.

"You love her—still?" she whispered incredulously.

He nodded. "I am afraid I always shall, Beatrice."

She looked at him with wide eyes. "Do—you want to marry her, Phil?" Her voice was piteous.

"She is already married," he said gently.

"A married woman," she said slowly, and then, with a sob in her throat, "if—if she were not married —would you have asked her to marry you, Phil?"

He had no thought of evasion or denial.

"Yes."

Beatrice stared down at the floor with eyes that saw nothing for the tears that blinded them. A great sense of loss and desolation surged over her. She loved Philip Territt with all her heart.

"And—now?" she said at last.

"I am engaged to you, Beatrice." He came over to her then and sat down beside her. He took her hand in his, pressing it gently. "If you wish it to end, tell me so, dear. I shall not blame you. But you had to know."

"Yes," she whispered, "I had to know."

Then she lifted her head. "It must have been someone in India," she cried. "You did not seem happy there and that was it. And that was why you went away so suddenly up into the hill country."

He said nothing, and she took his silence for an affirmative.

"Oh, *Phil!*" she cried suddenly, and she pressed her face against his rough sleeve and her voice hurt his heart as the pain in his arm. "I care so much that I am not going to think of her. Why should I?"

She paused, but he answered nothing.

"Why should I?" she resumed. "She is married. She is far away, and—and after a little while she will not count. It is because I am sure of that, of—of all that marriage and a home will come to mean to you, that I am not going to think of her any more." She rose and he rose also. They faced one another.

"Oh, Phil!" she whispered, and the tears came then, "am I not pretty enough to make you love me a little, just a little?"

"You are very lovely, dear." And he looked at her wistfully. He could not add that beauty was not everything.

"I would be such a faithful, loving wife to you," and her voice broke again.

"And I shall try to be a good husband to you." He had almost added, "If I come back from Flanders." For from the moment he left the War Office he had been haunted by a premonition. But of this to Beatrice he would not speak—not at this juncture anyway. He turned to her in remorse, took her hands in his. "Forgive me, dear. It shall all be as you wish. I leave all arrangements in your hands."

Beatrice drew a deep, sobbing breath. "Then—let it be all settled, Philip. We will not think of it again, or ever speak of it again. That is best. We will go on just as—just as if you had not told me. And I shall love you the more because you did tell me. Some day, Phil, I, too, will count before anyone else, I and your children," and she stood up very straight and tall then, and as if she saw a moment when she and not the other woman would count for most in his life.

He stood very still looking at her. Some of the hardness born of suffering went out of his face. He looked at her and began to understand that, after all, Beatrice might make life less unendurable and less lonely. Her words lingered in his mind—"I—and your children." The words thrilled him in an inexplicable way.

"I want you to tell me, Phil,' said Beatrice, and she laid both hands on his shoulders and drew his head down on a level with hers, "whether you don't think that our marriage will bring you some measure of happiness. I believe it will. I intend that it shall, as far as lies in my hands. Of her, that other woman, whom I have never seen—and never shall see, I suppose—we shall never speak again. But I want you to tell me, and tell me now, whether you think our marriage will, or will not, make for your future good, even if not at first for the happiness which, I believe, will come to you afterwards. If you do not wish our marriage to take place at all, tell me, Philip, now, while I can bear it."

CHAPTER XXIII

A Scrap of Paper

PHILIP TERRITT came to the decision then and there. He took both her hands and looked into her face, which was now more that of a woman than of the pleasure-loving child he had deemed her. If any one other person in the world in that desolated autumn of his life could make for happiness at all, that person would surely be Beatrice Byndham. Into that future he could not see. It might end on the fields of Flanders, or he might have to live out its years side by side with Beatrice.

Marriage, whether he lived or died, would give him a right to protect Beatrice, to make life less harassed with financial cares and worries than hitherto. For himself he hoped, if he hoped at all in that moment, that life would end for him, as he wished, in his country's service. Because of that half-hope, perhaps because of presentiment, he told himself that on leaving the house he would go straight to his solicitors and have a will drawn up, giving everything he possessed in the world to Beatrice Byndham. He put his arm about her in a spasm of remorse.

She drew his head down to her and kissed him, as Mrs. Byndham entered. The trouble slipped from her eyes as she looked at them.

"Not for worlds," she declared, "would I have

interrupted you two dear people. Really you look quite too wonderfully happy. Philip, an express letter has been travelling all over London after you. From the W.O., I expect. Though it looks quite unofficial. I suppose that is to disguise its importance. But no one else would send a message here, I suppose."

She held it out to him and he took it quickly.

"It will be from the W.O.," he said. "Excuse me!"

It was, as Mrs. Byndham had said, a large plain envelope, marked "Immediate," and anything but official-looking. Territt tore it open while Mrs. Byndham, frankly curious, waited, chattering aimless nothings to her daughter.

It was only a half-sheet of paper, within it an enclosure, a torn scrap of paper on which words were written. He drew it out, with a wondering frown.

"Someone's acting up to the crusade of economy," Philip began, and then he stopped with marked abruptness.

He stared at the words written on that sheet of paper, and his face went slowly white under the tan. He said nothing; just stood there and stared at the written words, as if he could not believe his eyes.

Beatrice's hand touched his arm twice before he noticed. "What is it?" she asked. "Bad news?"

"Is it—Flanders?" put in Mrs. Byndham. She looked perturbed. Supposing Philip had to go away at once! All her castles in the air began to rock and totter at the very thought.

"No!" said Territt, and unconsciously he moved away from them, as if nearer to the light of the window. He still stared at those few words written there. He saw then that it was but part of a letter, and on the torn scrap of paper was written:

"*That night, had I gone to Soho, and had Philip asked me to go away with him, I would have gone. Only for you I would have gone.*"

And there it ended. Just that and no more. A few words in Enid Marcourt's unmistakable handwriting, which someone had obtained possession of and forwarded to him. It was very obvious that she herself had not done so. The handwriting on the envelope was not hers. Good God! was it that of George? No.

All sorts of ideas, rejected at their birth, raced through his mind. Enid—Enid had written that, a confession as it were, and someone had sent it to him.

"What is it, dear?" Beatrice said, unable to bear the suspense any longer. "Tell me, Philip. You frighten me."

"It is—a message from someone," he answered slowly. "I don't think I understand what it means. But I am going to find out." He clenched the paper in his hand, picked up the envelope, and looked at the superscription and scrutinised it more closely.

It was like, and yet unlike, Lady Emma Beckendon's handwriting. He remembered the queer way she made those capital letters, slurred now as if in haste or anger. It was that of Lady Emma! Why had she sent that scrap of paper to him? Suddenly he recalled the face of the woman at the terminus last night, the woman who had looked like Lady Emma Beckendon, and yet not like her.

The conviction came that it had been she, after all. Why had she gone to the terminus? Why had she sent this? To let him know that she knew? Enid had told her. Enid had written words that made his heart throb, made him even forget that by his side in that very room was the woman who next week would be his wife. But why, *why?* The thought hammered at his brain.

He left abruptly, with a murmured excuse. He had answered Mrs. Byndham's question—no, he did not think it would make any difference to the date he would leave for Flanders. He said something to Beatrice, whose eyes were full of wondering tears. He never afterwards, as a matter of fact, remembered what he had said to either of them. Only that a sudden, blinding fear of he knew not what hounded him out of the house. He could not have stayed there another minute. Only one thought obsessed him: Enid had loved him, after all!

When he was in the street he jumped into the waiting taxi and gave the order for Lady Emma Beckendon's house.

"Drive fast!" he said, his lips set.

He recalled the words he had said to Mrs. Byndham—that the letter had no military bearing that would make any difference in the date of his going to Flanders. Would it not? Would it make no difference if Lady Emma, with her known reputation for interfering in other people's affairs, had somehow got hold of a letter Enid had written to somebody she trusted and had gone to George Marcourt about it?

She, Lady Emma, had sent no word with that

torn scrap of paper. The handwriting on the envelope was that of one troubled or angry. But it was a clear call. She had known that when he received it he would go straight to her. She no doubt intended to lash him with her sharp tongue, would be even then waiting; for the messenger had been to his hotel and probably to clubs he used to frequent, and the autocratic old dame would be all the angrier at delay. He pictured her sitting in grim state, her small eyes blinking as she waited. She knew he would come.

But when he arrived at the big house in Grosvenor Square the footman informed him with impassive face that her ladyship was not at home. He volunteered the further information that he believed her ladyship was still at Marcourt Place. She had been there all morning, he had added formally.

What was she doing there? Territt asked of himself. He thought he knew.

She was telling George all about it, and Enid was going through trial as a culprit before a merciless judge. Then, if George knew, and that terrible old woman knew, Enid would need him. She was the woman he loved, the woman who loved him. She was now perhaps in sore distress. The hot blood rushed to his face and he bade the chauffeur drive his hardest to Marcourt Place.

"Don't stop for anyone," he added. "I'll see you through."

As the car spun on, picking out the less crowded thoroughfares, Philip Territt leaned forward, deep in thought.

What were they saying to her, those two? How were they misjudging her, his little love? Let them think or say what they would! What did it matter now? Those written words sent the blood coursing through his veins, his heart pounding. Enid had written those words. The barriers were down for ever between them.

He would go into that house, if he had to force his way in, and whirl her away from them all.

What mattered the gossiping tongues of the world when two people loved each other? What mattered the laws men made? Laws could not fetter love. What could separate them now? *Nothing*. Then he thought of Beatrice, and the iron of remorse entered his soul. Because, as he neared Marcourt Place, he could not bear to sit still any longer, he stopped the taxi and got out, telling the man curtly to wait there. He would probably need him again in a few minutes, he had told himself grimly. Where one had come, two would go back. All else was submerged for the moment.

Unseeingly he went on, mechanically making for his destination. There was the corner of the street. Half a block farther down was Marcourt Place, and Territt went limping along the pavement, his stick tapping and making a sharp, audible sound in the curious and unusual stillness that to-day filled the street.

Another few yards and he would be at the house, walking up those well-remembered steps. He set his lips with determination and told himself he would not come down those steps alone.

Then all at once he stopped and began to tremble exceedingly. For the first time he noticed the curious silence, the line of waiting broughams in that street.

Suddenly the stillness had new and terrible meaning.

In front of Marcourt Place they had laid down straw on the street.

CHAPTER XXIV

'Twixt Life and Death

OVER the house itself since the day before had hung a strange, heavy stillness. The servants spoke in whispers and tiptoed about their duties. In the basement they gathered into groups whenever Mrs. Marcourt's maid, or Jevons, the footman, went downstairs.

There was nothing new to report. The doctors were still upstairs. George Marcourt was still in the library. In Mrs. Marcourt's sitting-room, Lady Emma Beckendon and Mrs. Whiteway sat in silence, their faces turned to the closed door that led to the room beyond.

There was nothing to do but wait. The slow moments dragged by, turned into hours. The morning died away and still the doctors' broughams stood waiting. Mrs. Marcourt was very ill. It was all so unexpected, and no one seemed to know exactly how it had happened.

The muffled sound of the door-bell and telephone called Jevons often. He shook his head in reply to all inquiries. There was a change apparently, whether for good or ill Jevons could only surmise. The vicar had been sent for.

George Marcourt went upstairs to the sitting-room where the two women waited. Even he might not pass beyond that barred door. He sat there for a little and then went back to the library again. That was how he had spent all last night, all this morning. He wandered incessantly about the house and garden mechanically smoking endless cigarettes that grew cold between his lips. Sometimes he forgot to light them at all.

Yet yesterday everything had been so different. Two of those very surgeons in Mrs. Marcourt's room now had, at this very hour yesterday morning, assured him that the slight operation was a complete success. They had beamed their satisfaction, shaken hands with him and vanished. They would call again towards evening. But they came long before the time appointed, and came as the result of a hurried message from the experienced nurse in charge. Something had inexplicably gone wrong. They explained to George Marcourt that "it meant another operation." All that he vaguely understood was that it had something to do with a tied artery—and that his wife was suddenly and very seriously ill.

They reassured him almost immediately. These things happened sometimes—one could not foresee them—but it was the last thing they had expected in a comparatively simple case like this.

But the doctors stayed the night. Towards dawn they suggested to Marcourt, still reassuringly, they would like another opinion, and another brougham rolled smoothly over the straw in Marcourt Place. An hour later it was followed by another. They were holding a consultation now. Five of the most famous doctors in London were in that room where Mrs. Marcourt lay, white and silent.

'Twixt Life and Death

The lingering, pungent odour of chloroform still penetrated the house, wafted at intervals into the big dark-panelled library, and crept downstairs. It greeted Territt in a sickening wave as Jevons opened the door.

Captain Philip Territt did not speak. His eyes asked a hundred questions his lips were unable to utter.

"Quite done in, he looked," Jevons said afterwards. "The war has broke him up completely. His left arm bandaged, and him limping as if his leg had been badly smashed. Good-looking he used to be, but you wouldn't think so this morning, his face was that drawn and haggard, and him looking as if he ought to be in hospital. I think he thought it was the master who was ill. He turned so queer-like. But I told him that he had just gone upstairs, and would no doubt be down in a minute if he cared to wait. He's sitting in there now. I went up and told the master, but he don't seem to understand anything at all." He shook his head. For the last hour Marcourt had not moved.

Captain Territt was in the library, as Jevons had said. He had gone in there, and Jevons had shut the door quietly as he tiptoed out. Then he seemed to have been forgotten.

Time went by and still Territt sat there, staring before him at the heavy, tawny carpet with its pattern of drifted autumn leaves. It seemed hours since Jevons had gone to tell Marcourt that he, Territt, was there waiting to see him and yet George had not come.

How still, how terribly silent was that house! Not a sound from above or below! The very windows in this room were shut. The sunlight blazed against them. In the trees of the square opposite, a bird began to preek and chatter. It sounded faint and far away.

What was it Jevons had said to him? He put his hand to his head. His forehead burned against his cold fingers. How stupid he felt—as if his brain had ceased thinking! Perhaps it was the smell of chloroform, that pungent odour already all too familiar to him. Perhaps he would wake in a moment and find himself back in hospital, for he felt as one who walked and talked and moved in a dream from which he must wake.

Something had seemed to snap in his brain as he came up those steps. He had seen Jevons's face but as a blur. In the background he had been vaguely aware of a maid, red-eyed with weeping, who waited by the great stairway.

"Mrs. Marcourt is very ill, sir," Jevons said. "The doctors are still here. I am glad you came, sir," and the fellow's face looked genuinely distressed; "the master hasn't spoken or eaten a thing since yesterday. I'll tell him you're here, and if you could cheer him up, sir——"

He had ensconced Territt in the library, found him a comfortable chair, and hunted for an ash-tray. Territt watched him unseeingly, as if he were a spectator afar off who had no part or place in these things.

Jevons hovered around for a moment.

"If you could just cheer him up, sir," he begged. He had been with George Marcourt for fifteen years. In his own way he suffered because his master was suffering. "He is nearly frantic about the mistress."

Territt spoke at that. "Is—she—very bad?"

"I'm afraid so, sir"—Jevons shook his head—"and yet she was all right yesterday. Quite bright and cheerful-like after the operation. It was just a slight one, I understand, sir. It took place in the morning, and early in the afternoon she was talking to the maid about some little things she wanted done, some flowers sent to the hospitals, some parcels to the East End for the poor. She was so well the master went on to the House, as she begged him to do. She had her mother and Lady Emma with her, sir, and everything seemed all right. But at four o'clock she took very bad. They say she has not known anyone since."

Territt stared at Jevons. His lips moved but no sound came. What he was about to say he did not know. His brain refused to formulate anything for his lips to utter.

"The master wouldn't see anyone, sir. But he'll see you, I know." Jevons knew how welcome Captain Territt had always been in that house. For years before Marcourt's marriage Territt had been a constant guest. Jevons would have said that the marriage had separated the master from the friends of his bachelorhood. He had become so wrapped up in his home, to the exclusion of almost everything and everybody else. But his friendship for Territt stood alone.

It was over half an hour since Jevons had gone.

Unbroken silence lingered in the library. Strange thoughts stole through Territt's mind. The world, he thought, had fallen away from him and left him in space, in an immensity of suffering almost beyond endurance.

He walked to the window, and stood with his back to the door of the room, his face to the sunlight that beat against the glass.

In the street below the trees rustled ever so softly. The sky was a blue Delft bowl, guiltless of cloud. It was a day for happiness, for dreams, for the green glory of the countryside, where two people who loved each other might wander, leaving behind them the world of fever and fret, the memories of struggles, of right and wrong, black sin and passionate pain.

He remembered with quickening pulse and a stabbing pain the thoughts that had thronged his heart as he came up that still street in the noonday sunshine. Mad dreams they were, as dust and ashes—less than dust. The wheels of Fate had passed over these dreams and crushed them into the earth. All other thought fled from his mind but this, that upstairs, in her room, the woman he loved lay, helpless, wounded, suffering, between life and death.

And he, who would have given his life gladly that she might live, could not help her. He had even no right to be in that house. He could not follow George up those stairs. It was not his to wait even outside the barred door of that room where men fought a hard battle. His head bowed low in the unutterable anguish of that realisation. In this hour he stood outside.

Then suddenly he straightened himself. Somewhere in that room the invisible wires of a message stirred, a message from spirit to spirit, a wireless flashing its mystical way, recording in his very soul.

"What is it?" he cried aloud to the silence.

"What is it?" But this time he spoke in a whisper. The beads of perspiration stood out on his forehead, chill and damp. The message came and he heard it plainly . . . knew in an anguish beyond expression what it portended.

There was a sound at the door and he turned. George Marcourt stood on the threshold, staring at Territt with a bewildered, dazed expression. His faithful, doglike eyes had a strange blur across their usual clearness. He looked an old man, a very old man indeed.

"It is Philip, isn't it?" He gazed at Territt as if he were not sure. "You look different somehow." He passed his hand to his head as if pushing back a heavy weight that pressed on his brain and made understanding difficult. The action was pathetic in its helplessness.

There was his friend, broken beyond belief, who needed him, all his companionship could give. It called upon all his strength to meet that demand at this hour when his own heart was torn, his own mind on the rack. But there came back to him days of the past, of good old George, not very intellectual, but good-natured, great-hearted, never failing any man or woman in any strait.

Territt went impetuously forward, took George Marcourt's hand and gripped it fast. It lay in his grasp, cold and limp. George sank unresistingly into the chair Territt placed for him.

He shook his head when Territt asked him to drink something, to eat something and pull himself together. But he drank at a gulp the brandy forced upon him. It was the first thing that had passed his lips since four o'clock the previous afternoon. He began to speak in that strange, dazed way.

"They're still there, Territt. Not one of them has come out to tell me anything." His tortured eyes had the look as of a dumb brute asking questions to which there could be no adequate answer. "What are they doing in there? They, who are strangers, and I, her husband, shut out."

He stopped suddenly and dropped his head on his outstretched arms.

Territt's lips twitched. He glanced away, and then back again at that outward symbol of most utter anguish and despair. The bowed shoulders heaved convulsively once or twice. The grey head, almost bald, was level with the table.

For a moment Territt stood hesitating, his jaw set, his mouth a grim line of pain. Then he walked to the window, came restlessly back to the middle of the room, and moved suddenly to Marcourt's side. His hand, trembling, rested on the bowed shoulder nearest him. He spoke huskily:

"George, old man, this won't do. You've got to buck up. She—she will need you in a moment. You must not go in looking like that. Do you hear? Pull yourself together. You must!"

He was mixing again a stiff measure of the spirit

and water. He pressed it on George authoritatively and bade him drink. It was strange that he, of all men, could do this in an hour when he, like George, could have flung himself into a corner, oblivious of all else in the world but his own overmastering grief.

But the need of another, and that other his friend, called for the best in him. It sapped nearly all his strength in that hour, for George began to speak of the incredible thing that had happened, the dark shadow that had suddenly fallen across the sunshine of his happiness. It took all Territt's strength to listen as he was compelled to listen.

"You came to me, of course, as soon as you knew," said poor George. "I shall always be grateful to you for that. And she will be grateful to you, too. It was only yesterday afternoon that we, she and I, were speaking of you. She looked so well then and everything seemed all right. I had been told on the 'phone that morning that the hospital ship from Kut came in the night before."

Territt sat down. He was crouching forward in his chair, staring blindly at the floor.

"So we talked of you," said George, "and how glad we were that you were going to settle down. At least I did most of the talking. Enid said she hoped you and Beatrice would be happy, that she was sure you both would be."

Territt said nothing. His lips trembled, that was all. But the most terrible moment was yet to come, when Marcourt began to speak of the happiness his own marriage had brought to him.

"Not a single hour of regret in those eight

years," he said, and his voice broke at thought of how trouble sat beside him and fear kept vigil now. "We were so happy. She was not like other women, who are never content unless they are flirting with some other man. She was faithful to me in thought and word and deed. I would trust her with my life."

Territt listened in silence. He had half averted his face while his friend was speaking. The light from the window sharpened the profile, the line of the jaw set sternly.

"We were talking about the future, too. Enid had planned out things that are too sacred to speak of, even to you, Phil, who are my best friend. God! How she had planned and dreamed!" He covered his face with his hands. "And now for a dream that could not be, her life has paid the purchase."

He began to walk up and down the room feverishly, and once or twice he groaned sharply. Territt sat like a statue in his chair.

Marcourt was grateful for his silence. Only sympathy and understanding would realise that silence was the best medium. It was something to have someone there, to feel the consciousness of another presence, in that room where fear kept pace with him.

So Territt sat still and waited, while Marcourt stopped beside him to speak at intervals and then fell again to stalking up and down the room, to and fro like a caged animal.

Once he stopped abruptly in front of his friend.

"Just one hour," he said incoherently, "one hour, and then she did not know me at all." His eyes kept on asking Territt why this thing should have happened. "There we were, an hour before, talking of the future. She was so bright, so well. And then I went away because she wanted to sleep. She felt suddenly so tired, she said. Because they told me it was all right and that she would sleep for a few hours, I went to the House. I had hardly reached there when they sent for me."

Again he stopped and again there was silence while Territt sat, the stoop of his shoulders plainly visible. The room was darkening, outside the sunlight fast beginning to fade.

"When I came back she did not know me," said poor George, and he spoke now to himself, as if he forgot any other presence in the room. "She spoke of places she had never seen . . . she said queer things . . . that the Road of the World began at Soho. Strange . . . strange. . ." He shook his head and began to walk on, muttering as he went.

Territt moved suddenly, twisted as if in bodily anguish. He drew his breath sharply. His eyes closed and his face went white as death. The words George Marcourt had spoken haunted him, clutched at his very heart-strings.

"The Road of the World . . . begins . . . at Soho."

He uttered an inarticulate sound. His white lips quivered. All his powers of endurance seemed at an end. He must rush out of that room, out of that house, lest he break down and the truth pour out in passionate flood.

A wild impulse came over him to tell Marcourt

everything, to say savagely: "We love each other, she and I. This is the hour that should be mine, the suffering that I shall bear alone. What have *you* to do with her? Has not she herself spoken? Fool! fool! why do *you* walk up and down like that? The law that gave her to you, what of it? Love is greater than the law, greater than you or me."

He could bear it no longer and, as he lumbered to his feet, his cane fell with a sharp sound to the floor. George turned to see him standing there, leaning for support against the heavy oaken table. His eyes blazed with fierce brightness in the white patch of his face.

"Marcourt," he began sharply, "Marcourt——"

He caught his breath as a hand tapped at the panel. The door opened and a woman came in. She was a little, thin slip of a woman, worn-faced, wan with vigil; she did not seem to see Territt. Her eyes were fixed on Marcourt.

"George," she said with a sob in her throat, "Enid is asking for you. . . . Come quickly!".

Marcourt looked at her face and read the infinite compassion in her eyes. He had turned dumbly to his friend Territt, who would understand. He had tried to speak, but words would not come. He saw Philip's face through a haze—a face all twisted and tortured, it seemed, the eyes staring at him with a new and implacable and inexplicable hate.

George made an uncertain step forward. He paused as if to gather strength, then all at once his big, burly form crashed heavily to the floor.

CHAPTER XXV

Into the Silent Land

In the quiet room upstairs the curtains were drawn back so that all the afternoon sunlight, now fading fast, might filter through in pale, crocus-yellow radiance. In the grate a fire burned as if the chill of approaching autumn had crept into the room. The aroma of chloroform still lingered, faintly interspersed with the fragrance of lavender.

Mrs. Marcourt lay very still on the big white bed, her hair streaming out across the pillows in a tangle of coppery brown. The firelight danced on the walls. A ray of sunshine, like a shining shaft of unspent gold, fell across the pink carpet, pale as the heart of a shell.

In the library the doctors were telling George Marcourt the truth. Mrs. Marcourt was dying.

Marcourt stood staring at them while they told him. His mouth opened in a queer way and shut again. He did not seem to understand.

"You mean—she is worse?" He looked at them piteously, as if begging them not to tell him. They looked away from him as they answered. The truth had to be told. Mrs. Marcourt was much worse. All that could be done had been done.

"Fetch more doctors," Marcourt cried hoarsely. "Don't think of the cost——"

All the doctors in the world could do no good, they assured him. He gazed at their strained, haggard faces, those of men who had gone down to the very gates of death and had fought a losing fight.

He stared at them with bloodshot eyes. As the truth beat its way into his soul, the blood receded from his florid cheeks and left them sickly white.

He turned dumbly from them to Territt—Territt whom he had begged to remain. He was standing by the window, his head bent. The outline of his bowed shoulders brought conviction to George Marcourt.

"Philip!" he called sharply, "you heard. Tell them it isn't true; it can't be true."

He began vaguely to stumble across the room towards his friend, his bloodshot eyes wide with terror and unbelief, a suddenly old man, bent and broken under the blow. It was very terrible to see.

Territt turned with a queer upward jerk of the head. "It is too true," he said. "Enid is dying."

That was the worst hour of all to bear that day, perhaps. It was Territt upon whom George Marcourt leaned in that bitter moment of realisation.

Afterwards, bowed and broken, he went lurching up the stairs to that room where Mrs. Marcourt lay so quietly.

One of the doctors stayed behind in the library with Territt. The broughams of the rest began to move out of the street. Once a door somewhere in the basement opened and the sound of a woman's weeping ascended; then the door closed again and shut it out.

Into the Silent Land

The doctor and Philip Territt stood by the window looking out at the sunset.

"He will take it badly," the doctor said, shaking his head. "We knew last night, of course, but it would have done no good to tell him. And we hoped against hope. Lady Emma knew. Most admirable woman that!"

"Lady Emma knew," said Territt involuntarily.

The doctor nodded. "It was she who advised us not to tell Mr. Marcourt." He sighed. "I am afraid this thing will break him up altogether."

There ensued some minutes of silence. Territt spoke suddenly, his voice hoarse. "You are sure nothing more can be done? Nothing?"

"Nothing; it is only a question of hours."

"Is she in pain?" The question seemed wrung from him.

"None whatever."

Territt turned sharply, sank into a chair in the background, and said no further word. Jevons came to the door immediately afterwards with a message. He gave it in a low voice. But Philip Territt heard it distinctly.

"The nurse thinks you had better come, sir."

The door closed again. The room was left to Territt and his thoughts. He bowed his head in his hands. Something cried aloud in his heart and forced him to his knees, praying as he had not done since he was a boy.

The light died suddenly from the room. There fell a dead silence as if all things therein slept. Something greater than life, colossal in its magnitude, awful in its sense of majesty, began to brood over that house.

Territt never knew how long he crouched there, motionless, waiting. Vaguely he knew the day had fled suddenly, a pursued thing, over the hills of Time. All its sunshine had vanished with it. Only the shadows remained, dark and cold, ever deepening. . . .

The room was a dim world in which he was alone and forgotten; the worlds of the past, of the present, had no place for him; they spun on outside his world of grief. He was unconscious of physical fatigue, of any dominant feeling except that of waiting, vaguely waiting for some message that would reach his tortured mind.

Sometimes he was as a spectator, standing on the road without, watching one window, knowing all too well that at any moment a hand might reach up and draw down the blind. Someone opened the door, but he did not hear.

It was Lady Emma, her wig awry, the untidy grey fringe of her own hair showing plainly. The paint on her old face was runnelled with the passage of tears. Her eyes, swollen with weeping, blinked fast.

She saw in that bent figure, its stooping shoulders, the naked soul of the man stripped bare of all else but suffering, suffering become anguish unspeakable because of helplessness.

All the bitterness she had ever felt towards Philip Territt slipped away from Lady Emma Beckendon then. They stood on the same ground, hallowed with suffering, with sense of loss, of futility, of life's emptiness, when the thing one loved one might not save.

She put her hand to her throat, swallowed abruptly, went out as noiselessly as she entered.

In the hall below waited Beatrice. She had just entered. With her eyes wide with disbelief she was listening to something Jevons was saying. She did not appear able to grasp its meaning. When she saw Lady Emma she ran towards her, stifling a sob.

"Tell me," she beseeched, "that it is not true." Her hands clung to Lady Emma.

The old woman uttered an inarticulate sound. Then she spoke.

"It is quite true."

Beatrice gave a low cry and began to tremble all over.

"Come!" said Lady Emma briefly. She drew the girl, unresisting, to the door of the library. "Captain Territt is in there," said Lady Emma. She closed the door behind her very gently.

In the room, far off in that dim world in which he revolved alone, Philip Territt stood. That tense moment of waiting, of expectancy, held him fast. Far off on the dark horizon of that dim world he saw the clouds slowly lift. The white minarets of another world in which the sun shone for ever rose before his eyes. His soul cried out to the dear, passing soul of another—cried out for one word, for one second's pause. He called her name in a sobbing whisper, and across the silence of the room a voice had answered.

"*Philip!*"

He heard his name whispered, no more than a breath. His heart leaped. · She was calling him, spirit had responded to spirit, the message halting, broken here and there, flashing its way. He felt no surprise, and bent his head to listen.

"*Philip!*"

There was a sharp click behind him which swung him back to the world in which men move and have their being, to the present, to the knowledge of something ominous. The Living, not the Dead, had spoken.

The lights had flashed on. Under the rose-coloured globes stood Beatrice, her hand still on the switch. The light flung its warm glow across her face, her eyes full of vague fear.

He did not seem to hear her voice, for he did not move. He remained motionless, his head half turned towards her, still bent as though in arrested contemplation. His face was blank and white and terrible.

"Philip!" she whispered. She dropped her hand from the switch and began to move slowly, uncertainly, towards him. Her eyes were questioning, still afraid. A new terror came into them as she saw him staring sightlessly beyond her into the lurking shadows. She saw his haggard face, his clenched hands. She stopped quite still. So for a minute they stood. Then he drew himself up shortly as if he had just become aware of her presence in that room. He spoke her name.

"Beatrice!" he said hoarsely. Their eyes met. With a stifled gasp Beatrice ran to him. Her hand touched his arm, her fingers pressed deep into his sleeve. She cried out and her voice rang loud in that silent room.

"Philip, Philip, what is it——?"

He interrupted her quickly.

"Hush! Beatrice," he said hoarsely. "Enid is very ill."

She looked at him pitifully, the tears began to rain down her cheeks.

"Oh, Phil dear," she sobbed. "Do you not know? Enid cannot hear. Enid is dead."

CHAPTER XXVI

To Be or Not To Be

OUTSIDE the grey mist of dawn still shrouded London. The holland blinds in the big hotel that looked out over the Thames were still drawn close. Against one of them, high up, the wan reflection of a light showed. A dark shadow moved now and again, flung against the pale yellow screen as if from a stereopticon.

Far below, on the Embankment, life and light began to creep into the City on the heels of dawn. A motor-lorry rattled on the grey road and a cheery whistled refrain broke the stillness. Eastwards a faint glow began to flush with colour the grey, tense face of the sky.

Life woke suddenly with the rush and the dull roar of a London that never sleeps. Queer, staccato pauses come suddenly and unexpectedly in that hour before dawn, a time of strange, eerie quiet. Then the rush and the roar sweep on uninterruptedly again, the throbbing of a great city, pulsing against its bars.

Philip Territt stood in thought. The chill grey of the dawn was on his face. His thin features, stern with the impress of a night's vigil, were silhouetted sharply against the flame of light that burned steadily above the writing-table.

On that table lay three letters, one to the War

Office, one to Beatrice Byndham, and one to the old family lawyer. Something else lay on that table, grey and sinister. The light gleamed on the shining barrel.

Philip Territt switched off the light and touched the cord of the blind. As it skirled up it flapped a little in the morning breeze that blew freshly through the open space at the top. A barge creaked in the river below. It went past, heavily laden, on the brown waters of the Thames. Territt's eyes followed it until it passed out of sight.

He had no sensation save of the monotony of things, and the dull, throbbing ache of his left arm. Soon even that would pass.

He would not be the only man who did the thing he was going to do. He wondered, in a dull, indifferent way, whether they felt as he did, bereft of all that life held sweet and worth living for.

He could not live and know her dead. While she lived, no matter how far they were apart, life itself linked them together, content with the knowledge of their love. It had been a bridge that spanned any distance, a communion in which they met and ate of the sacred bread of Love that had never been profaned.

Then he had his dreams, the dear vision of her, warm and breathing, her face turned towards him. Neither the widest sea nor the farthest lands could break the links that had held them.

Now the links were snapped, for ever broken. For him there would be but the memory of a pure, calm face, closed eyes, whose long dark lashes would never lift again in this world, and cold lips, shaped in the mystical fashion of death, silent about the solved Enigma.

For all his prayers she could not come back to him. She had gone so far on the Unknown Road that he could not catch even a fleeting glimpse of the dear vision which once had held him and made life a sweeter and purer thing, with joy pulsing through the minor *motif* of the days.

If he might only follow her along that Road! Somewhere, surely, at the far end of it, would be the Being Who made worlds and created souls for some set purpose.

Last night, when he had gone blindly out of Marcourt Place, he stumbled into a church. Late as the hour was, the sound of the organ throbbing through the quiet of a half-forgotten street lured him in, rather than any deeply religious feeling.

As with most men, the bonds of creed had long ceased to fetter him. The teachings of childhood had grown vague and blurred, the world in which he moved more real to him than the dim, visionary world beyond human ken. And, perhaps, like most men too, his mind, tinged with agnosticism or cynicism, because of the weird, empty reaches of ecclesiasticism, had long ago ceased to think of a future world at all.

Then suddenly he was brought up against that closed gate which no earthly key might fit, that grey wall that ever looms relentlessly before the wisest mind, a barrier the living may not pass.

What was beyond? Was there anything beyond, anything at all? How could he know? How could those men, leaning out over the pulpits, speaking of the Beyond so earnestly, how could they know?

> The preachers pray
> And the great seers pore
> Over their volumes of earthly lore;
> But all that science can give or teach
> Keepeth the Last Thing out of reach.

But the music of an old, old hymn pulsing through that almost deserted church, touched some long-forgotten chord of childhood, drew him by its mysterious, irresistible force, and brought him to his knees.

An old woman was whispering near him, her beads rattling metallically now and again. She was of the faith which had once been his own and that of all belonging to him, but which he had long ago discarded as puerile, superstitious, powerless to satisfy the innermost cravings of the soul.

The organ gave him more comfort, pouring its flood of melody upwards, throbbing as his heart throbbed, pulsing as the blood in his veins pulsed, sorrowing as he sorrowed.

Then it died away and he was alone with its echoes in the emptying church. As they put out the last light the last light in his soul seemed to flicker away and die, too.

If he asked that old, bent woman, hobbling out of the door before him, whose wrinkled face was already turned to that barred gate, what was beyond, she could not tell him. She would answer of a surety that Purgatory awaited.

Purgatory! He flung the thought from him!

Was not life itself the Purgatory through which men passed? Earth was crowded with suffering that crept close behind song, the note of pain ever sobbing beneath the laughter. When all things were evened there would be little need of Purgatory.

He came back to his room and locked himself in, and denied himself to all callers. Throughout the long watches of the night he kept vigil.

He had given his country almost all he had to give. It was a miracle he had not given life itself, for he had offered it more than once on the altar of Old England. His father and mother were dead, many years ago; he had no near relatives, but there were those who would keep up the old name.

He thought of Beatrice many times. She was young, a mere child, and would forget. She would marry someone else in days to come and be happier than ever he could have made her. For the shadow of one woman must for ever stand between them.

Beatrice would marry, and in the meantime he could lift the burden of worry, of hidden poverty from her young shoulders. He sat down and wrote to the old family lawyer, adding necessary instructions for the disposal of all he possessed. He left everything, except the estate which was entailed, to Beatrice Byndham unreservedly.

The light glimmered on the revolver as he wrote. He waited only for the hour when the will could be signed, made valid in the presence of witnesses. He wanted no hitch afterwards. Beatrice was to have everything, with as little fuss and publicity as possible.

Then she passed out of his mind, as she had passed last night when he had loosed her arms from about him, and walked out of Marcourt Place, awed and numbed of brain.

Looking at him now, in the growing light, there was nothing in that impassive face to show the stern resolve behind its quiet mask. The keen eyes held determination, the mouth was a grim line, that was all. The letter to the War Office dealt only with the matter of the instructions he had found awaiting him when he returned to his rooms. Someone had blundered or had changed his mind, for Captain Territt was courteously informed that the W.O. was of opinion he could be of more use in England, training recruits. His leave was extended for a period of two months. After that he would be called upon to take up his new duties.

They did not want him then, after all, said Territt bitterly. Their promise had been callously broken. The Big Man had, as a matter of fact, probably forgotten that he, Territt, ever existed.

There were hundreds of men who could fill the place they offered him. He was a soldier, a leader, a man who could do things in actual battle. To kick his heels about the countryside, to fill in his spare time with teas and matinées—he could not do it. The W.O. letter emptied life of everything. It was the last straw.

He looked at his watch impatiently. How slow the hours passed! He stood by the window, gazing with eyes that saw nothing at the river and its ever-changing freight.

Along the corridor, outside his room, Boots, whistling softly, was emptying the contents of his wicker basket. He paused opposite the door of Territt's room and the man at the window turned. The boots he had worn yesterday were still on his feet.

But the rustle of paper, and not of boots, was heard distinctly, and a white, oblong piece of paper slid under the door. Then Boots went on his way whistling unconcernedly. The hall-porter, who had forgotten to send up a letter the night before, had chosen this method of seeing that Captain Territt received it at the earliest opportunity.

Territt had little curiosity about it. Letters came at all odd times. It was probably a tout's circular or an invitation. Well, he was done with both. These things mattered no more to him. He had reached the stage when Life, that huge, slow-moving monster, crushing all before it in its relentless passage, mattered even less.

The letter lay on the faded carpet, but Territt turned his brooding eyes away from it and stared at the river again. But the white scrap of paper, lying there, twisted its way into his thoughts again and again with haunting persistence.

With an impatient shake of his shoulders he bent to pick it up and recognised the handwriting with a sense of shock. It was that of Lady Emma Beckendon. Why was she writing to him? Did not she realise that all was over and ended, that nothing she could do or say could have any effect? He held it in his hand uncertainly. Then he broke the flap. A tremor passed over him as he read. It was short and terse. Here and there it was smudged by anger or tears, perhaps both.

"I find it hard to write to you, but it would be harder to hold any conversation," she wrote without any introduction, "so I will just put down for the first and the last time the message I was asked to give you. There is no need to say by whom. That much, I trust, you will forget, as I will forget that ever the message was mine to deliver——"

He raised his eyes at that, and the hand that held the paper trembled violently. A message—a message from Enid—a voice from beyond that grey barrier. He seemed to hear it speaking. It was no longer the voice of Lady Emma, but of Enid herself, that spoke in the written words that followed.

"The message is that Life goes on and upwards and that we must follow it, nor swerve from the path, wherever it may lead. Death is Life without the limitations and without the bitternesses of earth. Life goes on—and upwards."

There was a smudge, a mark as if the pen had trailed in the proud old hand that had not shrunk even from this bitter task. He read on:

"We spoke of you the night before she died. Of what was said there is no need to speak beyond this, that because she loved Beatrice she desired her happiness—and yours, and that, whatever happened, you should always remember that she, loving and understanding Beatrice as she did, wished for the marriage above all things. She asked me to tell you also, knowing that you would understand, that the faded violets of this year will die, but the violets of a Spring-to-be will bloom fresher and sweeter for the winter that has passed."

That was all. The letter ended as abruptly as it began. The hand that penned it had shaken considerably in those last two lines, had blotted it with haste. He thought of the writer as a hard, worldly woman, selfish in most things, with the fierce pride of race fighting against a promise which had been given and which therefore had to be kept.

As he gazed at the written message in his hand, the words of the dear dead woman he loved burned into his brain.

"Life goes on—and upwards"; and again, "We must follow it, *nor swerve from the path,* wherever it may lead." Had she foreseen the dark night of storm and stress that had sent his mind almost rocking, that had seared his heart with its iron of regret? Had she known that the dawn would find him there, perchance, and on the writing-table before him that which would force the barred gate? She had said that she wished for the marriage above all things. She had looked to this hour, when he must stand alone, all his defences down; and so she had sent him a message knowing that, living or dead, the words had power to sway him. The voice from the grave had bid him live.

How the words haunted him! He heard her whispering those words to him, bending over him, as he bowed his head low on his outstretched arms. "Life goes on—and upward." "Nor swerve from the path."

Slow, hot tears from eyes that once would have scorned to shed them, dropped on his clasped hands.

To Be or Not To Be

He who would have died that she might live must live because she wished it. The letter brought her near, very near to him. Its words tore gently from his eyes the veil of doubt, bidding him see through those dear eyes that had never doubted life's continuance.

"Enid! Enid!" he cried hoarsely, and the living, and not the dead, again had answered.

Somewhere from the gardens near a bugle blared out suddenly. The shuffling sound of feet broke the stillness. A voice rang out like a clarion:

"Quick! . . . *March!*"

The man in the room above sprang to his feet.

Out of the garden below, into the grey street, shoulder to shoulder, men in khaki began to march. They swung along the Embankment, heads high, the band loud, triumphant, calling on the world to behold with pride.

Out from offices, from behind counters, from the ploughing of fields, from cotter's hut, mansion, and suburban villa, these men had come, new recruits rallying to the Union Jack that fluttered proudly on the breeze.

A great lump caught in the throat of the watcher. The answer had come. It lay there, on the faces of those men in the moving ranks, shoulder to shoulder, side by side, men who were willing to give their all.

Life went on and upwards, palpitating with love of home and love of country, and the glory of the British flag, the emblems of the unfading rose of Old England, the thistle of land, and the little green shamrock c Ireland yet to be.

"*Quick! . . . March!*"

Life went on. He must go with it. carry on.

CHAPTER XXVII

An Understanding

Mrs. Byndham's drawing-room was characteristic of its owner. It was crowded with a heterogeneous collection of furniture, and bore witness to her ideas on art in the shape of grotesque jars, a cubist picture or two, art curtains, a statue of Buddha in the vicinity of a Chinese mandarin, each and everything with the air of disdain for each other's company.

Beatrice sat in a low armchair by the fire, leaning forward, elbows on knees, her hands supporting her chin, her eyes on the leaping flame. Once or twice she moved wearily, glanced at the ormolu clock on the mantel, and shivered as if with cold. An hour had ticked slowly away.

Presently the bell rang in the hall, and a little later footsteps echoed outside the door, at which a hand tapped lightly. Beatrice, though she drew her breath sharply, did not move.

Philip Territt opened the door, closed it gently, and stood on the threshold waiting. The clock ticked loudly in the stillness of the room.

"Beatrice!"

Beatrice turned her face towards him as if only then aware of his presence. She looked older. There was no laughter lurking in her eyes or at her lips. She rose slowly and stood quite still watching him.

Her arm lay along the mantel, resting on it as if for support, her hand clenched against the ornate wood.

Neither spoke for a moment, intuitively conscious of the delicacy of the situation.

Beatrice was gowned in some dark material which showed up the fairness of her skin, the pale gold of her hair. It showed also the extreme pallor of her face, the dark shadows under her eyes. But the eyes themselves were clear and steady, her mouth a firm, sweet line. Whatever else the night had brought to Beatrice Byndham, it had given her resolution; but the anguish of the struggle had left its traces.

He saw this with a sharp pang of remorse, and saw also that Beatrice *knew,* that the night had brought enlightenment, even if his action of yesterday in leaving her alone when he went out of Marcourt Place had not already shown her the truth. Not for the first time he discovered the inadequacy of words.

He came towards her, held her hands for a minute in silence, held them tightly because suddenly they trembled so, quivering with emotion.

"You received my message, Philip?" She drew her hands away and looked into the fire leaping in the grate, flinging curious, reflected arabesques of flame across her dark gown.

"Yes, I was just coming to you, as a matter of fact, when your message came through."

He paused as he saw her face light up and suddenly soften. She was fighting hard to retain her composure that she might say all she had planned to say and set him free. Afterwards—she had not let herself think of the emptiness of that "afterwards."

An Understanding

He was speaking to her, and remorse gave his voice a new tenderness.

"Won't you sit down, Beatrice?" Almost unconsciously his hand went out to hers as in a gesture of mute appeal. He drew her to the arm-chair.

Her lip quivered as she mechanically obeyed him. She sat down quickly, but turned her face away abruptly. Territt stood by her, looking down on her bent head in deep perplexity, instinctively aware of the struggle through which her young, stormy soul was passing. He waited until she spoke.

"I sent for you, Phil, because I wanted to see you quite alone. Mother will be out until after lunch. She did not know you were coming, or that I telephoned to your hotel asking you to call." She lifted her eyes then, bright with the effort to keep back tears. "I felt that you and I had something to say to each other which no third person, no matter how near and dear, might hear."

He nodded gravely. He stood by the mantel, his tall figure a little stooped, the grey in his hair very noticeable this morning. His left arm, in its khaki sling, ached dully. But there was a greater ache in his heart.

Poor Beatrice! A flood of uncontrollable pity broke over him with overwhelming force. He remembered her as so young, so lovely, so gay, but a few days since. He thought of her proud face, the sweetness of her eyes, on a night months ago, when they stood on the steps of Marcourt Place and she had said to him, "Phil, I love you! I shall always love you, and you only."

What a child, an idealising, lovely child, she had been! He tried to make things easier for her now, though words were so hard to find.

"Dear," he asked gently, "need anything be said that had best remain unsaid, if things are to be as before between you and me?"

"Can they ever be as before, Phil?" Her eyes, moist with the fret of tears she would not shed, met his. They looked at each other a long moment.

"Only yesterday morning," she said, "I was so happy, only yesterday morning—and to-day all my world is at an end."

He was profoundly moved. Her words flooded his consciousness with a lucidity and insight, a terrible clearness of perspective, etched sharply on the road of sorrow which Beatrice, too, had trodden. She was no longer the child he had deemed her but a suffering woman.

In that moment of realisation his only thought was for Beatrice. It was part of his nature that he should put her before himself. He looked at her with new eyes, dark with pity as well as with pain.

"For God's sake, Beatrice," he exclaimed, "don't say such a thing! You are young. Life lies before you——"

She made a weary gesture. "It is the worst of all to bear," she said, "that life lies before me. Years, many long years of it, perhaps." Her hands worked unconsciously by her sides, and she looked the picture of veritable woe as the vista of emptiness spread out in imagination before her.

Then she saw his face and her own changed.

Would she place the burden of her sorrow on the bowed shoulders of this man who had already so much to bear? She stood outside his life—she must grasp that. Words were futile and inadequate—all she had to do was to set him free, to say good-bye and see him no more—for ever.

But the young, passionate heart of her cried out at that, and she turned her face from him. He could see nothing but her exquisite, almost flawless profile.

"Beatrice! Is it as bad as that with you?" he cried in uncontrollable remorse, and laid his hand gently on her shoulder.

"I—I feel it is too bad to bear, Phil." Her shoulders quivered for a moment. Then suddenly she straightened herself, rose and faced him.

"Philip, this is harder for both of us than I thought possible. It is best to get it over and done with. Then you must go away." She paused for a second, and then continued in a low voice. "It seems to me that words are of little use, that the only thing to do is to give you back your word and say good-bye."

"Beatrice, you wish that?"

She brushed her hand wearily over her forehead.

"It is what you wish, is it not, Philip? And yet yesterday——" and she burst into tears.

"Yesterday," he said, "is different from to-day, Beatrice." His own voice was far from steady. "I told you in the morning, in the little room adjoining this, all there was to tell."

"But—I thought it was—someone in India—far away."

"There is a country farther away than India, Beatrice."

"You mean——" Her voice was tremulous, eager in its questioning.

"I mean the dim bourne, Beatrice."

She sat quite still. As the light from the window fell full on her, he saw every feature of her small face, every phase of expression that passed across it. In the silence a voice, borne on a gust of wind, floated into the room, a voice singing of love and roses and spring. Without a word he went to the window, closed it and, standing averted from her, spoke a little roughly.

"There are some things, Beatrice, of which one cannot speak. If I ever spoke of them at all it would not be now. Yesterday morning I told you the truth, because it was only right that you who were to be my wife should know it."

"Between yesterday and to-day," she half whispered, "there stretches a great gulf. You stand on one side, I on the other. The bridge that spanned it has gone. It was only built of dreams, Philip."

"Dreams!" he spoke as if to himself. "Dreams are all that I have had, Beatrice. It is strange you should speak of them as a bridge and voice my unspoken thought."

The closed window had not altogether shut out the singer's voice, spending itself now in a last sweet note. Beatrice waited until it ended.

"I want you to be free, Philip," she said quietly. "It is what you would wish, I think. You will soon be in France and my friends will understand why our marriage did not take place. When the war is over explanations will be easier, though nothing will hurt so much—so much."

As she spoke with a note of despair, suddenly appeared to her mental vision the Mocker, cynically reminding her of the life of her set by way of solace. The whirl of the world would catch her up. She would fling herself into it and dance the mad dance of heedless pleasure. The moment, and the moment only, that was all that counted, with no time for thinking. What did it matter though people whispered and raised their eyebrows, shrugged their shoulders and asked what could one expect of those Byndhams?

The young mouth hardened as she faced in thought that future in which she must have no time for thinking. Remembrance! That way madness lay. She said strangely terrible things, for a young girl, in that desolate moment.

Suddenly Territt strode up to her, caught her hands and lifted her to her feet. They faced each other in a moment tense with hitherto unknown emotion.

"Beatrice," he said under his breath, "do you know what you are saying?"

Her eyes wide and still vague looked wearily into his. "Was I speaking aloud? I did not know. I am sorry, Phil. I hope I did not say anything to hurt you."

"Not to hurt me, but yourself." His hands tightened on hers.

She shrank as she threw back her head. "It can matter only to myself, anyway——"

"It matters to me also, Beatrice."

"No!" and her voice rang passionately. "For this moment perhaps, Yes. But when you go out of this room, No, No. You will forget; men are like that. It is only we women who remember, who break our hearts and often our lives on the rugged rock of memory. Oh! why do you stay? Why do you not go?"

"Because I wish to stay, Beatrice."

"I do not want your pity, Philip. Your only feeling as regards myself can only be regret. But you need regret nothing. It was all a foolish mistake, something that could never be."

"Why not?" he asked gently.

"Why not?" she repeated, with a poignant change in her voice. "Because I will not bind you, Philip. I will not ask you to do what you have no wish to do."

"And—if I wish it?" he suggested.

His eyes were looking at her with a new and inexplicable tenderness.

"If I wish it, Beatrice?"

She shook her head wistfully. "How could I believe that, Philip?"

"Because I wish you to believe it, dear."

He saw the change that came over her face, the revelation of its beauty, the light that crept back to her eyes. The tears came, too.

"Philip!" she whispered. "Oh, Philip!"

She leaned towards him as he came at her call. He knelt down beside her and her tears dropped fast on his brown hand.

"You—don't want me to give you up?" she said. She caught his hand and held it close against her breast. "O Philip, are you quite, quite sure?"

He bent his head until it rested against the dark sleeve of her gown. He thought of Enid, of the last message she had sent him. He set his lips in a firm, enduring line.

"I am quite sure, dear."

Her heart throbbed and beat fast as he knelt. In the grate the fire was dying, but in her heart leapt the clear, steady flame of her love.

"Then—it will make no difference."

"It will make no difference, Beatrice." He almost had added, "She wished it so."

But the anguish of his voice in those few words could not be mistaken, and he was glad she could not see his face. His brow was wrinkled, seamed with intolerable pain. He heard another voice than that of Beatrice Byndham which said over and over again:

"He will marry Beatrice and it will be for the best."

Beatrice, too, was thinking, for she clung suddenly to him.

"Philip, I have something to tell you. Had you gone away you would never have known it. But I'll tell you now. I feel intensely, so intensely that I do not think I could have gone on as before. I could not! Last night I felt as if I could not bear to live through another day that must for ever separate us."

"You—felt like that!" he breathed.

"Yes! I faced the other alternative. I saw the

empty years," and she sobbed a little, clung tighter to him. "It takes more courage to live, Philip, to love on when one is bereft of the dear hope of a lifetime."

He nodded, his left hand clenched involuntarily and sent stabbing pains through him.

"But now, O my dear, I know I will make you happy, I *know*. Whether you live or die, whether France takes you or leaves you, I will always know that you chose not to go away when you could have gone and left me."

She lifted her veiled, wistful eyes and saw only his grey head, still bent.

"I shall be the better woman for last night's suffering, Philip. It showed me life as it is, myself as I am. It showed me, too, that the one real thing in my life was you, that you filled my life to the exclusion of all else. And that to lose you would leave my life empty as nothing else could. We must help each other."

He rose and kissed her on the proud brow, above the eyes that, for all their tears, shone now with a serener light.

"Yes, we must help each other, Beatrice." But his eyes looked over her little head, and far away.

"And when you are away," she said, "I shall not be unhappy. I do not think it wrong or unwomanly to tell you, Philip, how strong and sure a thing my love is; that I want to be your wife. I want to be mother of your children." Her voice dropped into a whisper. "Philip, marry me before you go to

Flanders. Let me go with you to the old home of which I have heard, where you were born, and which must be hallowed with your boyhood's memories. Marry me soon!"

"It shall be as you wish, dear. We shall go when and where you wish. I have gone to my old home, alone, for many years. It was peopled only with dreams." He straightened up like a man who shook these things from him. "But you shall go there, Beatrice."

As he walked to the window, Beatrice's voice followed.

"I, too," she said, "have peopled that old house with dreams. Yours were dreams that could not be; mine are possible."

Her voice thrilled.

"You will find me there, waiting, when you come back from Flanders. The words 'home' and 'wife' shall have new meaning for you."

She lifted her head bravely, "And if you do not come back I shall have memory."

He saw her transfigured face, heard her sweet voice, strong with a reborn happiness, beheld her eyes lit with the vision of a future he could not see.

She stood there in the glory of her youth and beauty, challenging, unafraid. Her eyes looked beyond the man she loved, and the radiance of her vision reached out to him and drew him nearer.

She met him halfway across the room, held out her arms as to a little child stumbling along a dark road, sobbing silently. All that was best in her, all that was maternal, went out to him. She put her arms about him as if he were her little child indeed.

She drew his head to her breast, pressed her young warm face against his cold one.

"Boy, *dear,*" she whispered. . . .

CHAPTER XXVIII

At Bugle Call

THE rain was falling gently like slow tears, and in the old grey flint church, with its tall square tower, the sound of the organ rose and fell with a majestic pathos that thrilled the small congregation.

The vicar spoke without faltering, strong and sure in the faith that gave the body bravely to the dust, "in the sure and certain hope."

His voice was triumphant, although the new mound by the pathway would be all that was left to him of perhaps the most dearly loved of his children.

"I am the Resurrection and the Life. . . . he that believeth in Me . . . shall never die."

How strong, how sure was a faith that rang like that, stirring echoes even in souls that kept religion far in the background as a shadowy thing to be paraded only on Sundays! The words echoed in the arches and rang with surety and hope eternal.

Lady Emma Beckendon, in one of the pews, heard them. She had been thinking how plain and severe the church was with its simple altar, furnished but with a shining cross; she thought also that for the service of a Marcourt it would have been fitting and most touching to have acolytes, the swinging of a censer, the misty veil of incense.

But there came all at once into that simple church

a power which she had never known and which shook her worldly and selfish heart as nothing else had shaken it.

Beatrice sobbed audibly. Territt, stern and very still beside her, heard the sob and turned. His hand went out and touched hers reassuringly. The old woman saw that action. They sat directly in front of her. She stared before her and thought of words she had written:

"The faded violets of this year will die, but the violets of a Spring to be will bloom the sweeter."

Enid had been right, then. This was what she meant and only George would remember. George who sat by her, so stupid and so silent.

Duly they filed out of the church into the churchyard, where the trees bent low over the quiet, leaning tombs, from which the moving finger of time had erased the names.

The rain was falling still, but the clouds were slowly dispersing, their ragged edges rimmed with the light of departing day.

George crossed over to Territt in those last few moments that held them all with the mystery of something beyond human ken. The vicar had brought the majesty of an unshakable faith to the graveside.

"There shall be neither sorrow nor crying. . . ."

His beautiful, sweet face was lifted towards the heavens. One knew then how men had died in the past, had been burnt at the stake because of this thing they held fast, this simple, childlike faith that felt not flame or fire, nor the works of the earth, nor corruption of the body, but raised itself on invisible wings and followed the path of the pale Galilean who walked among the hills of God.

The rain stopped abruptly and the sun came out. The words of the vicar ceased for a moment, and a shaft of sunlight struck across that black pall that the wind was lifting ever so slightly. Then earth covered the things of earth. . . .

George Marcourt shook his head in a dumb, puzzled way. He spoke to Territt.

"She never knew me at the last. . . . The doctors knew, but they never told me . . . she spoke of places she had never seen . . . she said queer things . . . that the Road of the World began at Soho. . . . Strange, strange!"

Then Lady Emma called him and they walked to the waiting car. Beatrice went with them because Lady Emma looked so tired and aged.

"Do you get married to-morrow, Beatrice?"

Beatrice answered in a low voice, "Yes." She looked at Lady Emma, and her voice quivered.

"To-morrow! That's sudden and scarcely decent." The old woman spoke with rapid fierceness.

"I thought you'd say that," Beatrice rejoined, "and I agree with you. But there's no help for it. A war wedding is not like any other wedding, and we are to be married at the registrar's with the utmost privacy. We both loved Enid too dearly for any fussy ceremony, and we feel that she wouldn't have minded in the circumstances. You see, Philip goes to Flanders, after all. He had a letter stating he would be wanted for Home Defence, but it was sent to him by mistake. Only this morning the War Office notified him about Flanders." She added, a little less defiantly: "Philip needs me—and I need him."

Lady Emma stared grimly before her. She wondered how much Beatrice knew, whether she knew anything at all. Her own lips were for ever sealed. She had done her duty as a Marcourt, had stood by George's wife from the time she came from this village to London until she left it again for the last time. She had done her duty.

She always saw the future, years ahead, with those queer, blinking eyes of hers. She had all the pieces, as it were, set on the chequer-board. Had you bent over it and looked through her eyes you would have seen the pieces in their places, that her masterful hands had already mated George Marcourt and had set his house in order.

George spoke to Beatrice now and shook his head. He looked queer and stupid, and as if he had not slept for many nights.

"She never knew me at the last," he said, and he looked at her as if she had asked why. "She spoke of places she had never seen . . . she said queer things . . . that the Road of the World began at Soho. . . ."

There stirred in Beatrice's mind a dim recollection that the Marcourts, like many other ancient families, showed now and again signs of mental decadence. She stared at George's face so changed, the eyes so pathetic. He was fumbling helplessly in his pocket as if he searched for something. He shook his head as if not remembering what it was.

"*George!*" cried Lady Emma sharply. "Come! It is getting late. You must not keep Beatrice."

They got into the carriage, and the chauffeur shut the door after them and climbed into his place. The car turned and swept down the road. Beatrice stood and watched it out of sight. Philip Territt, who had been walking alone, up and down that broken grey-flagged pathway, where the green grass flourished in the interstices, had gone back to the grave.

There was no one there now but himself. The little children who had been so strangely quiet were indoors. The vicarage door, always so hospitably open, was shut for this day.

He looked down at the mound on which the wreaths of flowers were already wilting. They had laid her under the brown earth, had shut her away from sight—the dear hands of her, the dear eyes of her. He felt as if he must throw himself down beside her, tear from her all that weight of earth, those fast-dying flowers with all their terrible significance.

In the sky a lark began suddenly to sing. It sang on and on, filling the world with melody. He raised his haggard face and watched that dark, palpitating speck as it sang of life unending.

The door of the vicarage opened. The mother, turning her face towards the churchyard, saw the solitary figure there. He was not looking at the sky-lark now but at the new-made grave at his feet.

"Sleep well, my dear, sleep well," he was whispering.

As she gazed there came to her a memory of that day by the green glades of the beech wood. The knowledge that was denied her then was given her now.

Something swept across the quiet harbour of her life and shook her with its force. Mary, the mother, went indoors and slipped on her knees.

Across the velvety turf of the churchyard to Philip Territt came Beatrice. He had been standing a long while there, and Beatrice had suffered much in the waiting. She looked at the grave, at his face, and then down at the grave again.

"Come, dear," she said pitifully. She laid her hand on his arm, and so they went across the grass; and as they went the lark sang high in the sky, louder and sweeter, flinging his message abroad that the world might hear and heed.

Beatrice heard it and turned her face to the pale sunshine. She saw the grey clouds, sombre with rain, scuttling away with the wind at their ragged heels. Life would be like that, she told herself. Patience, and in a little while the clouds would pass away out of sight. The radiance of the dying day made a new world. She walked into its radiance, head high, believing because she wished to believe.

"Listen, Philip!" she said. "The skylark is singing of hope and joy, of sunshine that follows the rain, of happiness that follows sorrow as night the day. Listen, dear!"

They stopped by the gateway and tears filled Beatrice's eyes, tears for the dead woman whom she had loved, tears of joy for the morrow. To-day—ah! it belonged to the Dead, but To-morrow——

"A song of hope and love that shall triumph over all things," she whispered. She clung to him suddenly.

At Bugle Call

The glow of the sunlight flung its radiance across her face. "Listen to the song, Philip. Listen——"

Mechanically Philip Territt turned his head. He heard the song of the lark far away and very faint. But very clearly he heard one other sound calling him forth, calling him insistently—high and shrill and loud above the song of the lark, above the voice of Beatrice—the blare of a bugle across the fields of France.

Printed by
Cassell & Company, Limited, La Belle
London, E.C.
F30.217

Lightning Source UK Ltd.
Milton Keynes UK
UKOW01f0614031017
310287UK00004B/295/P

9 781330 877364